CAROLINA BAYS

By

DAVID C. TERRY

First published by Dog Ear Publishing
4010 W. 86th Street, Ste H
Indianapolis, IN 46268
www.dogearpublishing.net

ISBN: 1-59858-241-0
Library of Congress Control Number: 2006936723

This book is printed on acid-free paper.
This book is a work of Fiction. Places, events, and situations in this book are purely Fictional and any resemblance to actual persons, living or dead, is coincidental.

Printed in the United States of America

Acknowledgements

On February 24, 2005, a close and dear friend of mine was tragically killed in an automobile accident while returning to work from lunch. The roads were wet from the heavy rain and a truck crossed the center lane hitting Rick Parker in his small pickup truck. He was killed instantly leaving behind his one and only pride and joy, daughter Clair. I was perhaps the last person to speak with him before his accident.

Rick was the type of person who wasn't afraid to take risks and would do anything he could to help anyone who needed his assistance. He never asked for help in return. His life wasn't always glamorous, but the one thing he remained true to was his daughter. Clair was his life and he dedicated everything to her. Through his rough exterior, he possessed the heart of an angel and it showed every time he looked at Clair.

I named the main character in my book Rick Parker in honor of his memory, and he will live on along with Clair.

Many times, we take for granted our friendships with others that we have developed over the years. It is very rare that we have a true friend that we can see inside of and know his or her feelings without saying a word. Such a friendship was between Rick, Robert "Bob" Livingston, and me. The three of us would many times tear up from laughter we shared during lunch. Rick always tried to hide or keep himself from losing it, and all it took was a look from me to get him started again.

When we worked together, it was Rick who offered assistance whenever I needed it. He was one of the smartest people that I have ever had the pleasure to work with and he took his job seriously.

I will always be thankful for the times we shared. It was my privilege to call him a friend, and he will forever remain a part of me.

I would also like to thank my wife, Charlene, for being my editor and proofreader. Without her, it would have been difficult to write the book. She allows me the opportunity to express myself through my imagination.

Others that I think need mentioning are: my good neighbor, Joan Hill, for providing me the proper grammar corrections; Brian Terry, my oldest son, for giving me suggestions throughout the book; and my mother, Lois Capps, who also gave me inspiration and encouragement to write.

TABLE OF CONTENTS

Chapter 1

I Didn't Want to Act Stupid

I'd just settled down in my seat having received a complimentary glass of champagne from the flight attendant, when I heard the voice of the captain welcoming everyone aboard.

"Good afternoon, ladies and gentlemen, and welcome aboard United Flight 2161 from Miami International to Chicago O'Hare International with a stop in Charlotte Douglas International. Our estimated travel time to Charlotte is two hours and 12 minutes, and one hour, 37 minutes once we depart for Chicago. The weather in Charlotte is 57 degrees and partly cloudy. Chicago is 34, with rain and windy conditions. Sit back and enjoy your ride, and if there's anything we can do to make your trip more enjoyable, please don't hesitate to ask one of our flight attendants."

Having heard the weather conditions in Chicago, I was glad to depart the airplane in Charlotte, because the weather was much nicer. I'd been in Miami for two weeks writing a story on the disappearance of a charter boat and all its passengers. I'm a freelance writer who was writing the story for the *Charlotte Observer*. Since my specialty is investigating disappearances, they wanted me to go to Miami and find out the facts related to this story. My investigation led me down a road that came close to getting me murdered, and I was glad to be going back home to my place of serenity on Lake Norman near the small town of Comelius, North Carolina.

As I felt the rumble of the plane taking off, I thought more about the story I'd written for the paper. Because of the deadline I'd been placed under, I'd sent it to the editor earlier and it was to be published in the following morning's paper. Reading over the article made me sweat from the danger I'd placed myself in a few days earlier.

The investigation started at the local Coast Guard Station where the first reports of a missing vessel had been reported. The *"See Adventure"* had not returned to its berth for more than two days, and the captain's wife was the one who reported them missing. She said in the report that it was a fishing trip for some executives visiting Miami from Dallas, Texas. It was supposed to be a one day trip and the last word she received from her husband, was they were about 90 miles out in the Gulf Steam and the fish were biting. There wasn't any indication of trouble aboard this vessel and it just disappeared without a trace.

The Coast Guard searched for the *"See Adventure"* for two days and was not able to find any evidence of its whereabouts. There were other boats in the area, but no one reported any suspicious activities. The report did say that a mid-afternoon storm was in the area and they presumed the vessel took on water and sank. Yet, there wasn't a single call for distress or any debris found, and even the Coast Guard stated that was unusual.

Continuing the search, I investigated the known drug areas on the south side of Miami. These areas were known for bringing in illegal drugs from Columbia on pirated boats. So, my hunch told me this could be what had happened to the *"See Adventure."* Pretending to be an interested buyer from the north, I was able to contact Juan Sanchez. Juan wasn't what I would call an upper-level drug dealer, but more of the street-level type. The upper-level dealers are the ones who have direct contact with the drug lords and it's hard to get inside their network. Juan was more of a deliveryman and transported the shipments from the boats to the various locations in the country. But I knew Juan would be a good place to start, because through our conversations I found out he'd been involved in the transportation of a shipment of Cannabis, also known as pot, Grass, Ganja, Wacky Weed, etc. …Also in the shipment was some Rohypnol or *"Roofies."* This drug is commonly known as the "date rape" drug. The *"Roofies"* had a particular distaste in my mouth because it had been used on my sister while she was in college at Appalachian State University. She'd attended a party and her escort slipped some pills in her drink, then raped her later back at her apartment.

Juan was very careful at first in our meetings and I knew he was sizing me up to see if I was the man. Since I was not familiar with the area, he surmised I seemed sincere in my efforts to purchase some drugs. He took me to a bookstore in a rundown area south of Miami. At first, I was nervous entering the place, because it felt like there were people staring at me and I couldn't see anyone. As we walked in the front door, an older woman was sitting at the counter and she didn't smile or say a word to me. Juan said a few words to her, which I didn't understand, to which she started to smile, and this made me even more nervous.

At the back of the room, Juan pushed on a bookcase and exposed a hidden door. He pushed on the button beside the door and I heard several knocks followed by a different series of knocks from Juan. When the door opened, I saw a huge Cuban-looking man dressed in an old T-shirt. He slapped Juan's hands and stared at me.

"Who is this guy and why did you bring him here?" the man replied.

"It's okay, man! He's with me," Juan said, still slapping hands.

Juan told him I was a buyer from the north and I was okay. He said he'd vouch for me and led me into the hidden room. Once inside, I noticed a lot of tables and boxes labeled, "*Frozen Fish*." There were two other men in the room and they were busy packing metal cylinders inside the boxes, covering them with ice.

"Está ganando mucho dinero," shouted one man.

"What did he say?" I asked Juan.

"He thinks you have a lot of money and they want some of it," he said laughing.

Juan took me to another room and there were all kinds of different types of drugs stacked on shelves. He just pointed at them and told me to pick out what I wanted, and we'd negotiate a deal. I didn't want to act stupid, but I did not have a clue what any of the drugs were that I was looking at. However, I didn't want Juan to know. Picking up a plastic bag containing white powder, his eyes lit up as if he'd hit the jackpot.

"Okay, my friend,…how many bags do you require?" he asked in his Cuban accent.

"Let's talk price. How much for a bag?" I replied, trying to act knowledgeable.

"For you, a special price, because you are my friend," he spoke, and the other men laughed hearing his reply. Twenty-five thousand for a kilo, and that's half the cost you'd find anywhere else."

Juan was smiling and for a moment, I thought I was dealing with a used car salesman from the way he was grinning at me. He started bragging that this was the finest nose candy on the market, so I knew I had a bag of powder cocaine in my hand. He took another bag from the shelf, opened it and asked if I wanted to sample the goods. I replied that I trusted him and declined his offer.

Juan showed me some other bags that I had no idea what was in them, but I acted as if I understood everything he was saying to me. As we continued walking around the area, I noticed some items in a different room that appeared to be nautical. This could be what I was looking for, I thought to myself and asked Juan if I could have a look. He again smiled and told me everything in there was for sale. All I had to do was pick out what I wanted and we'd negotiate another deal.

"Los ricos hombre," I again heard from one of the men packing the boxes.

"My homies think you are a very wealthy man," Juan spoke as we entered the room.

The room was full of items that I knew came from yachts, and I saw everything from silverware to instruments. One item caught my eye and it was a small wooden box that had some lettering scrapped off the top. What I could make out were the letters "S— ——-ture." I told Juan I wanted this box and asked him how much it was. He immediately took the box from me, saying it wasn't for sale.

"I thought everything in here was for sale," I said to him.

"No! ... No! ...Nothing is for sale in here!" and he grabbed my arm and started escorting me out of the room. I tried to stop, but the niceness he once displayed, turned to anger and he led me out of the building into the street.

"There's nothing for you to buy here!" he snapped at me.

"What's wrong? I thought we had a deal!" I replied.

"No deal for you! You leave and don't come back," he stated and turned, heading back into the bookstore and leaving me standing in the street.

I had no clue what went wrong inside the room. He suddenly became angry when I picked up the box. This must have come from the "*See Adventure*" and would prove my theory that the boat had been used in a drug shipment. My only problem was how to get more information.

For the next two days, I hid around the corner of the bookstore watching for any activity. On the third day, several strangers entered the store and at first, I assumed they were buyers. It was getting later in the day and the sun was setting, when I noticed a small delivery truck come from behind the building and Juan was driving. I could make out one of the strangers I'd seen earlier riding in the passenger seat. So, I started the car and followed as far behind as I could and still be able to see what direction they were going.

After a few turns, we ended up on Highway 821 heading south. Maintaining a safe distance behind, we traveled about ten miles until they turned onto Galloway Road and headed toward Biscayne National Park. Within twenty minutes, the truck turned onto a small dirt road. I drove past the road so as not to be seen, and saw a small sign that read, "*Black Creek Canal.*" Just a few feet ahead, I turned off my lights and pulled to the side of the road. In the darkness of the night, I could make out the headlights of the truck from a distance. Using a small flashlight, I headed down the same dirt road the truck had gone down. The dust from the tires of the truck lingered, and a few times it was difficult to see my way down the path. As I got closer, I turned off the flashlight, slowly making my way toward the noise I could hear from a distance. Walking down a dark road in south Florida next to a canal made me hope nothing moved around me. I knew Florida canals were full of alligators and poisonous snakes. Hopefully, the recent movement of the truck coming down the road would have scared anything away.

With my heart pounding from either the excitement of the adventure or the fear of being attacked by a vicious creature, I soon reached a clearing not far from the men. The truck was backed in next to the canal and it was obvious they were unloading something from a boat to the truck. There wasn't much to hide behind, but I made my way closer and hid behind a small bush. The three men continued carrying large items that looked like bales of marijuana. After several more trips, they stopped and started drinking some beer. One of the men seemed to look in my direction and for a minute, I thought he saw me. However, he continued drinking and they began laughing and telling jokes. Juan went back on the boat and started taking things. He held up a man's watch and was dancing up and down with joy while the others gestured their approval.

About that time, I heard a splash in the water next to me and I was sure it was an alligator attacking. I gasped aloud and the two men came running over to me, hitting my face with a bottle one still had in his hand. Falling to the ground, they both jumped on top of me and I thought they were going to break my arm.

"Who are you and what are you doing here?" one screamed at me.

"He must he a FED," the other spoke, and they pulled me toward the truck.

"I know this man," I heard coming from Juan as he too joined in hitting me in the stomach. "He's the guy who was in the bookstore the other day."

"Well, let's just shoot him and be done with it," came from one of the men, and I thought my life would soon be ended.

The men continued discussing my fate and finally Juan suggested I take a boat ride, to which they laughed and agreed. I didn't understand what he meant at first, but they tied my hands and led me aboard the boat. Juan told them to meet him at the normal place and started up the vessel. Before leaving, they bound me to a handrail inside the boat.

Juan carefully navigated his way through the canal and I could tell this wasn't the first time he'd made this trip. After about thirty minutes, we headed into the open waters of the ocean. I asked Juan where he was taking me and he replied, "To the graveyard."

"What is the graveyard?" I reluctantly asked.

"Oh, it's where all the boats go when we are finished with them," he replied, smiling.

"What happened to the passengers on this vessel?" I questioned him.

"They have no more problems," he stated, and opened the small door leading below.

Inside I saw a man and woman lying on the floor. They had been shot in the head. I could tell they had been shot at close range, because blood was splattered all over the cabin. I knew Juan was going to plan the same type of death for me, so I began to question him.

"Juan, how many times have you done this?" I asked.

"Man, I lost count. ...Maybe twenty times. I don't know."

"Are you planning on shooting me," I asked him.

"No man, you get to hold your breath and if you are real good, you might last for five minutes," he said laughing at me.

Thinking I wasn't going to make it anyway, I asked him about the "*See Adventure*" and what happened to her. He seemed surprised that I knew of her, but started telling me all the details of the night they seized the vessel.

"That was an easy kill," he said. "They thought we were out of gas and came over to help when I put a bullet in the head of the captain. Then Jose` finished off the others," he bragged.

He told me they used the boat to transport a shipment of dope that had been dropped from an airplane.

"The "*See Adventure*" is laying in the graveyard along with its crew," he said, and started slowing down the vessel. "Well it's time to go diving," he stated after coming to a complete stop.

Juan pulled a rifle from underneath a nearby blanket and started firing rounds in the bottom of the boat. He must have fired fifty rounds into her and water poured into its cabin. From a distance, I could see a small boat approaching fast, and Juan said it was his ride home.

"I hope you have a good time with the fishes," he said laughing.

As the boat came closer, I heard someone shout out, "Freeze and don't make a move." Juan started to move toward me and I heard the sound of a gun firing. Juan fell below my feet from the impact of a bullet hitting him behind his right ear.

Not knowing who these people where, I tried to slide down the wall for any protection I could find, thinking they would be firing more rounds at the vessel. But soon, two men jumped aboard the boat with guns and I could see they were wearing U.S. Customs jackets.

"Are you all right, Sir? Is there anyone else aboard?"

Still terrified, I could barely speak the words that I was all right and I had not seen anyone else. I did point to the cabin below and one of the men shined his flashlight there, displaying the gruesome findings. Water was gushing in and after they untied my hands, they moved me to their small boat. While pushing away from the sinking vessel, I asked them about the people still aboard. They assured me the U.S. Coast Guard was on the way and they shot a flare into the air to help locate the position. From one of the handheld radios, I heard the captain of the Coast Guard ship reply that they saw the flare and would be on the scene within minutes.

The customs agents took me back to their office to debrief me and wanted to know how I had managed to get myself in that predicament. I explained why I was there and the events leading up to my rescue.

"Mr. Parker, you are very fortunate that we were tracking that vessel or you wouldn't be here," they informed me, and I agreed.

We talked further on how they had been following that shipment of drugs from Columbia ever since it had reached the United States. They were watching from afar and saw me be abducted. Capturing the other men, they found out where the vessel was being taken. I thanked them for saving my life and one of the agents asked me if I was the same Richard Parker who wrote articles for the *Beaufort Herald*. I told him I was a freelance writer, and I had written some articles published in that paper. He said he was from that area and had read my report on a family that was murdered. The family members were close friends of his and he'd saved the article.

With the customs agent's assistance, I was able to follow up with the Coast Guard in finding the "*Graveyard*" that Juan mentioned. Down below, resting on the bottom, were several boats that had been seized by the drug runners. One of the boats was the "*See Adventure*." What was left of the remains of the captain and his crew were found and turned over to their families for burial.

Chapter 2

ANOTHER FAMILY DISAPPEARS IN SINGLETARY LAKE

It wasn't very long before the captain came on the speaker and told us we would be landing in Charlotte. The flight attendant removed my trash and asked me to stow away my gear to prepare for the landing. After complying with her request, I picked up the national newspaper I'd been given when I first sat down in my seat. Reading it, I noticed a small article saying, *"Another Family Disappears in Singletary Lake."* At first, it didn't appeal to me, but as I continued reading the article, it mentioned this was the fifth family to disappear at this lake in the last three years. There wasn't any more information except all the other previous disappearances had not been solved, and the local authorities were mystified. As soon as I finished the article, we landed in Charlotte.

It's always good to drive up and see your place when you have been gone for a while. The drive from Charlotte up to Comelius took about 45 minutes, and I'd stopped along the way to pick up something to cook for dinner. I knew my wife, Janet, wouldn't be home for a few more hours and our daughter Clair was still in school. When I opened the door, Lady, our Lhasa Apso, jumped up to greet me. She was excited to see her daddy once again and after placing my luggage in the bedroom, we sat down in our favorite chair out on the deck overlooking the lake. She knew I'd brought her something to eat and sat next to me waiting for her surprise. While feeding her a treat, I stared at the peacefulness of the lake and enjoyed the beautiful sunny day.

Having been gone so long, there was a lot of mail and newspapers

Janet had saved for me to review. Most of the mail was bills, and she had taken care to ensure they were paid. She handled all the money in the family and this made it easier for me, since I was on the go so much covering stories. A few checks from articles I had written needed to be signed, and I took care of it so she could deposit them in our account the following day.

With the business of the mail finally behind me, I began reading two weeks of newspapers. Janet knew I liked to catch up on all the local happenings. Lady loved to sit in my lap while I read, with me slowly stroking her back. Lady had settled down when I saw an article on the missing family again. This time there was more detail, because Singletary Lake was only located about 100 miles from Charlotte. The writer described how the family was camping with a church group and went canoeing on the lake. Several others went on the adventure and returned to the campsite. The Jenkins family told them they were going to explore a little more of the lake before heading back, but they never returned. They were camping at the state park and the park rangers searched for hours and did not find any clues to their disappearance. Local law enforcement searched the lake for days without any evidence. Sheriff Ed Bailey made the statement that this was the most unusual case he'd ever been involved with.

"Normally in a case like this, there's evidence of mischief or accidental death," he stated. "But there's not any evidence anywhere in that lake, and we've had divers and sonar devices looking. The only thing in that lake is an old boat the rangers once had, and they knew where it was located," he continued.

The sheriff made references to the other disappearances and even talked about closing the lake to visitors until the mysteries had been solved. He also stated, none of the rangers had ever seen anything suspicious and they did not think there was any foul play involved. One ranger indicated he thought they may have flipped over, their bodies washed ashore, and the wild animals carried them off. But this would not explain why no debris from the boat was ever found.

As I gazed out at the lake, I began to wonder how a family could completely vanish without a trace. Then I thought about how the "*See Adventure*" disappeared and it was from drug runners.

Could this be the same sort of disappearance? I thought to myself.

"But they vanished in the daylight hours," I spoke aloud, and Lady raised her head to see who I was talking to.

About this time, I heard the voice of Clair as she came running onto the deck to give me a hug. She was very excited to see me home again, and the noise caused Lady to jump up barking.

"Hi Daddy! I'm so glad you are home. ...I've missed you." Clair kissed my left cheek.

"Well hello, Pumpkin. I'm so happy to see you, too," I spoke as I kissed the top of her head.

Clair and I had always been close, but she seemed especially glad to see me and I wondered why. I didn't have to wait long to find out, because she immediately started telling me about some trouble she'd gotten in at school two days earlier.

"Dad, don't get angry…" and I knew I was about to hear a good story. "I got in trouble at school, but it wasn't my fault," she pleaded. "I was in math class and this boy pulled my hair, so I slapped him up beside his face," she blurted out with emotion.

"Why did he pull your hair in the first place, Clair?" I asked her.

"I don't know, but I bet he won't do it again, Dad," she responded.

I know, as her father, I was supposed to be upset with her actions, but I had to catch myself from smiling at her reply. She had always been one to stand up for herself, so I wasn't surprised to hear she'd slapped a boy.

"What did your mother say?"

"She told me I should not have hit him, and to just ignore these things when they happen," was her answer.

This was funny to me, because I once saw Janet stand up to several mothers during a soccer game when one of the other team's players knocked Clair down. When I grabbed her arm and asked her to return to our side of the field, she told me to let go and stomped away, turning as she walked, pointing her finger at the player who pushed Clair. I told Clair I'd talk with her mom about the incident and assured her everything would be fine.

"But Dad, she won't let me go anywhere and I'm on restriction for two weeks," she again pleaded and I just told her to accept the punishment.

When Janet got home, I'd fixed dinner and had the table set and ready to include candlelight. Clair had eaten earlier and was in her room doing her homework.

"Hi honey,… how was your trip?" she asked as she kissed me.

I told her it went well, because I didn't want her to know how close I came to dying. She was a worrier, so there was no need in giving her any more reasons to be concerned. She seemed to except my answer and smiled as she noticed the dinner and candlelight.

We sat down at the table and I poured her a glass of wine I'd purchased earlier on the way home from the airport. She told me about her day and after dinner, we both gave Clair a kiss goodnight and retired to the bedroom. Janet wanted to take a shower and I began the process of putting away my clothes and luggage from the trip.

Removing my clothing, I entered the bathroom and I could see Janet's naked body through the glass door covered with the suds from the body wash. She didn't hear or see me enter the room, and I slowly slid the door aside and stepped into the shower. It startled her at first, but she quickly wrapped her arms around my neck and gave me a wet kiss.

"I've missed you," she said, continuing the kissing.

"I missed you, too, and I'm glad to be in your arms once again," I replied.

Janet began to rub her soapy body against mine and the passion inside me started rising. It had been a while since we'd made love, and she was feeling especially good at that moment. The smoothness of her wet breast rubbed across my chest and I quickly responded. My manhood was erect and she smiled at me as if she was proud she made it happen. She turned my body toward the showerhead to block the spray from hitting her face. Then to my delight, she slowly slid down until she'd reached my place of enchantment. The water seemed to get warmer to the point I had to turn it off. I pulled Janet up from her position and grabbed a towel from the cabinet, while leading her by the hand to the bed. Still soaking wet, I placed the towel on the bed and lowered Janet down. The soap from the bath was still on her body and I could taste it as I kissed her breast. She moaned when I gently used my tongue to lick her nipples and I knew she was ready for me. Still very excited with passion, I lowered myself down and made love to her. The only light in the room came from a candle I'd lit prior to going into the bathroom and as I continued my lovemaking, I could see her beautiful face and she was smiling at me.

I fell in love with Janet the first time I saw her, and I knew she was the woman of my dreams. We'd been married for 15 years and this evening I found her more beautiful than ever. Maybe it was my recent experiences, but I never wanted her more than I did at that moment.

Janet seemed more into the lovemaking than usual, and I assumed it was because I'd been gone, but I wasn't about to complain. She suddenly pulled my arm, rolled me over onto the bed, and climbed on top of me. The light from the candle flickered off her luscious body as she rode me, and it wasn't long before we both exploded from the passion.

"Man, that was wonderful," she said while gasping for a breath.

"It was that, my love," I responded.

We lay in bed for a while with her wrapped in my arms, and I gently rubbed her body with the tips of my fingers. She loved for me to stroke her in this fashion because it relaxed her. She kissed my chest from time to time, told me how much I meant to her, and said she didn't want me to leave her anymore. We'd talked about my traveling on several occasions in the past, but she still wanted me to find a job that would allow me to be home every night. I told her that my job required me to go on the road, and maybe the next trip she and Clair could go with me.

"You know it's hard for me to take off during the school year," she said. "There's a shortage of teachers and there's no way Clair or I can go until the summer break.".

The school year was ending in two months and I suggested we try to go somewhere during the summer months, and she appeared to be pleased with my statement. After another shower together, we retired for the night and I was ready for some sleep in my own bed.

Chapter 3

THIS SHOULDN'T TAKE VERY LONG

The following morning, I couldn't wait to go to the paper box and retrieve the newspaper. I was expecting to look for my article somewhere in the middle of the paper, but instead on the front page I saw a picture of some sunken boats.

"*Major Drug Bust In Miami*," was written in big bold lettering across the top of the picture. Under the title was "Richard Parker", staff writer. They knew I was a freelance writer, but it didn't bother me seeing my name on the front page of the newspaper. The editor had printed my report and findings word for word. The article continued on to the second page and I'd forgotten that I had written how close I'd come to dying.

I can't let Janet see this! I thought to myself.

Janet was finishing her makeup, ready to rush off to work. She was running a little behind, because we'd both slept longer than we should have. Clair was eating cereal and I hid the paper inside a kitchen cabinet so as not to be in view for Janet while on her way out of the house. As she came rushing through the kitchen, she kissed Clair and I, and hurried to her car.

"That was close," I inadvertently said aloud.

"What was close, Daddy?" Clair asked.

"Mom's pushing it close," I replied. She agreed and gathered up her things, heading out the door to the bus that was waiting for her.

All day I thought about Singletary Lake and the semblance of the disappearances with the boats in Miami. I'd convinced myself that I needed to go to Bladen County and do some investigating of my own. The only problem was, I knew Janet wouldn't be happy, since I'd been gone for two weeks. Nevertheless, my instincts were telling me there was more to this story and I needed to investigate it.

The remainder of the afternoon was spent doing research on the Internet to find out as much information as I could on Singletary Lake and the surrounding area. It was still my belief the mysteries were drug related, and I needed to know all I could about the nearby towns and road systems. If someone had abducted the family, then there must have been a road or path they used to exit the lake. The one thing that continued to haunt me was why would someone go to the trouble of seizing a small boat and killing a family in broad daylight?

While doing more research, I found out Singletary Lake was a state park located southeast of Elizabethtown, North Carolina. There were several other lakes located nearby, to include the popular family vacation spot, White Lake. The lake lies within the 35,975 acre Bladen Lakes State Forest. Singletary Lake is not the biggest of the lakes in this region, but is rather large, being 4,000 feet long with a shoreline of almost four miles. It was listed as the deepest of the lakes and that seemed unusual, since streams or springs do not feed it. Its water level fluctuates with the rainfall and runoff from the surrounding land.

Looking at a map of the area, I could only imagine how large it once was, because the data said it was only 44 percent of its original size. The reason for this reduction over the years is that vegetation completely surrounds the lake perimeters taking root in the dead organic matter that accumulates on the edge. These trees and brushes grow into the lake, slowly reducing the size. This is a normal occurrence in the ecological process.

The lake was named for Richard Singletary, who received a grant in Bladen County in 1729, then settled and logged its Longleaf pines for turpentine pitch and timber. This, and all the other lakes, became popular, and in 1827, the North Carolina legislature established that it would become property of the state and benefit all people, and would not be privately owned. By the early 1900's, the human population surrounding Singletary Lake increased beyond the soil's capacity to support it. In 1936, the National Park Service bought portions of the land surrounding the lake. In October of 1954, it officially became the property of the state and the state park opened that summer. Since that time, the Boy Scouts, 4-H Clubs, church groups, and similar organizations have primarily used it.

Having some background information on the lake helped me understand what activities took place there. I knew there had to be a road system of some sort surrounding the lake, and this fueled my suspicions that the disappearances could be malicious. Again looking at a map of the local area, I only saw one main road, Highway 53, traveling next to it. So, I knew I had to visit the area to get a better look for myself.

When Janet came home, Clair and I had prepared a good dinner for her. We'd fixed a roast in the oven and Clair did most of the preparing of the meal. I enjoyed cooking and she liked to help me. We were a good team and sometimes I felt Janet was a little jealous of our relationship, but she didn't say anything.

"Mommy, look what I've fixed for you tonight!" she blurted out as soon as Janet stepped in the door.

"Oh, it smells good, sweetie," and they gave each other a kiss.

"Hey,... what about me?" I spoke up. "I did have something to do with this meal."

"The only thing you did was get in the way, Daddy," Clair said, laughing at me.

"I know what you mean!" Janet said, and they both started laughing at me.

I didn't mind them having a good laugh at my expense. It was good to see them smiling and having fun. We had always been a close family and shared a good laugh when we could. I loved to see Janet smile, because it enhanced the dimples in her cheeks. When she'd laugh hard, her eyes would also squint and her nose would wrinkle up. She didn't like it, but I thought it looked cute.

The dinner turned out great and we both praised Clair several times throughout the meal. She loved to be the center of attention, especially when she did something for someone. After all the plates were cleaned, I looked at Janet and told her I wanted to discuss something with her.

"Where are you going now, Rick?" she immediately questioned. "I know that tone and it means you are going somewhere again, doesn't it?

The smile previously on her face was gone, and I could see that she wasn't happy. She stepped out onto the deck and stared at the lake with her back turned towards me. When I approached her and placed my hand on her shoulder, she twisted away from me.

"Janet, I haven't even told you what it's all about," I said to her.

"It doesn't matter, if you are leaving me again," she snapped at me.

"But listen to what I'm about to tell you before making such a stand," I said sternly.

"Okay, what is it? And just how long is it for this time?" was her cold reply.

The article from the paper was in my hand and I read the piece about the missing family at Singletary Lake. Explaining that I thought I could solve the mystery fairly quickly, she still didn't want to hear of me going away again. That's when I put my arms around her and said I wouldn't be going by myself.

"What do you mean by that?" she questioned.

"Like I said, this shouldn't take very long and I thought it would be a good trip for all of us to go to White Lake for a weekend vacation," I replied.

Janet had not heard of White Lake and wanted to know why we would go to another lake when we lived on one. But when I explained it was a family-oriented lake with lots of things for Clair to do, she finally smiled. I suggested that we look into getting a place that even Lady would be welcomed, and she thought it would be fun. Now her curiosity was getting the better of her, and she wanted to know more about White Lake and all the things to do. We looked on the Internet and found a site that showed a variety of fun things to do. When she found out the beaches were white sand and the lake was listed as one of the most beautiful lakes in the country, she was ready to go.

My plan was for all of us to go on a holiday weekend, but the next one wasn't until Memorial Day, and that was two weeks away. I didn't want to wait that long, but I knew I'd better if I wanted to keep my wife and family. So, the next day I called my travel agent and booked us into a cabin next to the water and close to all the activities. This rental allowed us to take Lady with us, so we were set.

Continuing my research, I wanted to know if there had been any other disappearances or strange occurrences in the nearby lakes. Bay Tree Lake was located 20 miles north of Singletary Lake, and it had a state park on it as well. The park did not surround all of it, as did Singletary Lake State Park. I wanted to know if there had been anything suspicious reported there. Going through all the information I could find, there had been deaths in the lake, but they were from accidental drownings and all the bodies were recovered. The same applied to the rest of the lakes I researched within the area. Everything I saw made me believe that I could solve the mysteries of Singletary Lake and still have fun with my family.

Chapter 4

YOU AIN'T GOT NO BUSINESS
AROUND HERE SNOOPING

Janet agreed to let Clair stay home from school the Friday we departed for White Lake. She'd talked with her teachers to get her schoolwork for that day in order not to miss anything. She was also able to get a substitute for her and we left early for the 140-mile trip. Following the directions given to us by our travel agent, we soon found the cabin and it was just as it had been described. Clair and Lady jumped out the car and ran to the water seeing how beautiful it was. Janet was smiling. She kissed me and said it was perfect.

That evening we cooked some steaks on the grill provided and enjoyed eating on the picnic table next to the lake. There was a gentle breeze blowing across the water and a few boats pulling skiers. Not very far away, we could see the activities of the amusement park and a Ferris wheel turning. Clair wanted to go, so we cleaned off the table and headed in that direction.

"I want to ride!" Clair said excitedly, seeing some of the thrill rides.

"Will you ride with me, Dad?" she asked, and I wasn't very happy hearing her request.

"Yes, why don't you,… Daddy?" Janet quickly said, knowing I didn't like riding rides at an amusement park.

Once while I was in high school, my best friend and I were riding a ride called, "*The Bullet.*" This was a two-seat ride that you were totally caged within and it turned in a clockwise motion as it also rotated like a Ferris wheel. This was the ride of all rides at the county fair, and I would not have even gotten on the ride if it had not been for a dare from my friends.

At the age of sixteen, you sometimes do things on a dare that you normally would not attempt.

As we were in full motion and I could feel my body turn in more directions than I wanted to feel, there was a loud noise of the main chain breaking and the ride shook violently. The chain was what made the ride move and stop, so now we were in perpetual motion with no way to stop us. Several of the workers started banging the sides of the carts as they passed by them next to the ground, hoping it would eventually slow the ride down enough to stop each cart, allowing everyone to get out. It took them almost ten minutes to free us from the nightmare we were living through. With each bang on the side of the carts, it felt as if the ride was falling to the ground.

It had been in high school and my terrifying experience, since I'd last ridden trill rides. However, Clair was excited and I didn't want to disappoint her, so I agreed to ride a few with her. On the Ferris wheel, I kept my eyes closed and Clair pulled at my hands trying to scare me. I wasn't afraid, but she found it funny when I pretended to be. Janet laughed and took many pictures while we were riding. Most of the rides didn't bother me, but when Clair talked me into riding the Teapots, I just knew I was going to lose my dinner. This ride did circles and the more I tried to slow down the movements, the more it turned. Janet said I looked white as a sheet when I stepped off and back onto solid ground. Clair loved it and wanted to ride it some more, but I knew I was done for the evening. We continued playing games at the arcade and Janet loved the competition of tabletop tennis. Clair found a new friend about her age to ride with and I thought that was great, because that meant I would not have to anymore. Janet and I played all the competitive games in the arcade and we ended up almost equal on who had won the most. She argued that she had and I told her it was I, but it really didn't matter. We stayed until the place closed, grabbed an ice cream and walked along the beach back to our cabin. Clair was exhausted from the evening's activities and fell asleep with Lady by her side as soon as her head hit the bed. Janet and I were tired, but I asked her if she'd like to take a midnight swim in the lake.

"I don't know what's in that lake! Aren't you afraid an alligator might eat me!" she said smiling.

"The only thing in that lake that will come close to biting you is me," I said grinning ear to ear.

We were pleasantly surprised to feel the water was only cool instead of cold as we dangled our feet off the edge of the pier. The night was still and the moonlight flickered on the rippling waves. It felt good to relax and enjoy a moment of silence. Like small children, we kicked our feet in the water and held hands while talking about how much fun Clair had at the amusements. Kissing Janet, I slid down into the cool water inviting her to follow. I didn't want to tell her I was freezing, because I wanted her to find out for herself. Within seconds, she jumped in beside me and screamed from the surprise. I laughed at her and she didn't think it was funny. She held on next to me looking for something warm, and that fell right into my plans.

The water depth wasn't deep and I was able to stand up, but Janet was shorter at 5' 3", and she had a difficult time keeping her head above the water. She clung to me and I didn't resist, feeling her body next to mine. She shivered for a while and I rubbed her arms, trying to make her warmer. After about ten minutes, she and I got used to the water and it didn't feel that cold anymore.

With her still wrapped tightly close to me, I kissed her passionately and she returned my kiss with one of her own. Her legs were tightly around my waist and I was holding her up in the water. My hands reached up and began rubbing her right breast as she moved with excitement. All the while, I was getting aroused myself. From her position, she could feel my excitement and reached down with one hand, pulling off her panties. I quickly followed her lead and removed my swimming trunks as well, placing them on the pier. Janet once again wrapped her legs around my body, only this time she guided my penis inside her. I looked around to see if anyone could be watching and felt secure knowing we were safely hidden by the pier and the darkness of the night. Using the buoyancy of the water, we moved together and it was as if we'd become one with each other. I always enjoyed making love with Janet, but tonight seemed more emotional rather than passionate. The passion was there, but we were truly experiencing a euphoric state. We continued making love for a long time and without any warning, both erupted in pleasure.

On Saturday morning I woke up early, because I wanted to begin investigating the area around Singletary Lake. It was less than ten miles from where we were staying, so I didn't think I'd be gone long. Janet rolled over and I kissed her goodbye, saying I'd try to be back in time to take them to lunch. She smiled at me and thanked me for the wonderful evening and the water sports. As I closed the bedroom door behind me, I winked and told her the moon would be dark tonight for us to do some more water events. She smiled, rolling back over to go to sleep.

The first thing I did was head down Highway 53 until I saw the lake from the road. Stopping, I pulled off the main road and made my way through a small opening near the edge of the lake. From my vantage point,

the lake looked very isolated and large in area. What caught my attention
was how dark the water looked, and I couldn't see the bottom. White Lake
was very clear and you can see the bottom almost everywhere on the lake,
but Singletary Lake was dark and did not have the sandy texture. I could see
why it was 44 percent smaller than it originally started out to be.

There's no way Janet would ever get in this lake and play water sports,
I thought, laughing to myself.

Walking around the edge of the rim, I looked for any signs of evidence that other people could have been there recently. If the disappearances happened next to this highway, then I should find clues of tire tracks
or footprints. Walking for about a mile, nothing looked suspicious. In fact,
the lake looked undisturbed. As I approached my vehicle, I saw a local sheriff's car and an officer standing next to my car. It looked to me as if he was
searching it and I startled him as I came walking through the brush.

"Stop right there!" he hollered at me with his revolver pointed.

"I'm just looking at the lake," I replied.

"You ain't got no business snooping around here!" he again hollered.

As we exchanged a few more words, I tried to explain my purpose for
being there. I became relieved when he lowered his pistol. He told me that
he was concerned when he spotted my vehicle and no one was around it.

"At first, I thought it was someone stopping to take a piss," he jokingly said. "But after I didn't see no one, I thought you either ran out of gas
or something was wrong."

We talked for another hour, standing next to the highway discussing
the disappearances. He had been one of the officers called to the scene the
night it was reported.

"I knew they weren't going to be found," he stated. "Ain't no one ever
been found in this lake," he said, "and this ain't the only lake people disappear in!"

I quickly questioned him on what he'd said. He told me he'd lived in
Bladen County all his life and knew of more disappearances that weren't
always reported. He said his second cousin went fishing with one of his
friends back when they were in their teens and they didn't come home.

"Them boys just vanished without a trace," he said in a terrified tone.
"I ain't been fishing or swimming in none of these lakes since that time.
The only lake around here that's safe is White Lake," he stated and that
made me feel better knowing what I'd done the night before and what I had
planned for the evening.

I wasn't sure why he opened up to me the way he did, but it was as if he
was trying to get help from me. Telling me of other lakes with mysteries in the
area, I asked him why there had not been a better investigation conducted.

"The government knows what's going on and they ain't telling," he just looked at me and said.

He wouldn't say any more and indicated he'd told me more than I needed to know. I informed him where my family and I were staying, and he indicated that I needed to go back to them, enjoy White Lake and go home.

The sun was getting hot on us standing next to the road and he excused himself saying it was past his lunchtime. Looking at my watch, I realized it was late and Janet would be upset with me for not returning to the cabin as I'd promised, so I jumped in the car and raced back only to find that she and Clair were not there. Janet left a note on the kitchen table telling me they'd gone to the amusement area to eat and if I could find the time, I could join them. From the tone of her note, I knew she wasn't very happy with me. Instead of going to try to find them, I fixed myself a sandwich, and Lady and I sat down on the pier watching the skiers.

Looking at the beauty of the lake and enjoying the peacefulness of the moment with Lady sitting in my lap, I pondered what I'd seen, or had not seen, at Singletary Lake. The deputy's words ran through my head over and over.

"The only lake that is safe around here is White Lake."

Before making the trip, I'd researched what I could find on the surrounding area lakes and there wasn't any information of strange disappearances. When he made reference that the government knew what was going on, it just didn't make sense to me. If what he was saying was true, then what would the government be hiding from us? The day was passing by and it would not be long before the sun went down, so I wrote a note for Janet to let her know I'd gone back to Singletary Lake.

Janet, I'm sorry I didn't make it for lunch, but I got tied up talking with a Deputy Sheriff about the disappearances. I'm taking Lady and we have gone back to the lake to look around some more. We'll be back in time for you, Clair and me to have dinner and enjoy the amusement park again tonight. I love you and look forward to our swim later.

I knew Janet would understand what I meant about the swim later, but I didn't want to go into more detail, just in case Clair read the note. Knowing she was angry because I wasn't back in time for lunch, I hoped she'd be over it by the time Lady and I returned.

Lady was happy to know she was going with me on a trip. She always wanted to go whenever I got into the car, and she loved to stick her face in the wind as we drove down the road. As I opened the car door, she jumped in, ready for the adventure.

The shadows of the forest made it difficult to see as I slowed down in front of the lake. This time I drove past the place I'd stopped at previously and saw a dirt road turning toward the lake. This was the entrance to the State Park, so I turned and made my way down it until I saw a chain blocking the road. On the chain was a sign that said the park was closed until further notice. I assumed it was because of the recent disappearances and they were not taking any more chances. Lady had to go to the bathroom, so I stepped out of the car and she immediately jumped down to the road. The car was still running and my headlights were on, but I couldn't see any activity. Lady quickly did her thing and suddenly perked up as if she heard something. I turned off the engine to the car to see if I could also hear it, but there was only a dead silence. However, Lady tuned into something and she didn't move. In the trunk of the car, I kept a high-powered flashlight and I retrieved it, shining the beam in the direction Lady was looking. Scanning the forest, I could not see anything that looked suspicious. Without any warning, Lady darted into the woods, barking as if she was in pursuit of something.

"Lady!" I yelled. "Get back here, now!"

She didn't slow down and continued running and jumping through the brush chasing whatever she had seen. I tried to stay on her with the flashlight as long as I could, but she quickly vanished out of sight.

"Dammit!" I said aloud. "Now I've got to chase her through these woods."

With flashlight in hand, I turned on my flashers to the car and stepped over the chain that was blocking the road. Although Lady had run into the woods, I figured my best bet was to head toward the ranger's station and ask for assistance. As I walked down the now very dark road, I could still hear Lady barking in the distance. At least I knew she was all right and as long as she continued to bark, there was a chance of finding her.

The road was longer than I'd anticipated and I assumed I'd walked about a mile when I finally saw some buildings ahead of me. Shining my light in that direction, it looked as if no one was there. Arriving at the first building, I knocked on the door hoping someone would answer. As I had suspected, no one responded to my repeated attempts for attention. The same was true of the rest of the buildings in the area, so I knew I was alone. The lake was directly in front of me, so I walked to the boat ramp and stepped onto the small pier next to it. At the end of the pier, I could hear Lady and she seemed to be going away from my direction, as the sound of her barking was getting weaker. I called out to her as loud as I could in hopes she would hear me and come to my position. For a minute, it seemed as if it had worked, because I could tell she was running toward me. Still yelling to help her find her way, she stopped barking.

"Lady!" "Lady!" I screamed and she didn't respond. "Come here, girl!" I pleaded, and there was nothing but the quiet stillness of the night.

I shined the flashlight toward the last place I'd heard any noise, hoping that she was just tired from running. There wasn't any sign of her and I became worried that maybe a wild animal may have attacked and killed her. The area was known for black bears and bobcats, so my imagination ran wild with the possibilities of losing my companion and member of the family. My first reaction was to head into the woods to try to find her.

Maybe she needs my help, I thought. She could be injured and can't find her way back.

The thought of losing Lady gave me a sinking feeling and I didn't want to believe she could be gone. We treated her like one of the family, and I knew Clair and Janet would take it very hard. So, against all sense of danger to myself, I started my way down to the edge of the lake toward the place I thought she could be. Next to one of the cabins was a boat, and I retrieved an oar to use as a weapon for defense if needed. It wasn't much, but at least it was something.

The thing I found disturbing was the silence of the night. The lake was black and there were not the normal sounds I should hear in the forest at night. I'd spent a lot of time in the woods conducting investigations and there were always noises from the forest occupants, but I didn't hear a sound as I walked along the banks of this lake. Even the crickets were silenced and I felt an eerie sense that I wasn't alone, but I couldn't hear or see anyone.

I was disoriented from the darkness, having walked two miles through the woods. Still calling out to Lady, I tried to make some sort of contact with her. Nothing, not even a whimper, could I hear. As I continued walking, I began to hear the sounds of cars passing on the highway next to the lake, and I followed them until I saw the headlights of a truck coming toward me. It was a welcomed sight and I knew I was back on Highway 53. It took me a while to walk down the highway to reach the place I'd entered before, but I soon saw the taillights still flashing on my car ahead of me. With a sadden heart, I turned around on the dirt road and headed to the cabin knowing Janet and Clair would not be happy with the news of Lady's disappearance.

Seeing the headlights of my car driving up to the cabin, Janet was standing at the door and I could see she was furious. She immediately stepped out of the cabin and closed the door behind her. I knew that was so Clair wouldn't have to witness the verbal abuse I was about to receive.

"Just where in the hell have you been all night?" she blurted. "Do you even know what time it is?" she again questioned me.

Looking at my watch, I saw it was two in the morning. I had not realized that I'd spent almost six hours in the woods looking for Lady.

"I'm sorry, Janet," I spoke in an apologetic voice.

"You should be sorry!" she said again, attacking me with her words.

"Lady... ran into the woods and I couldn't find her," I said, and she suddenly called for her to see if she was still in the car.

"What, you didn't find her?" she replied in a tearful tone.

"No,... baby! I couldn't and I looked everywhere." I said remorsefully.

Janet knew how much I loved Lady and I'd never leave her if I didn't have to. Explaining what had happened and how she suddenly ran into the woods, she seemed to understand my dilemma and turned her anger into sorrow.

"Do you think she's dead?" she asked through her tears.

"I don't know, but I think so," was my reply. I couldn't hold back my sorrow any longer and my eyes filled with tears.

Janet and I sat at the table outside as I told her of the events that evening. The more I talked about the eerie silence, the more she became frightened. We knew it would be difficult to explain why Lady wasn't there in the morning when Clair woke up. I wanted to return to the lake when I'd have daylight to look for her. Janet didn't want me to go alone, so she suggested Clair go spend the day with her new friend while she and I searched for Lady. This was the only way she would agree to the search, so I went along with her wishes.

Clair was the first to wake up and she came running into our room wanting to know were Lady was. We didn't want to lie to her, but also didn't want her to know she was missing. Janet spoke and told her I'd taken Lady to a nearby veterinarian because she acted like she was sick. She wanted to know when Lady would be coming home and Janet told her we were going to get her that afternoon. She seemed to be fine with the answer and Janet suggested she go to her friend's cabin so they could enjoy the amusement area. Clair indicated she would like to do that and Janet went with her to make sure it was all right with her new friend Becky and her parents.

As soon as Janet got back, we headed to Singletary Lake to look for Lady. Traveling on the same dirt road as the night before, the chain had been removed and we continued to the ranger's cottages. At the station, there was a truck that I had not seen the night before. When we stopped, a man in his late forties and wearing a state park uniform stepped out on the porch.

"Hi, folks.... How may I help you?" he asked us.

I explained how I'd been there the previous evening and that our dog ran off into the woods. Janet told him we wanted to look for her and he didn't say a word, only stared at us.

"Sir, may we look for our dog?" Janet asked again and he didn't reply.

"I'm afraid your dog more than likely got eaten by one of our wild animals in the park, or perhaps bitten by a poisonous snake," he finally said. "These woods are protected and full of rattlesnakes and water moccasins," he stated. "I can't have you wandering through the woods and possibly bitten by a snake, so I'll look for your dog."

We pleaded with him to allow us to search and I even explained how I'd walked through the forest without any harm, but he still wouldn't agree to let us look for her. Finally, he told us the park was closed and we'd have to leave. I figured I didn't have much to lose, so I told him I was a writer and I was doing a story on the disappearance of the Jenkins family.

"There ain't nothing to investigate here!" he said hostilely. "Now the park is closed and you'll have to leave," he said pointing at the road and turning to go back inside the cottage.

"But, what about our dog?" I asked one more time.

"Your dog is probably dead," he said as he entered, closing the door behind him.

We got back in the car and headed to the main highway. Janet wasn't one to cuss and it caught me totally by surprise when I heard her say, "What an asshole!" I looked at her strangely. She had a little tear coming down her cheek, and I could tell she was enraged with this man. Once we got back on the main road, I told her I wanted to stop next to the lake and search for Lady. Once we'd stopped, we crossed over a fallen fence and entered the forest. Under her breath, I heard her mumbled, "Just let that bastard try and stop us." Again, her language shocked me, but I was proud she wanted to take the adventure.

We searched the forest for about an hour and there weren't any signs of Lady. Trying not to be too loud, we called out her name hoping she would hear us. The longer we conducted the search, the more we realized she was gone. We walked in the direction of the lake and all of a sudden...

"Stop right there and don't make a move!" came from behind us. Janet and I froze in place throwing our hands in the air. "All right, slowly turn around and don't make any sudden movements," was the next command we heard.

When we turned around there were two armed men with 9 mm revolvers pointed straight at us. I tried to tell them we'd lost our dog, but they didn't seem to care what our reasons might be for being in the forest. One of the men ran up to me and pulled my arms down behind me, putting me in handcuffs, while the other still held a bead on me with his gun. Janet

screamed when he grabbed her and I told them not to hurt her. Hearing me
holler, he struck the side of my head with his gun sending me to the ground.
The impact dazed me and all I remember was hearing Janet scream as I fell.

"Rick! Rick! Are you all right?" were the first things I could remember hearing after I fell.

Janet was standing above me as my eyes began focusing in her direction. The two men who had attacked me were behind her and it concerned
me knowing I'd been struck by one of them.

"Are you okay," I mumbled to Janet.

"Yes, I'm fine, and everything is all right," she said, smiling at me.

One of the men apologized for hitting me and explained they had been
called by the ranger and were told some people were in the forest and were
armed and dangerous. He told us they'd seen our car parked on the side of
the road and pursued us into the woods. Janet seemed pleased when they
said they were sorry for hitting me, but that didn't relieve the throbbing
pain from the large knot on the side of my head where I was struck with the
butt of his revolver.

We found out they were deputies with the local sheriff's office and
hearing the dispatch of hostiles possible in the state park, they responded
immediately. The recent disappearances made them assume we were up to
no good in the forest and they were not taking any chances when they saw
us. But after hearing we were only in there searching for our dog, they
treated us differently. I told them about my conversation with one of their
deputies the day before and they said they'd heard about it.

"You are the writer guy, aren't you?" one of them asked, and I told
them I was. "Well the best thing you can do is take your family, go back to
where you came from, and leave this story alone," I was told and they both
got back in their vehicle and drove away.

Janet and I headed back to our cabin and it struck me odd that this was
the second time I'd been instructed by the local police to leave and forget
my story. I'd looked at Janet while she was driving and she had a worried
look on her face. I knew some of her concerns were for Lady, but I knew
she wanted to say something else to me.

"Rick! I really don't think you need to continue this story," she
pleaded. "There's definitely something strange and wrong with this place,"
she continued preaching. "I want to go home tonight and I want you to forget about writing this one."

I did not say much during the ten-mile drive and I never agreed to her
request. We didn't talk about the subject anymore and began packing to
make the trip back home. As we had anticipated, Clair took the news of

Lady's demise very hard. All the way home, she cried and lay down in the back seat of the car. It was a lonely ride for Janet and I as well, because she knew I wasn't about to give up my research and pursuit of this story.

It was hard on all of us walking into our house and seeing Lady's bowl and playthings lying around. Janet picked them up and put them away so as not to remind Clair of Lady. None of us mentioned her as we got ready to begin another workweek.

Chapter 5

MOM'S BLOWED UP LIKE A BULLFROG

O n Monday morning after Janet left and I'd gotten Clair on the bus for school, I sat on the porch and pondered the weekend's events. Something just didn't add up. The more I thought about it, the more it seemed obvious that someone wanted to hide something. Was the government involved? I wondered as the first deputy I'd talked with had suggested. I couldn't understand what they would be hiding, so I knew I needed to do more research.

Searching the Internet for further information on Singletary Lake, I found out it was part of a unique geology of the Carolina Bays. I'd never heard of this phenomenon previously, so I wanted to know more about them. My instincts told me there was more to the Carolina Bays that would once again require me to return to the area. I knew this would not go over well with Janet, but I knew I had to complete my investigation.

Carolina Bays are oval-shaped depressions found in coastal North Carolina, South Carolina, and northeastern Georgia. Some reach as far as New Jersey to Florida. There are approximately 500,000 of them present in groups and aligned almost universally from the northwest to southeast. The most concentrated numbers of depressions or lakes are in the southeastern end. The further I dug, the more intrigued I became.

The bays are especially rich in biodiversity, and include rare and/or endangered species. Many of the bays have filled themselves in over the years, but many of the larger bays are still visibly present to include Singletary Lake. White Lake is another example of a Carolina Bay. Only about 10 percent remain, because over time loggers and farmers have drained these sites to cut trees or plant crops. All have ecological systems of their own and many contain Cypress trees or Bay trees, to which it was named. The rich soil has long been a favorite of farms for centuries.

The origin of the bays has long been a subject of controversy as to whether it was a meteoritic impact or extraterrestrial. Many researchers have formulated their own theories as to how they came to be here on this planet. I was surprised to find out more than 350 bibliographic entries and more than a century of investigations has been done related to their origins.

The number one theory was the formations were a direct result of a comet, which may have exploded and produced the depressions. This would explain why they were symmetrical in nature. Others supported the ideas the bays were caused during the great floods, either by marine or sub-aerial processes. They believed eddies, current and undertow created the depressions along with underground springs.

The theory that struck me was the hypotheses they were created by extraterrestrial origins. At first I thought it was some author's attempt to sell books, but as I dug deeper into their findings, I realized what they were saying made sense. What made them formulate their theories was found in the characteristics of the bays.

"Mathematically and physically, it doesn't add up," stated one professor.

"It's impossible and even improbable that meteors caused these depressions," was another researcher's opinion.

The studies showed no sub-aerial mechanisms could have produced the bays, because some bays are 346 to 260 feet above sea level. No marine terraces are known to be at elevations over 350 feet above sea level along the Atlantic Coastal Plain. This may have proved the dismissal of one theory, but the possibilities of meteors still seemed viable to me. So, why couldn't meteors create the bays, I thought as I continued the research.

The characteristics of the bays showed the southeastern portion of many bays are more pointed than the northwest end, and the northeast side bulges slightly more than the southwest side. The major axis dimensions vary from approximately 200 feet to seven miles, with only minor fluctuations or deviations from the systematic northwest-southeast orientation. The deepest depth was around 50 feet and offset to the southeast portion of the center. They all have an outer rim that varied in height from zero to 23 feet. The odd thing is, some overlap other bays without destroying the morphology of either depression. So, one bay could be completely contained in a large bay. Bays occur in linear arrays, in complex clusters of as many as fourteen bays, as scattered individuals, and in parallel groups that appear to be aligned.

My research was leading me more and more in a direction I wasn't truly prepared to go. What started out as a simple disappearance that I was sure related to perhaps drugs seemed to be a lot more complex. Before I realized the time, Clair came through the door and she was crying.

"What's wrong sweetheart?" I said, kissing her on the forehead.

"I got in a fight on the bus," she said through the tears.

"What were you fighting over?"

She told me a girl heard her talking on the bus about the loss of Lady and called her a name. Continuing, she stated the girl laughed at her because she was crying, and that's when Clair slapped her.

"Daddy, Mrs. Provost stopped the bus and she was mad at me." By now she was almost shaking. "She told me I would be suspended from riding the bus for a week."

The crisis for the moment took precedence over my research. Although I wanted to continue reading more information, Clair needed my attention and I devoted my time to her. Explaining fighting was not the correct method of handling her issues, she seemed to understand.

"But she made me mad, Daddy, when she called me a name."

Clair said she felt like I was disappointed in her and I reassured her that I wasn't, and told her how much I loved her. We sat outside on the deck and I helped her do her homework. She had more to do, because we had taken her out of school on Friday. We were almost finished with her last math problem when Janet stepped out on the deck.

"Hi,... Mommy, I got in trouble today," Clair blurted out to her mother and Janet wasn't surprised by the news.

"Yes, I know. Mrs. Provost called me and she explained what happened on the bus," Janet stated.

She wasn't pleased with Clair, but she seemed to understand. Janet told Clair that Mrs. Provost would continue to allow her to ride as long as she agreed to behave herself on the bus. Clair was relieved to hear the news and said she would from now on. We finished her homework while Janet took a shower. I felt like the family needed some excitement, so we went to Clair's favorite place for dinner. The pizza place had an arcade and we all played games for about two hours. Clair beat me in all the games that I played against her, but Janet and I got in a heated battle when we played a game of air hockey. Clair loved to see us compete, because she said we looked like kids. Janet was extremely good and it took all my skills to beat her by scoring the last point of the game.

"Okay, it's time to go," she said immediately after I scored.

"How about one more?" I suggested, followed by Clair saying the same thing.

"No, I've had enough, so let's go!" Janet said as she headed out of the restaurant.

Getting into the car, Clair and I could tell Janet was upset because she lost the game. As I backed out of the parking space, I looked at Clair. She was puffing her cheeks out at me and I started laughing aloud. This was what we would do whenever someone acted mad.

"Okay, what is so funny?" Janet spoke hastily, and I continued backing the vehicle, laughing.

"I said, what is so funny?" she yelled at us.

As I began pulling away, Clair joined in with the laughter and this truly did anger Janet. She turned abruptly in her seat and stared out the side of her window. I wasn't about to say anything, but Clair didn't feel quite the same way I did at that moment.

"Mom's blowed up like a bullfrog," Clair chimed out.

Hearing Clair, Janet couldn't contain her laughter either and we all started laughing aloud. This just encouraged Clair even more, and she made frog noises all the way back to the house. After a few minutes, we ignored her and Janet appeared to be over the resentment of her loss to me in the first place.

The next day, I continued with my research. I wanted to know more about the similarities of the bays. In my mind, I still considered the bays might have come from terrestrial causes like meteors, etc. ...It made good sense to me, seeing the locations, that a group of meteors hit the earth and formed these bays. This may have been the meteors that caused the demise of the dinosaurs, I thought to myself. By all accounts, these meteors struck the earth 10,000 to 15,000 years ago and it was a logical explanation. But it wasn't until I read the bays lacked the elevated structural rims associated with known meteorite impact craters, that I once again entertained the idea of other possibilities. A normal meteorite crater tended to be deep and round, whereas the bays are shallow ellipses.

Other possibilities mentioned were asteroids and comets. However, with all of the objects, the impact velocity and size would indicate the basic crater size and depth. The basic formula for calculating crater impact was documented by Baldwin in 1963. The results of his experiments showed the relationships of the impact and explosions. The size of a crater was directly proportional to the velocity, mass, and texture of the object.

For a Carolina Bay with a major axis of one mile and regarded as an impact crater, the expected depth should be approximately 1,000 feet, the rim height 159 feet and the rim width, 1,000 feet. The closest bay to this size is the Junkyard Bay located in Clarendon County, South Carolina. It is almost one mile in length along the major axis and the rim height is less than ten feet, whereas the expected rim height derived from Baldwin should be around 150 feet. This was a huge difference, so I got more information on other bays to see how they applied. Lake Waccamaw, not far from Whiteville, North Carolina, has a rim height of 23 feet. According to the formula, the rim would equal 200 feet. With all the bays I researched, the same factors held true. Every single bay I examined, the rim heights were over 50 times smaller than they should be according to Baldwin.

As if this wasn't enough data, I wanted to know what angle an object from space must have been traveling to create the distinct northwest-southeast orientation of the bays. Studying the projected paths, the azimuths for 12 different bays from Virginia to Georgia, I realized an object from space, such as a meteor shower, could not have struck the earth at the same time. Using the earth as a backdrop, I plotted the known trajectory paths. What I was expecting to see was a variation of paths, because the objects would have become deflected entering the earth's atmosphere. But as I plotted, I saw there was almost a straight line of trajectory, as if there had been no interference.

"There must be something wrong with my math," I considered and recalculated my figures. "This can't be correct," I spoke aloud, scratching the top of my head.

Each time I redid my calculations, they always showed the same results. The paths of every bay indicated that whatever created the Carolina Bays came from a straight trajectory path, and from all the research I'd found, this seemed impossible.

"How is it that I'm the only one who has come up with this theory?" I asked myself. Either I'm wrong, or everyone else just missed it! I considered.

Many researchers with scholar degrees have investigated the mysteries of the bays and nowhere in their findings had anyone documented my results. My background is that I'm a graduate of the University of North Carolina at Charlotte, with a Bachelor of Science in Business Administration as my major degree. I'd double majored in Criminal Justice and this was what got me started in the investigative field. My first job was working for a private investigator and I followed a cheating husband for two weeks. It was the excitement of the hunt for the truth which hooked me, and I've never wanted to do anything else.

I've always had a sixth sense that's led me in the right directions in the past, and now I was feeling my senses tingling. But I still couldn't believe my sampling of data was precise enough to come to a conclusive result. There had to be something I'd missed, and the only way to find out was to go back and visit the area again. This was not going to set well with Janet, and I knew a battle would take place once I told her my intentions.

Chapter 6

HOW WILL I KNOW THAT
YOU ARE OKAY

For the rest of the week, I continued doing as much research as I could on the Carolina Bays. The more information I was able to come across, the more I felt my data might be correct. Janet knew I was working on it and she was giving me the cold shoulder. Finally on Friday, I asked her out on a date. Janet started this dating game shortly after we got married. She said she always wanted to keep our relationship alive, and sometimes I would find notes or receive letters in the mail from her inviting me on a date. I must admit it has helped keep our romance alive for the past 15 years of marriage. When I was off on trips, I'd do the same by sending her a card with an invitation to meet me for dinner or a movie, and she enjoyed being asked as well.

On Friday morning, I sent Janet some flowers at work with a note attached. The note was simple and all it said was, *"A Man Who Adores and Loves You, Requests Your Presence For Dinner At Capital Grille—Time 8:00 p.m."* This was Janet's favorite restaurant and I knew I needed to use all my charm to convince her of the next trip I was about to take. Shortly after lunch, she called and thanked me for the flowers.

"The flowers are beautiful," she told me over the phone.

"They don't come close to your beauty," I responded, still trying to butter her up.

"And dinner sounds wonderful. I'll be home as soon as I can," she said as we hung up.

Clair spent the night with one of her neighborhood friends. I'd cleared it with the parents, so I knew Janet and I would have an evening alone, and I was looking forward to it. We made the trip to Charlotte as soon as she got home and was ready. She looked as beautiful as I'd seen her in a while. Dressed in a long red satin dress that conformed to her body, she truly was the woman of my dreams. I'd been on many trips and had seen many beautiful women, but none equaled Janet in my eyes. Walking into the restaurant, I couldn't help but notice many of the men watching Janet being escorted to our table, and that made me even prouder that she was my wife.

The dinner was perfect, and we laughed while enjoying the fine wine with the juicy steak and desserts. Several times Janet leaned over, kissing me while thanking me for the lovely evening.

"The pleasure of this evening is all mine," I said to her while pouring more wine.

"No, this is just the beginning of a pleasurable evening," Janet spoke as she gave me a naughty smile and I knew what she was thinking.

The trip home seemed longer, but I didn't mind, because Janet sat next to me like she did when we first dated. She laid her head on my shoulder and nodded off to sleep. At that moment, nothing in the world was more important to me.

Because the dinner and ride home took longer than I'd expected, it was after midnight when we arrived. It had been a long day, but I was not finished romancing my wife. Janet went into the bedroom to change her clothes and I placed a bottle of *Chateau Margaux*, with two wine glasses, next to the spa on the deck. I'd removed my clothes and was sitting in the spa awaiting her arrival. When I looked around to the door leading onto the deck, Janet walked through only covered by a towel. Just prior to stepping into the spa, she dropped the towel, exposing herself to me, and I gracefully assisted her as she settled down nestled in my arms. We enjoyed the warm rushing bubbles from the water jets and I held her as if it was going to be the last time. Janet reached for the controls of the jets and turned them off, stating she wanted to enjoy the peacefulness of the night and the beauty of the lake. The spa was shielded from view of the neighbors, but because Clair could sneak up on us at any time, it'd been a while since we'd been naked in it. The sounds of the night enhanced the moment even more, and Janet repositioned herself so that she was sitting in my lap facing me. She put her arms around my neck and slowly placed her lips upon mine. Her lips were soft and wet from the water, and she knew how to make every desire within me rise. Her kissing became more intense as she slowly began moving her body against mine, and I could feel her breasts next to my chest. I reached out to caress her and she pulled my hands down to my side, continuing her passionate kissing. Janet knew I liked to be in control when we made love, but she was directing this show and all she wanted me to do was enjoy the ride. At first I found it difficult to keep my hands off her wonderful body, but whenever I made a move, she pulled me away.

The moon was just bright enough that I could see the light twinkling off her wet body. She had a body most men would kill for, and I was the one who was enjoying all her pleasures. She continued her assault until she knew I could no longer hold myself back from the passion boiling inside of me. As if she was directing a movie scene, she placed me in such a way that allowed her to position herself so we could make love.

Because the evening was so wonderful, I'd decided not to say anything to Janet about my plans. The following morning, I fixed her a wonderful breakfast on the deck for us to enjoy. I knew Clair would not be home until the afternoon, so this would be the time to tell her.

"Thank you for a wonderful evening," she said, greeting me as she sat down to breakfast.

"You are very welcome, and I was the one who experienced the pleasurable evening," I said, giving her a kiss.

The conversation during breakfast was going well and we talked about Clair and our work. Janet told me how the school board was changing some policies and I pretended to listen, but my mind was on the speech I was about to give.

"Janet, there is something that I need to discuss with you," I said, trying not to alarm her.

"Don't do this again!" she said with some concern in her voice. "Don't you tell me that you are going back to that lake again!"

"Baby, I've got to go," I said, and she stood up and walked back into the house without saying a word.

I sat there a while staring at the lake and a few sailboats taking advantage of the morning breezes. Janet came back and sat down beside me, and I could see she wasn't happy.

"Why do you have to go back there?" she questioned. "Don't you have enough material to write your article?"

Explaining about the research I'd done during the week, I told her of my theories that the bays were created by extraterrestrial origin and I needed further information. She looked at me like I was insane, but I continued to tell her how I'd come to my conclusions and she appeared to understand what I was saying. She'd heard my theories before from some of the other investigations I'd been on, so I guess hearing me talk about the possibilities of extraterrestrials didn't surprise her very much. As I talked, Janet just stared at me and I knew she must have considered calling the paddy wagon to come get me. Then I took her by the hand and led her into the study, showing her the calculation of the trajectories that must have created the bays. Janet was a math teacher and she began her own calculations using the data I'd collected. When she'd finished, there was a blank look on her face.

"Rick, if your data is correct, then you are right. Are you sure of your data?" she asked, and that's when I used the opportunity to tell her that was why I needed to go back and do more research.

For the first time, Janet seemed to understand why I needed to go. She admitted this story could be the biggest story I'd ever written if all the facts were correct. We continued going over the data and with her help, I was able to get a better representation for the projected paths of the entity that may have created the bays. Although the paths were not in a straight line, they definitely came from the same source.

The plot thickened with each new detail I found related to the bays. The history of the bays added further to the puzzle. Based on the timeline data, they were not formed at the same time. A single meteorite shower could not explain the fact that there are ghost bays that overlap and contained within other bays. These ghost bays generally have the same rim heights as those bays that were impinged upon. The origin of the bays has been a long debate, but more scholars agree they were formed 10,000 to 15,000 years ago. However, several researchers have dated many of the bays over 20,000 years old, based on the radiocarbon tests conducted on the artifacts and organic materials that were found preserved in the sandy matrix of the bays.

My research shifted to study one of the largest of the bay lakes and that was Lake Waccamaw. Not far from the town of Whiteville, North Carolina, it too was the typical elongated oval shape oriented with its axis northwest to southeast. The lake was dated to be somewhere around 15,000 years and originally thought to be created from a meteor, but did not display the characteristics associated with a meteor crater. Instead, its highest rim height is 23 feet and it has a flat bottom of approximately one foot of mud on top of two feet of dark sandy silk. The water has an unusually high pH and alkalinity levels. There are several reasons given, stating the cypress trees contributed to the intense scavenging of phosphorus sediments and the human inputs of phosphorus or nitrogen.

Comparing this information with the other bays, I found about every 500 years, the major bay lakes have been changing in shape. While most have decreased in size in the last 500 years, Lakes Waccamaw, Singletary, White Lake and a few others, have expanded. This did not alarm me in the beginning, but the historical data showed they changed at the same rates. It's normal for rivers and lakes to shift shores and depths over the years through the erosion processes, but not in a consistent manner as the data suggested.

The final finding in my research that didn't make any sense was none of the lakes had any evidence of fragments from meteors, asteroids or comets to indicate a strike. This factor alone made it hard for me to understand how anyone would believe they were impact craters created by meteor showers.

Now that Janet understood I needed further information that would require me to go back and visit the bays, she was less defensive with me. She knew I was on to something and wanted to know more as well. The day before I was leaving on my trip, she took off from work and we grilled steaks on the deck. We knew I might be gone for a while and she didn't want to talk about it all through dinner. Instead, we sat almost saying not a word to each other and I could not stand the tension any longer.

"Janet, we need to discuss this before I leave," I finally spoke.

"What's there to talk about, Rick? We both know you need to go, but that doesn't mean I have to like it," she said, and I saw a tear fall from her cheek. Why can't you wait until school is out in a month and Clair and I will go with you," she pleaded.

I tried to explain that I would be traveling to the different bays and might be spending many hours doing my investigations. "Janet, I really need to know that you and Clair are all right so I can devote my time to where it needs to be," I explained to her.

"But…what about me?" Janet screamed. "How will I know that you are okay?" she said and openly started to cry.

We talked for the rest of the evening and I reassured her that I'd call whenever I could, but she still was concerned for my safety. We knew there was potential danger associated with investigating this story, and all I could do was tell her I'd be careful.

Chapter 7

HE SURE DID SCARE
THE HELL OUT OF ME!

Once Janet and Clair left in the morning, I packed enough clothes to stay for two weeks. I didn't figure I'd be gone longer than that and I wanted to be home in time to go to Clair's end of school graduation to the next level. With all my travels, I'd managed to make it home to attend all of her graduations and I wasn't planning to miss this one. Before driving off, I wrote Janet a note and slipped it under her pillow.

> *Janet, I just wanted to let you know that you and Clair mean more to me than anything in this world. I love you with all my heart and will miss you while I'm away. Although I know it's not me, look in the closet underneath the towel. I love you, Rick.*

In the closet, I'd placed a large teddy bear that had his arms open and written on his chest was, "*My heart belongs only to you.*" Just below the inscription, I'd attached another note that read, "*Sleep with him and pretend it is me, and he will keep you company until I return.*" Janet loved for me to give her surprises, so I was hoping this would cheer her up once she found it later that evening.

My investigations would lead me back to Singletary Lake, but I wanted to study the layouts of other bays for myself to get a better understanding of their origins. I'd read a lot about Lake Waccamaw, and this lake sparked interest due to the small differences in its water content and size. It wasn't far from Lake Singletary and straight down Highway 74 from Charlotte just past Whiteville, North Carolina. According to the lake's data based on its size, the rim walls should have been close to 200 feet if a meteor had created the crater. The highest point of the rim is 23 feet and that is a huge variance factor. So, I just wanted to get a good look at the lake and its surroundings.

My first stop was at the bed and breakfast inn I'd reserved for the night. I wanted to check in and talk with the owners to find out their perspective on the lake. Being locals, I knew they must know some of the folk lore that may have been passed down through the years.

The inn was nestled among some trees next to the lake. As I drove up the long driveway, I could see the lake and it was large. It displayed the same tea-colored water that Lake Singletary had, and even looked similar. Extending out onto the lake was a long pier that was covered at the end. There were several boats tied up and I hoped I could find time to enjoy an evening sailing. Next to the pier, I could see a large, Atlantic white cedar tree standing tall in the water with its branches hanging over the pier shadowing it from the sun. Stopping in front of the inn, it looked like some of the Colonial Inns I'd seen in magazines. In my room was antique furniture with a Victorian working hand-pump that supplied water for the dry sink. Out my window was a beautiful view of the lake, and I couldn't help thinking that I wished Janet was there with me to enjoy the atmosphere.

After settling in, I went to the office where I met John Mallard. John owned the inn and he told me it'd been in his family for centuries. His grandfather was the one who'd turned it into a bed and breakfast house in 1934. He was very friendly and seemed willing to talk about the local history, so we sat on the front porch in some rocking chairs. John was knowledgeable on the history of the lake and from what he was telling me, it could apply to any of the bays in the area.

"You know before the white man came to this lake, the Indians lived on the eastern shore at a place called, Indian Mounds. We still call it that to this day. On one of the mounds, nothing will grow," he stated while pointing to the right. "Did you know that Indian Chieftain, Osceola, was born here at Lake Waccamaw?" he said with excitement, and I had to admit that I had heard of the name, but wasn't too sure who he was.

"Well, he became a great warrior who led the Seminoles of Florida in their war against the whites. Even the government has a heroic statue of Osceola on exhibition in the City of Washington."

John continued for hours talking about how Charles the Second of England originally granted the land to one of the Lord Proprietors to settle in the new world. In the 1700's, John Powell purchased the land and brought cattle in from Virginia, and some of his descendants still owned property in the area. In 1852, Josiah Maultsby was the first to begin a township, calling it Flemington. But in 1890, the name was changed to Lake Waccamaw.

"My great-grandfather bought this 35 acres of land in 1895 and built one section of this inn," he said, pointing at a section.

"It was my grandfather that added the remaining part that you see today."

John talked until the sun began to set and from our advantage on the porch, it was beautiful and almost directly across the lake. His wife, Betty, came out to invite us to supper, and I was ready to eat. Some other guests joined us, and Betty served a full course meal followed by freshly baked peach cobbler with ice cream.

Following the meal, several of us returned to the rocking chairs to enjoy the wonderful view of the lake. The stars were visible and the moon was about at quarter lumination. John seemed eager to tell more stories of the lake and this was exactly why I was there, so I encouraged him by asking, "Are there any stories of strange disappearances?"

He looked at me with a puzzled look and for a moment, I thought I'd said something I shouldn't have. However, he just stared out at the lake for a while and finally spoke. "There are many stories of strange things that have happened on this lake over the years. This ain't the only lake around here that's had something go on and no one knew what happened," he said, still staring out at the lake. "My father told me once of the lake swallowing boatloads of people and there weren't no traces ever found of them."

John's voice almost began to quiver as he told the story, and I could see there was something about the lake he feared. But as quickly as he began telling stories, he stopped and excused himself, saying he had some chores to do. One older lady named Mabel, seemed a little concerned about John's tales, but I reassured her that those types of stories were normal for lakes. She smiled at me and said, "They may be normal, but he sure did scare the hell out of me!"

The hours slipped into the night and I didn't want to go snooping around in the dark in areas that I was not familiar with, so I retired to my room to begin a fresh start in the morning. Before turning out the lights, I called Janet to let her know I was doing fine and tell her how much I was missing her. She had settled down for the night and by talking to her I could tell she was upset about something. When I questioned her, she said she felt sorry for the way she had acted the night before I left. Janet's heart is as big as the world, and she sometimes takes thing too seriously. I told her of the place and its beauty, while describing the sunset earlier. Before we hung up, I agreed to bring her back for a romantic weekend. She felt better and wished me a safe adventure the following day.

The next morning I awoke to the aroma of bacon filling the inn. I quickly showered and got ready for the day's events. Betty saw me as I loaded up a few things in the car, and asked me to join them for breakfast. After smelling her cooking for the last 30 minutes, I was ready to eat. Once again, she put out a great meal and I thanked her as I left.

I didn't drive very far before I saw a small sign directing me to Indian Mound that John had talked about. The curiosity from his stories made me want to see for myself the phenomenon of the mound that would not grow anything on it. As I approached the small village of various shops, I could see a few people walking around. One placed looked similar to a gift shop, and I asked the clerk where this mound was located that could not grow anything. She politely smiled and pointed to a spot about 200 yards further down the lake. Looking at the bare area, it just seemed to me as if it could have been a tourist attraction, because it appeared man-made. Next to the mound was a plaque telling the history of how the early Indians believed it was the devil's mound. Again, I thought this could pass as a tourist trap and wondered whether I was wasting my time.

Walking back to the car, I saw an old man sitting on a block of wood carving animal figures. Figuring I didn't have anything to lose but time, I went over and sat down next to him for some conversation. At first he was hesitant to talk with me, but when I appeared interested in his carvings, he opened up. The piece he was working on was a wood duck that he said did not live around there anymore. Wanting to know more about the duck, he said the lake was once full of these ducks and over the last ten years, they had all disappeared. He was attempting to carve a replica of every animal that had vanished from the lake. I asked how many carvings had he done and he pointed to a small building. I could see many different animal types within it. I didn't know how many I saw, but I knew there were more than 20 different species.

"Sir, I assume those are from the beginning of the lake's history," I said and he nodded his head no.

"I've done all those animals in the last fives years. Each one has disappeared in the last ten years just like this duck," he said back to me.

"Why have they all disappeared and where have they gone?" I questioned him.

"The lake swallowed them," he said as he stared at the lake in the same manner that John had done the night before.

Is everyone here strange? I thought to myself.

John gave me the same explanation about the missing boatload of people. I was even more convinced that this was a folklore created by the locals for stupid tourists. Excusing myself, I headed back to the car, but not before looking at the carvings. Seeing them, I just knew I was right, because there were squirrels, rabbits, bobcats, and several kinds of birds. Shaking my head as I drove away from the village, I felt like a fool who had wasted his time.

The map showed a road encircling the lake. I continued driving until I noticed a small patch of thick woods hiding the view of the lake. Stopping, I grabbed a stick from the trunk of the car and some bags in case I found evidence that I wanted to save. The woods were covered with small brush making it hard to navigate, but I made my way toward the lake beating down the brush before me. My concern was the possibility of poisonous snakes hidden in the many branches and leaves along the path I was taking. The trees were thick and shaded the sun, which made it difficult to see where I was walking. When I'd traveled almost halfway through the woods, I stopped, because something caught my attention.

"Who's there?" I hollered. "Is anyone there?" I yelled again, but I got no reply.

Then the hairs on the back of my neck stood up as a dark shadow of something quickly moved to the right of me and I just knew I was being attacked by a bear. Turning sharply with my stick ready to defend myself, the object disappeared. Without warning, from my left side something moved once again at a fast pace. I swung the stick around to strike whatever it was that was lunging at me. My weapon did not hit its mark. I was knocked to the ground with a strong force of wind, and I knew I was done for. Too terrified to even scream for help, I lay on the ground motionless, hoping the attacker would not come back to finish the job.

Remaining still, I could feel something warm flowing across my left shoulder and neck. I didn't want to move, so I continued to lay in the thick forest floor on my right side. All of a sudden, the hair stood up again and I could feel warmth as if something was breathing on my neck. There wasn't any sound, but I could feel the breath of something, even though I couldn't see what it was. My mind was full of possible scenarios, but Janet popped into my head and I knew she was going to be upset with me if I died after she told me to be careful.

Even during a time of death, all I'm thinking about is how upset Janet will be, I thought, and almost found myself laughing about it.

The hot air became more intense. I figured it was ready to end the standoff and enjoy me for its dinner. So with nothing to lose, I quickly swung the stick upward hoping to get the first hit and maybe get lucky enough to stick it in the eye, or at least scare it away. Swinging as hard as I could from my position on the ground, I wasn't able to make contact. As I turned toward the predator, to my amazement, nothing was there.

"Where did it go?" I questioned myself and stood up prepared for a second attack.

My heart was pounding hard and sweat was pouring off my forehead into my eyes. The stick rose, and I waited for another sign that it was attacking again. Knowing I'd been attacked from behind, I constantly scanned the area all around me. For more than ten minutes, I held my stance, hoping I would be able to swing if it attacked, all the while listening to any movement in the forest. That's when I had another eerie feeling come over me again.

Where's the noise? I thought to myself. "It's just like the forest around Lake Singletary," I found myself saying aloud.

There weren't any normal noises of the forest. In fact, there wasn't any noise at all. Even the trees were silent from the wind that normally blows in the tops of them. I continued to stand there vigilantly for a while longer, and all of a sudden I started hearing the sounds of birds chirping and crickets. It was as if someone turned on a sound machine full of forest noises. Whatever it was that had attacked me appeared to be gone and I made my way back out of the forest as fast as I could go through the thicket.

Exiting the forest near my car, the sunshine was bright and almost blinding. It was hard for me to understand how just a few seconds earlier, the forest was dark to the point it was difficult to see. Now, I was back out and felt lucky to be alive.

Something attacked me in there and I know I wasn't dreaming, I thought to myself.

About that time, I started wiping off some sweat from my neck and I saw blood on my hands. I'd felt some pain on my left shoulder, but considered it was from the fall. Taking a better look at the back of my shoulder through the car mirror, it looked like a lion, or perhaps a bear, had clawed me. The back of my shirt had blood on it and I knew it wasn't from the fall.

Trying not to get blood on my seat, I drove back to the inn to clean myself up. The pain was becoming more intense, but I didn't want to go to the hospital. Entering the inn, I tried to hide the fact I was injured, but Betty saw me.

"Mr. Parker, what happened to you?" she screamed and came toward me. "John! John! Come here quickly," she again yelled, and I tried to tell her that I was fine.

John came running in from the back of the inn and immediately escorted me into a small room in the back. Betty made me pull off my shirt and she almost screamed seeing the damage to my shoulder.

"We need to get him to a doctor!" she gasped.

"No! No doctor, please!" I begged her.

"You have some deep cuts that may need stitching," she replied, and John agreed.

Knowing I didn't want to go anywhere, John called his friend and physician, Doctor Raymond Thomas. John said he only lived a few miles down the road and he would be there shortly. I didn't want him to have to leave his office for me, but John informed me that he was retired and loved to come to the inn to visit anyway.

Within a few minutes, Doctor Thomas was there and he began to examine my injuries. He poured alcohol to clean the wounds and for a moment, I thought I saw Jesus. That hurt more than the injuries themselves.

"Now you've got to be still, young man," he instructed me. "You've got some bad scratches here and I need to clean them out," he said as he poured more alcohol.

Even though the burning of the alcohol was painful, I felt better hearing him say they were scratches. He began questioning as to what animal did that to me. Doctor Thomas stated he'd treated many wounds over the years, but none matched the pattern of the marks on my back. He pointed to them and explained to John how they were different.

"Remember when that camper was attacked by the bear back in 1987?" he asked, moving his hand across my shoulder. "The wounds of a bear would look like this." He again moved his hands in a certain direction. "Now a panther or bobcat would make these kind of tears on a body," he said as he pulled sideways on my back.

For a moment, I felt as if I was a lab rat in a medical experiment and Doctor Thomas was instructing John. With each explanation, he would dramatize the method of attack used by animal.

"This ain't like any animal I've ever seen," he again said, and asked if he could take pictures of my back.

Betty got an old Polaroid camera she had and started snapping shots of my back. I felt uncomfortable having my back on display, but I was thankful he was giving me medical attention. After a few more pictures, he stuck a needle in my shoulder to numb it for the stitches he soon applied. During all of this, John called the sheriff's department. It wasn't long before the same deputy I'd seen at Lake Singletary walked through the door.

"Well Sir, we meet again," he said as he greeted me, and Doctor Thomas and John appeared puzzled.

"Do you know Mr. Parker, Jeff?" asked John.

"Yeah, I met him a few weeks a go at Lake Singletary snooping in the woods."

"What were you doing wandering in some place you shouldn't be?" he asked and laughed.

"Just take a look at his back!" Doctor Thomas spoke.

The deputy looked and he wanted to know about the injury. I wasn't too sure I wanted to explain the truth, so I told him I was walking through the forest and an animal attacked me from behind. When he asked what kind of animal, I told him it happened so quickly that I wasn't able to see it.

"Well from the looks of it, you're lucky he didn't have you for supper," he said, and everyone in the room agreed.

After the doctor had finished sewing me up, we all sat on the front porch. The deputy took a report on the incident and said he would take a look around for any suspicious animals. I thanked him and Doctor Thomas for their help, and offered to buy them dinner. Betty had left us earlier and was cooking another wonderful dinner. I didn't have any problem talking Doctor Thomas into staying, but Deputy Hawthorne said he had to go.

Chapter 8

I FELT THE HOT BREATH OF SOMETHING ON MY NECK

That evening while in my room, I went over in my mind what had happened earlier in the day. It was obvious that something attacked me in that forest. The wounds on my back were created by something, but I never saw what it was. Using my notepad, I wrote down the known animals in the area, and I remembered what Doctor Thomas had said about the kind of wounds I had.

Why didn't I see it, if an animal was responsible? I thought to myself as I took notes. But I never saw anything. What was breathing on my neck? I again wondered. Without realizing it, I was shaking.

The fears I'd experienced in the forest made me question whether or not an animal had actually attacked me. The wind was blowing rather strong, and maybe it was possible it blew me over and I injured myself on a fallen branch. Being an investigator, I knew I had to review all the possibilities, and the last explanation made more sense. The more I thought about it, the more it sounded like something from a horror movie and I started laughing, realizing how stupid I must have sounded telling this story. Examining the wounds through the bathroom mirror, the telephone suddenly rang and I jumped from the sound.

"Hello!" I spoke as I picked up the receiver. It was Janet.

"Hi, Honey! How was your day chasing big foot?" she said, laughing. For a second, I thought someone had told her of my situation.

"Well, he's still safe," I replied, and gave a little smirk over the telephone.

We talked for a while and I never mentioned the fact that I'd been hurt. She was worried enough. I wasn't about to add to it by telling her I'd been attacked by a mysterious monster in the woods. Instead we talked about the inn and when she asked what I'd found out during my adventures that day, I just told her some folklore.

It had been my intention to move on to the next lake the following day, but I asked John and Betty if it was all right to stay an extra day and they seemed pleased. Morning found me very sore and it was hard to get my shirt over the reddening wounds on my shoulder, but I managed. During breakfast, Betty questioned me on what I planned to do that day, and I told her I was going exploring.

"You need to stay here and relax!" she said harshly, yet caring.

"John, make him stay here so I can take care of his wounds," she spoke to her husband.

"Betty, he's a grown man and if he wants to go exploring, then let him go," he snapped back at her, and she didn't appear to appreciate his words.

Making my excuses to depart, I made my way back to the forest where I'd been the day before. Standing and looking into the darkness of the woods gave me an eerie feeling as if I was being watched. I'd brought with me a recorder to place in the woods to see if I could capture any usual sounds. With stick in hand, I entered at the same place I had started the previous day. Knowing how dark the forest was the last time I was here, I scanned the area with my flashlight as I slowly walked through the brush.

I wasn't far from the spot where I'd been attacked when the forest noises became silent. The recorder was on and I sat it down on a log next to me. Turning to head out of the woods, I felt the hot breath of something on my neck from behind, and I froze in place. From the direction of the breath, I knew it had to be something large, because the air was coming down my neck from the top of my head. The only thing I could think of which would be that big was a bear possibly standing on two feet. But I could not hear any grunts or noises coming from it, only the feel of the hot air down my neck. I didn't move a muscle and the breath shifted from side to side, then it quickly moved away from me. The wind pressure from its departure was strong and almost knocked me over. Reaching for my recorder, I snatched it up and ran as fast as I could in hopes of exiting the woods without getting caught. Ahead I could see the car through the opening, and I made my way as fast as my feet would carry me. Then without warning, something hit me from the left side and I flew 20 feet, tossing the recorder and stick into the air. The impact was so strong I was having trouble catching my breath. It knocked the wind out of me and I was gasping as hard as I could to breathe.

Whatever had struck me would surely finish me off now, I thought as I lay there in pain.

"Mr. Parker! Mr. Parker, are you in there?" I heard, and I thought I was dreaming. "Mr. Parker, this is Deputy Hawthorne. Are you all right?"

Still not being able to holler to let him know my location, I started making noise by kicking the brush around me. The strange thing was, I heard the forest noises again. There was a lot of comfort hearing the birds singing in the trees, and I didn't feel threatened anymore. Deputy Hawthorne found me and helped me to my vehicle. He wanted to call for an ambulance, but I pleaded for him not to call. Instead, I asked him to find my recorder and within a few minutes, he walked up to me carrying the broken case.

"What is this?" he questioned me. "And what happened to you?" he said while pointing at my left side.

Looking down, I saw my side was bloody, so I pulled up my shirt to revel scratches similar to the ones on my shoulder. They didn't appear to be as deep, but they looked like an animal had done this to me. My ribs were hurting and I knew why after seeing the damage to my left side.

"Mr. Parker, I think you need to come with me to the station for a complete report and I'll have someone look at your injuries," he insisted, and I agreed to follow him.

The deputy took the remains of the recorder with him and the trip took about 30 minutes. The soreness settled in my side and I was having difficulty catching my breath as I got out of the car. Deputy Hawthorne noticed my predicament and called for help, and within a few seconds, several other officers assisted me into the building. The EMT units shared the building at the police station, so I was taken to their area for medical attention.

"Man! What got a hold of you?" one of the medical attendants questioned after pulling off my shirt.

"I really don't know. Some sort of animal, I assume," was my reply.

"Well I ain't seen none of the animals around here do anything like this before," he stated. "What did it look like?"

"I don't know, because I didn't see it," was my answer.

Deputy Hawthorne was standing next to me and wanted to know how something could attack me in a way to cause the injuries it did and not be able to see my attacker. He appeared to be a little angered and also questioned why I went back to the place knowing a wild animal had already attacked me.

"I told you I would get back to you after I'd done some investigating, so what were you doing there?" he forcefully asked.

The evidence of my injuries told him something had happened to me, but I wasn't too sure he'd believed my story the second time. I figured I'd tell him why I was there in the first place.

Explaining I was an investigative writer who was doing a story on the disappearances of the family at Lake Singletary, he wanted to know why I was at Lake Waccamaw. I explained about my research and that I was only there to get a first hand look at another one of the Carolina Bays. He gave me a puzzled look and I could tell he didn't have a clue as to what I was referring to when I mentioned Carolina Bays. One of the other medical personnel in the room said they had heard of them, but weren't sure what they were. While I was being wrapped with a bandage around my ribs, I started telling them of the mysteries associated with the Bays.

"Are you suggesting there are monsters around here?" I heard, and someone started laughing at my expense.

"Yeah, that's why my wife's uncle ain't come home yet! One of them monsters ate him up and all this time we thought it was another woman," I heard, and even Deputy Hawthorne joined in with the laughter.

"Maybe that woman had long teeth and claws," one more person stated, and the laughter continued.

"Well Hell, they all have long teeth and claws," the first man spoke between the laughter, followed by the sound of his wife, who also was a medical EMT, slapping him.

Everyone in the room was laughing and several other deputies entered the room wanting to know what was so funny. When they were told the joke, all but one of them joined in and made some commits of their own. This one deputy didn't smile at all and seemed to stare at me as if he knew what I was talking about. Finishing my medical treatment, I thanked them and headed back to the police section of the building. Deputy Hawthorne called to the deputy that had not joined in the humor, for him to take care of me.

"Hey Jack, this is your kind of story, so why don't you get his report," he stated, directing me toward an area of the room, and I thanked him for rescuing me in the woods.

"Just stay out of there until we kill that animal," he sternly stated without a smile as he departed through an open door.

"I'm Deputy Jack Wilson and would you please follow me, Sir?" he politely asked and I walked closely behind him.

In a small room that I knew was an interrogation area, we sat down and he started asking me questions about my accident. I went over the same details I'd told earlier and I figured he too, would think I was crazy or humorous. Not one time during the questioning did he smile or make any remarks to my answers. For the first time, I felt like someone understood what I was talking about, so I started asking him questions.

"Deputy Wilson, you do not appear alarmed by my statements. I sense that you know what I'm talking about,... correct?" I asked and he didn't respond. "You don't think I'm crazy, do you?"

Deputy Wilson continued writing and I could see he wasn't comfortable with my questioning, so I ended my probing. When we'd finished with the report, Deputy Wilson informed me that the police department would do an investigation and asked me not to return to that area. This sounded as if he was giving me the standard speech that all victims receive after a statement.

Leaving the police station, I returned to the inn, hoping to get some rest. John and Betty met me as I drove up, and it was obvious they had heard what happened to me. Doctor Thomas was sitting on the porch and I felt like I was going to be placed in a police line-up for identification. Seeing I was sore, John helped me to the porch and sat me next to Doctor Thomas.

"Okay, Rick,... tell us what really happened to you," Doctor Thomas questioned.

The story was getting old having repeated it several times, and I wasn't in the mood to revisit it. I just wanted to go to my room and get some rest.

"I got attacked by a bear and that's all there is to it!" I snapped and started getting up from my seat.

"There ain't no bears big enough to do the damage I've seen," the doctor replied and reached for my shirt. Before I could stop him, he pulled it up revealing my bandages.

He pleaded to have a look at my side, but I didn't want him to touch me, because I was sore. John and Betty also begged for me to allow him to see my injuries.

"Rick, Ray knows what he's doing, so let him take a look," John said as he grabbed my arm to stable me as I stood up.

At this point, I figured it was easier to let him examine me, so I pulled up my shirt exposing my left side to him. He gently removed the bandage and I heard him almost gasp as he looked at my wounds.

"Mr. Parker, this is not from a bear," he said to me. "Whatever caused these wounds did the same damage to your shoulder, because it follows the same patterns. I've never seen marks like the ones you have and I'm a little concerned."

After completing his task, Doctor Thomas said he wanted to call a good friend of his at North Carolina State University. He explained she was an Associate Professor who taught Veterinary Medicine at the university. He stated he was the one who got her into medicine and had remained good friends with her, so he wanted her to take a look at my wounds.

"Marsha Johnson is one of the best in the country for solving animal related attacks," he said, bragging on her abilities.

"She's been called in on a lot of cases, and her specialty is identifying the species and defining the strategies for ameliorating problems."

The thought of more people probing me didn't appeal to me, and I told Doctor Thomas that I really didn't want him to call his friend. He asked to take some pictures of the wounds and I agreed, hoping this would pacify him. Once the pictures were taken, I went to my room to get some rest. When I didn't show up for dinner, Betty came to my room and she'd fixed a plate of southern fried chicken and mashed potatoes. Thanking her for the hospitality, I told her that I'd be checking out in the morning and she was concerned. She asked if I was going home and I informed her that I would be, even though I knew I wasn't. My plans were to go back to Lake Single-tary for a few days to recuperate and reflect on the recent occurrences. But Betty didn't need to know of my plans, as she seemed happy knowing I would be going home to Janet.

Chapter 9

IT JUST DOESN'T MAKE SENSE

The morning sun was bright as I awoke the next day. I hadn't realized how tired I was, because I slept for over 12 hours. Luckily, I wasn't supposed to call Janet, so I knew she wouldn't be upset if she didn't hear from me. Gathering my things, I rolled my suitcase out of the room to my car. The ribs were sore and that made it difficult for me to pick up my bags to load them into the trunk. John was doing some yard work and noticed my dilemma.

"Here, let me help you with that," he said as he placed my bags in the car for me.

"Thank you, John," I replied.

"Well, we hate to see you leave us and we hope your misadventures don't keep you from coming back," he said while shaking my hand.

"John, you and Betty have been good to me and I thank you for your warm hospitality. I plan to bring my wife and daughter back here real soon," I said.

He wished me a safe trip back home and as I drove down the long driveway, I could see him and Betty waving goodbye. Although the stay was marred by injuries, staying at the inn was wonderful, and I knew I'd be coming back with Janet soon.

The night before, I'd made arrangements to stay at the cottage Janet and I stayed at the last time we visited White Lake. It was close to where I wanted to be, and I knew it would be a private area. Since I'd stayed there before, the key to the place was under a rock next to the picnic table. This was the arrangement the owner and I made, because he was going out of town.

Inside the cottage, I found a note from the owner that said I needed to call 555-6745. I had no idea to whom the number belonged, but assumed it was the place the owner was going. Since I was comfortable and did not have any problems with the place, I didn't see a need to call. Instead, I put away my things and walked down to the lake. Sitting on the bench made me miss Janet and I wanted her to be there with me at that moment. Looking at the end of the pier and remembering the night she and I made love made me homesick. But I was there on a mission and I knew I needed to focus my energies, so I started thinking about that forest at Lake Waccamaw.

What attacked me and how could I not see anything? I pondered over and over. It just doesn't make sense that I sustained the type of wounds I had on my body without seeing my attacker.

The more I thought about it, the more puzzled I became. The first time I could believe a strong gust of wind knocked me to the ground, but not a second time.

"And what was breathing on my neck?" I spoke aloud. "There was something there and I know it!"

For dinner, I fixed a sandwich and drank a cold beer I'd placed in the freezer earlier. I usually do not drink alcohol, but I felt the need to have a few beers to ease my sore body. My nerves were on end thinking of my brush with death, and I wanted to calm down and relax before calling Janet.

"Hello, dear," I said when she answered the phone, "and how was your day?"

"I'm fine and you sound like you are doing pretty well yourself," she answered. "Have you been drinking?"

Janet always could tell when I've had a few and even though I tried to hide it, I knew I'd been busted. So, I said the first thing to come to my mind. "Why yes I have, sweetie," I replied. "Me and some of the locals had dinner and I guess I drank a few more than I should have," I admitted, trying to justify my situation.

She knew it wasn't uncommon for me to socialize with people when I was doing an investigation. That was one of the techniques I used to get information and she was fully aware of it.

"Did you drink and drive, Rick?" she asked, and I assured her that I had not driven.

"Are you still at the inn?" was her next question.

Explaining I'd completed my investigation at Lake Waccamaw, I told her I was at the cottage and wished she was there with me. This tactic seemed to work, because she stopped asking me questions and began telling me how much she missed me and wanted to be there as well. We continued talking for about 10 minutes more and the last thing she told me was to be careful. Still not telling her of my injuries, I promised I wouldn't do anything stupid. In my mind, I had not done anything stupid, only a stupid thing happened to me.

Once I hung up the phone with Janet, I remembered the tape recorder I had taken with me into the woods. The recorder itself was broken, but I was hoping the cassette tape would have information and still be functional. My first thought was the recorder must have struck a tree when I went flying through the air. However, looking at the pieces, there were not any signs of tree bark or marks that I would expect to see. Instead, it looked like the machine had just blown apart from within. The screws holding the case were stripped as if they'd been forced out. Impact with a tree could not have caused this, so I wondered how the damage occurred. Pulling the tape out of the unit, the case was broken, but it looked like I could salvage it with a little glue. In my tool kit I always carried with me were the necessary items required, so I fixed the cassette.

In the cottage was a stereo system with a cassette player, so I inserted the tape to see if it had picked up any sounds. Listening carefully, I heard all the normal sounds of the forest that I would expect to hear. The clarity was good enough to allow me to hear the sound of my feet as I stepped through the forest crunching leaves and branches. The birds were singing and I even made out some other animals in the background. I had not realized when I entered the forest how much the wind was blowing, but the recorder easily picked up the wind whipping through the tree branches. Also on the recorder, was me mumbling as I walked, and I didn't remember saying anything.

"Over there!" I heard myself say and I tried to think what I was looking at. "I don't see anything and that's a good place to leave the recorder," I again heard.

A smile came across my face, because I could hear myself grunting as I bent down and placed the recorder on the ground. Then all the sound stopped as if the recorder had been turned off. The only sounds I heard were me standing back up and suddenly a gasp. There was nothing else heard at this point and I thought perhaps the unit had stopped working. As I listened for any kind of noise, I didn't hear anything. Then I jumped up out of my seat when I heard something that sounded like a strong gust of wind. Immediately after this, I heard myself flying through the air and the noise became loud from the sounds of the cracking case and silence. I knew this was when the unit broke into pieces.

Playing the tape made the hair stand up on the back of my neck again, and it was as if whatever attacked me was there with me in the room. My heart was pounding so hard, I thought I would have a heart attack. I was scared and truly felt the presence of someone or something there with me. Looking around the room, all I saw was the shadows cast from the light of the lamps.

"Boy, do you realize how stupid you must look right now?" I spoke aloud. "There's not anyone around here!" At that point someone knocked on the front door, and I know I must have screamed like a little girl in a horror movie.

"Pardon me, Sir!" was coming from a young man standing on the deck as I opened the door. "I'm sorry to bother you at this late hour, but I've run out of gas and I saw your light was on. I wanted to know if I could use your telephone," he requested, and at that point I was kind of glad someone was there.

Instead of allowing him to use the phone, I offered to take him to the gas station. He didn't want to inconvenience me, but I really needed to get some fresh air. While on the way, he told me he'd just dropped his girlfriend off and was heading back home. He said he thought he could make it because he wasn't far from home. During the conversation, he disclosed his father was a park ranger at Lake Singletary, so I took the opportunity to ask him some questions about any stories his father may have told him about the lake.

"Dad doesn't say much about it, but I know strange things have happened there," he began to tell me. I asked him to explain what he meant.

"Sometimes he comes home and mom and I can tell he's upset. Mom doesn't like for him to work there, because she also knows there's something weird about the place. Dad won't let us go there and enjoy the facilities." As he said this, he appeared upset, and for a moment I thought he wouldn't tell me anymore.

"You said weird things happen there. What are you referring to?" I asked.

"Dad told us the lake is changing and the wildlife are leaving the forest," he said, and I couldn't help but think of the old man at Lake Waccamaw and his wood sculptures. "Dad wants to shut the park down, but they won't let him."

I asked, "Who won't let him?"

"The government!" By now we'd put gas into his vehicle and he wanted to head home.

We didn't say anymore and I didn't want to scare him away with my questions, but I did ask if I could visit him at his home the next day. He indicated that he wasn't too sure his mom would approve, but he'd call me later if it was all right. He thanked me for helping him and I let him know I'd been there myself and didn't mind assisting him.

Returning to the cottage, I again felt an eerie feeling as I stepped into the living room area. Searching every room, no one was there, but I still felt as if I was being watched. By now, it was getting late and I wanted to go to bed, hoping to get a good night's sleep. When I removed my shirt and the bandage covering my ribs, I was horrified to see my left side was completely bruised. Whatever hit me gave me a good smack, because I was black and blue. Making myself as comfortable as I could, I finally laid down and before I knew it, the sun was shining through the window.

Looking at the clock sitting on the nightstand next to the bed, I couldn't believe it was almost 11:00 a.m. I never slept pass 8:00 am, so I was alarmed to see how late in the morning it was. My body felt as if I'd been beaten during the night and I had difficulty getting out of bed. I managed to take a shower and get dressed, but it wasn't an easy task. On the table were some donuts I'd purchased the night before at the convenience store that we'd gotten gas from.

Thinking about the tape, I replayed it while I ate a donut. When it reached the part that became silent, I turned up the volume. There was a noise that I couldn't tell whether it was static from the tape or something creating it. Therefore, I replayed the tape over and over trying to pick out any usual sounds. The eeriness that I'd felt the night before came over me again, and I could sense the presence of something in the room. Figuring it was my imagination, I continued analyzing the tape.

Allowing the tape to run to the part where I'd placed the recorder on the ground, I heard what sounded like someone breathing. It was faint and barely audible, but it was there. Trying to hear better, I moved toward the speaker sitting next to the stereo and suddenly felt hot air brush across the back of neck. It startled me. I turned quickly to see what it was, and nothing was there. As the tape played the part where I was knocked through the air, a strong gust of wind pushed me to the side. The force knocked over the lamp and the front door suddenly flew open shattering the window. Whatever had been there was now gone and I didn't feel its presence any longer. However, I knew it wasn't my imagination, because I could see the damage that was caused from the entity.

Whatever was in the forest was for some reason following me and I could tell the sounds on the tape angered it. The proof was on the tape, and I felt that I finally had some clues. Fearing the thing might come back, I was afraid to replay the tape. However, I knew I had to prove to myself I was not hallucinating and rewound it. This time I set up my video recorder to give me visual evidence if something happened. As I pushed the play button on the stereo, there wasn't a sound. The unit appeared to be working, but there wasn't any noise other than normal speaker sounds. It was as if the tape had been erased.

"What happened to the sounds?" I yelled aloud. "This is impossible!" I again screamed in an angered voice.

There was nothing left on the tape. I let it play for a long time and rewound it several times, hoping I'd made a mistake. It had been completely wiped out as if someone had recorded over it. To make sure the stereo was functioning correctly, I played another tape that was lying close by. This tape played fine. I couldn't understand why my tape was erased, yet this one worked. If an electrical interference caused the problem, then both tapes should have been affected.

The first thing I needed to do was go to town and get a pane of glass to repair the one that was broken in the door. It took me most of the day to make the repairs, and my sore body caused me to slow down the process as well. It was close to 5:00 p.m. when I finally finished. I felt as if the whole day had been wasted. Not having anything to eat, I went to the local restaurant for dinner. As I entered the restaurant, I saw the young man I'd helped the night before sitting with who I assumed was his mother and father.

"Hello, how are you doing today?" I spoke as I was led to my table.

"I'm doing fine, Sir, and thanks again for helping me last night," he said, and his father stared directly toward me.

"You must be the person who assisted my son in his time of stupidity," the man said. "Thank you for helping him. I owe you a great deal of gratitude," he again replied.

I let him know that I was glad I could help and he asked me to join them for dinner. They had all ready ordered and he called the server over and asked her to put my order on his bill.

"No, that's not necessary!" I said, but he insisted.

The server didn't argue with him and I gave her my order. Thanking him, I introduced myself and he did the same with his family.

"My name is Frank Class and this is my wife, Judy. I believe you've already met my son, No... Class!" he said while laughing at him.

"Dad, stop calling me that," the young lad spoke harshly.

"Okay, this is my son, Chad." This time he tapped him on his head and that angered his son even more.

We talked a few minutes about his son's situation and his dad made a couple more jokes. Finally, Judy told him to stop and he smiled, saying he hoped Chad had learned his lesson. Frank asked me what I did and for a moment, I wondered whether or not I should tell him the truth.

"I'm a writer and I write articles for various magazines," was my response.

"Are you on vacation?" he questioned me, knowing I was staying at White Lake.

"No, actually I'm here investigating a story for my next article," I said, and they all looked puzzled.

"So, do you write about vacation stops and are you going to write about White Lake?" Judy asked.

"Not really. ...I'm writing about the strange disappearances like the family who vanished at Lake Singletary," I replied, and everyone became silent.

I knew I was taking a risk, but I'd hoped this would gain me access to some inside information knowing he was a park ranger. Several seconds passed by and I could tell everyone felt uncomfortable.

"I heard about the mystery while returning from Florida and that's what I do," I said to break the tension. "Every mystery that I've ever investigated, I've been able to solve." I told them how I'd solved the drug case.

"This is one mystery you ain't going to be able to solve," Frank said and asked for the check. I knew I was about to lose my chance for information.

"Please, Frank! I know you work at Lake Singletary and I'm not trying to make you or the park look bad. I'm only here to find the truth as to what happened to that family and from what I've seen, something very strange is going on."

"Frank, maybe you need to talk to him!" Judy insisted. "Tell him what is going on," she said.

"There ain't nothing going on and you need to stop this investigation if you know what is good for you," he snapped.

With that, he got up and headed to the checkout counter to pay the bill. I apologized to his wife and she nodded her head acknowledging my gesture. Chad thanked me again and followed his parents out the door. Still sitting at the table, the waitress came by and told me she had heard our conversation.

"Mister, you really don't need to be stirring things up around here," she said while cleaning off the table. "We are a peaceful community and we don't want to make them mad," she uttered, and I asked her who would get mad. "They would," she replied, and went to the back of the restaurant without saying any more.

My dinner plans didn't turn out as well as I'd hoped, and now I was even more confused. Everyone seemed to know more than they were willing to tell.

What were they trying to hide and why wouldn't they talk about it? I wondered as I watched the waitress stare at me from the back.

Finally, I left and headed home to the cottage. Along the way, I picked up some beer and chips for later. As I drove up to the cottage, I could tell something didn't look right. The lights were on and I thought I'd turned everything off prior to leaving earlier.

There was a lot of concern as I slowly closed the door to my car and made my way up to the cottage trying not to make a sound. Being a Friday night, I could see other cottages had guests that had arrived for the week-end. I had been told all the cottages along my drive would fill up for the weekend and it appeared some had. My first thought was someone had gone into the wrong place thinking it was his or her rental. So trying to be polite not to walk in on someone, I knocked on the door. No one replied, so I knocked the second time a little harder.

"Come in!" I heard vaguely from a woman's voice, and I knew then someone must have mistakenly rented the cottage.

"Ma'am, I believe we have a problem," I said as I opened the door and entered the premises.

"No Sir, there's no problem here," I heard coming from the bedroom and to my surprise, Janet walked out in a shear black negligee.

"What are you doing here?" I questioned, and I immediately knew that was the wrong thing to say.

"Well, I'm happy to see you, too!" she snapped at me.

The shock of seeing her in the place made my reply seem to her like I wasn't glad to see her. Realizing my mistake, I apologized and told her I had not expected her, and explained how I thought a stranger was in the cottage.

"That's good, because I thought you may have been hiding another woman in here," she said as she ran over to give me a hug.

When I reached for her, she put her arms around me and squeezed. The pain shot through my ribs as if someone had stuck a knife in me and I hollered. This alarmed her. She jumped back and wanted to know what she had done to me.

"Nothing, darling," I said, still trying to catch my breath. "I had a small accident and bruised my ribs," I said as I pulled up my shirt to reveal the injuries.

"Oh, My God! What happened to you?" she screamed while throwing her hands up to her face.

The best answer I could think of for the moment, was to tell her I'd fallen off the front porch while changing the window in the door. I hated to lie to her, but I really didn't want her to know the truth and worry to any further extent. Janet stood there, stared at my ribs for a second, and then slowly put her hands gently on my face to give me a big kiss. At that moment, I didn't feel the pain anymore. Seeing her and feeling her lips again, was the best healing medicine I could have wished for.

Janet told me she'd arranged for Clair to stay with some friends for the weekend and thought it would be romantic to join me at White Lake. She wanted to surprise me and it was more of a surprise than she could have imagined. I sat down on a kitchen chair and grabbed her by the waist as she stood in front of me. She was so beautiful dressed in her sexy negligee. I pulled her close to me and in a small opening, I kissed her stomach. It truly felt so good to touch her once again and I was glad she was there. She tried to pull away, saying she didn't want to hurt me, but I hung on tightly as I kissed her more and more. With each kiss, I became enraged with passion and all I could think of was making love to her. My hands didn't waste time exploring her body and she didn't seem to mind me touching her. She helped me stand up and grabbed my hand, leading me into the bedroom. With her help, I was able to remove my clothes and lie on the bed. There was only the light of the kitchen shining into the bedroom, but I was so excited when Janet let the negligee slide off her shoulders to the floor, exposing that wonderful body of hers. With the precision of a surgeon, she lowered herself to me and we made love. Only a few times during the love-making did I feel any pain, and the pleasure made me forget it.

Janet lay on my right side and gently rubbed my sore ribs. She wanted to know how the scratches got on my ribs and I said it was from the edge of the boards as I fell to the ground. That seemed to pacify her until she reached for my back and felt the same marks on my shoulder. She jumped out of bed and turned on the lights to get a better look. When I'd removed my clothes earlier, she had not seen my back and wasn't aware of the wounds.

"Okay, what happened here?" she questioned, turning me to get a better look.

"It happened during the fall and I hit the steps," was my quick thinking reply.

"Bullshit, Rick!" Janet barked at me.

Janet didn't cuss and I knew she was mad at me, so I figured I'd better tell her the truth, knowing she would get even angrier with me if I didn't. By now, she had sat me up in the bed and was comparing the wounds.

"They look like the same wounds to me," she said. "It looks like some woman has clawed you."

I started to laugh, because I'd just realized she thought I was having an affair and this infuriated her. Seeing me laugh, see slapped me across the face and called me a son-of-a-bitch.

"How could you cheat on me? How could you do this to me and Clair," she screamed and started crying.

She was yelling so much that I couldn't get a word in. Every time I opened my mouth, she hollered at me more. I tried not to laugh any more, but I found it funny that she thought a woman caused the wounds. Finally, with all my strength and pain shooting through my body, I grabbed her, pulling her to the bed. She struggled and I informed her to please be quiet and listen to what I had to say. Her stubbornness continued to make her fight me, but I used my body to pin her down.

"Okay, get off of me!" she demanded.

"Are you going to listen to me?" I replied.

"I'll listen and it better be good, you bastard!" she snapped.

Releasing her, I grabbed my ribs, because I was in a lot of pain from the wrestling match with Janet. However, I began telling her of my adventure in the woods at Lake Waccamaw and how something attacked me. I could see she wasn't buying it at first, but when I told her about the second trip and how the deputy rescued me, she started to understand. Janet sat up in the bed and listened to my words, and I could see she was concerned. Finally, she kissed me on the cheek and told me she was sorry for believing I was seeing another woman. Now she laughed at the idea and I wasn't smiling. Again, she kissed the reddened cheek from her slap and apologized.

"Janet, you mean more to me than anything in this world, and I can't believe you'd think I'd want to have an affair with another woman. There's not another woman in this world that comes close to you," I said and her eyes filled with tears.

The rest of the night, I explained more about the events of the last few days and she got mad again because I had lied to her. Telling her of the attack sequences, she wanted me to forget the story and go home. Janet and I had been married for 15 years and she knew I would never back down from a story. But this wasn't the normal cops and robber type investigations that I was used to working on. Through the glimmer of light shining into the room, I could see the tears sliding down her face.

"Rick, this really scares me and I'm afraid for your life. The marks on your body tells me there is something dangerous lurking in those woods and I don't want you going back in there, especially alone," she almost commanded.

I had not told her of the close encounter I'd had earlier at the cottage when I played the tape. This would be the very thing that put her over the edge and I didn't want her to feel uneasy about staying there. Whatever triggered the anomaly to appear had to be related to the sounds on the tape. I was sure of that. So, I felt we were safe or I wouldn't risk Janet staying there in the first place.

In the morning, Janet and I went to the restaurant for breakfast and sit-

ting in the corner was Judy and Frank Class. As we walked by, I spoke and
they looked at me funny. I knew it was because the night before I had been
alone and I told them my wife was back at home. They must have thought
I'd picked up a woman and was cheating on my wife.

"Good morning and it's good to see you again," I said as I stopped in
front of their table. "I'd like to introduce my wife, Janet, to you," and they
both acted surprised it was her.

Judy, understanding Janet was my wife, invited us to sit with them.
Frank didn't look as thrilled about the offer, so at first I declined the invitation. Judy was very persistent and I could tell she wanted to talk to me.
Janet, not knowing any better, smiled and sat down next to Judy, so I followed her lead.

The women started talking as if they were friends and had known each
other for a while. Judy wanted to know how long she would be visiting the
area and Janet told her only for the weekend. I'd told Janet about helping
their son, and it wasn't a surprise when Judy started praising me.

"We wanted to tell you how grateful we are that your husband came
to the aid of our son," she said, smiling at me. "Most people would have run
him off at that time of the morning and around here that could prove to be
dangerous," she said and looked straight at Frank as she spoke.

"Don't start with that again!" Frank snapped at her, and Janet and I
felt a little comfortable.

"Frank, you need to talk with him and get this out in the open," she
replied, and he became irate.

"What goes on around here is none of their business and the best thing
he can do is take his lovely wife back home before someone dies!" There
was fire in his eyes as he spoke.

Frank stood up and walked out of the restaurant, leaving Judy sitting
there with us. No one said anything for a while and finally Judy apologized
for her husband's actions.

"I'm sorry, but he's under a lot of pressure from his boss because of
the disappearance of the family. He was working that day and I know he has
an idea what happened, but he will not talk about it. I'm worried for his
safety and I'm trying to get him to quit his job, but he refuses." We could
see the fear in her eyes.

Knowing Frank was waiting in the car, Judy excused herself and
wanted to pay for their breakfast on her way out. I grabbed the bill and told
her it was on me and she thanked me while heading to the door. Hearing
Judy state she was concerned for her husband's safety didn't fare well for
me, because now Janet was directing an assault toward me to leave and forget the story once again.

"Rick, we don't need the money enough that you should get yourself killed! Let's get out of here today and go home!"

I listened to her speech during the course of our breakfast without replying. She was clearly pleading her case and I could see the frustration on her face, because she knew I wasn't listening to her. Finally, she stopped and stared at the food in front of her.

"Fine! If you insist on continuing this quest, then I'm quitting my job and joining you," she said in a defiant tone.

"Oh no, you're not!" I quickly replied. "I'm not going to have you risking your life on one of my stories and besides, who will take care of Clair?" I asked.

We argued for 30 more minutes and neither one was gaining any ground. Explaining she needed to finish the school year, she finally shook her head in agreement. There was only two weeks remaining, and I knew she wanted to finish what she'd started because she was that way.

"Okay, you win!" she snapped. "But I'm coming back after the school year has ended and this time you won't get rid of me so easily," she said, and I finally saw her smile.

The remainder of the day we stayed at the cottage. Janet brought our bathing suits when she came and we went for a swim in the lake. The water was a little cool, but it really felt good on my wounds. The swimming also seemed to loosen me up more and my muscles were not as tight. That evening, I grilled some steaks and we enjoyed another wonderful evening of lovemaking. On Sunday, she headed back home and I knew I only had a week to try to solve the mysteries of the bays. Therefore, I began making plans for the week to include returning to Lake Singletary and the forest of Lake Waccamaw.

Chapter 10

THERE WAS SOMETHING OUT THERE

Monday started out pretty simple. A quick trip to the local mall to pick up a couple of recorders and I was off to Lake Singletary. My plans were to place a recorder in the woods and proceed to Lake Waccamaw to do the same thing there. It was still early in the morning and I figured I would be safe entering the woods. Stopping close to the same place as I'd entered previously, I made my way into the thick section of woods. The recorder was turned on and the forest was alive with sounds. Traveling about halfway through to the lake, I stopped and placed the recorder on the ground. Still feeling safe, I started leaving the woods and suddenly the eerie feeling came over me again. The silence of the birds and insects was almost deafening instead of quiet. Not stopping until I reached the edge of the woods, I got into the car and started pulling onto Highway 53. Then as if a freight train had struck me, a strong force hit the side of the car, pushing me to the opposite side of the road. A semi-truck was coming directly toward me and I managed to gain control of the vehicle at the last moment to pull out of his way. He wasn't happy as he drove by giving me a hand gesture, but I was still a little shaken up by the sudden jolt and didn't care.

Since the park ranger's station was close by, I turned down the long dirt road heading toward the lake. About halfway down the road, a sudden gust of wind blew branches and brush across the road in front of me. There was a small breeze blowing in the treetops, but nothing like what I saw. Seeing the ranger's shack just ahead of me, I quickly stopped and ran to the door, knocking loudly. As the door opened, I was surprised to see Frank standing there, and he didn't act glad to see me.

"Can I help you, Rick?" was his first statement to me.

"Frank, I'm sorry to bother you, but something strange just happened to me," I stated, and he didn't seem interested.

Standing at the door, I explained how I'd placed the recorder in the woods and the close call on the highway. When I mentioned about the strong gust of wind on the entrance road, another man stepped from behind Frank.

"You must be that man I've heard about snooping around my lake," he directed toward me. "Well Sir, this is government property and you are trespassing when you enter the woods without permission. I suggest you leave here and don't come back, because the park has been closed and we don't know when it will be reopened," he said and shut the door.

The look on Frank's face while the other ranger was talking made me think he was terrified and couldn't speak to me. This wasn't the place to have a confrontation, so I headed back to the car. As I approached the vehicle, there was a sound of a dog barking near one of the other buildings and I thought that was odd. It must belong to the rangers, I thought to myself and started to open the door. The dog's bark became louder as if it was trying to get my attention. Looking around, I couldn't see anyone, so I walked over to investigate for myself. Looking inside the window of this building, I saw Lady in there jumping up and down.

"Lady!" I screamed, trying to open the door.

The ranger that warned me to leave came running out with a pistol drawn and pointing it straight at me. He ordered me to back away from the building and I tried to explain that was my dog. He wasn't interested in hearing my plea and warned me one more time to move. Slowly stepping back, I made my way toward him with my hands raised high in the air.

"Sir, this is my dog. Just listen to her barking at me," I begged. "I lost her several months ago when I stopped to allow her to go to the bathroom," I said.

The ranger lowered his gun and told me to drop my arms. I was relieved, because it made my side and shoulders hurt. When he heard me say I'd lost her several months earlier, he acted differently toward me. He said they found her wandering around next to the lake and assumed someone had abandoned her. I explained there was a collar on her when she ran into the woods, but he said she was found without one.

As he opened the door, Lady ran straight to me and jumped into my arms. The force hurt at first, but I didn't care, because I had my friend back. The ranger witnessed the affection from Lady and he was certain she belonged to me.

"We are going to hate to see her leave, because we all have gotten a little attached to her," he said and started rubbing her head.

Thanking them for watching over Lady, we began our exit of the park. At almost the same point I'd seen the wind blow in front of me as I was coming into the park, Lady jumped down to the floor of the car and I could see she was terrified. There was something out there that she could sense and it scared her. This time nothing happened and when I turned onto the main highway, Lady jumped back up in my lap.

On the way to Lake Waccamaw, I stopped and got Lady some treats and water. As I got back into the car after purchasing the items from a small country store, a man drove up and stepped out of his car. Lady started barking at him. She'd never barked at strangers before, but I figured it was because of her trauma from being lost in the woods. Lady barked louder at the man who just stood there and stared at us without saying anything. He didn't appear afraid of her and he never entered the store until I'd backed away from the building and made my way down the road. Lady still watched the man through the back window as we drove off, and it wasn't until he was out of sight that she stopped barking.

"Are you better now?" I asked her as she jumped back into my lap wagging her tail. "What's wrong with you? Was that bad man trying to get you?" I asked her, and she looked at me as if she knew what I was saying.

At Lake Waccamaw, I stopped at the public access area next to the lake so Lady could have some water and a snack. With a piece of rope I had in the trunk of the car, I tied her to one of the tables while giving her some water. She was thirsty and drank most of the water I'd placed in front of her. We'd been there for about 10 minutes when she stopped and started staring at the lake toward the patch of woods I knew we were headed. She didn't move and I could tell she was sensing the presence of something. The more I watched her, the more she became nervous with her motions. I went to the car and retrieved the second recorder to see if there could be any sounds that I might be able to pick up and analyze later. Just as I'd returned to the table where Lady was tied up, she started barking as if she could see something. Looking all around me, I couldn't see anything, but turned on the recorder as I placed it on the table. There wasn't a second to spare, because once again I began feeling something breathing down my neck that made the hair stand up. Lady stopped barking and tried to pull the rope off from around her neck to make her escape. She could see or sense something standing behind me and she was terrified. She struggled and struggled until she managed to break loose from the rope. Without thinking, I hollered at her as she ran away from me.

"Lady!… Stop!" I screamed.

At that point, the force behind me pushed me out of the way, sending me 10 feet in the air, striking a trash barrel. Tables went flying and I could see whatever it was, was going after Lady. Several more tables and trash containers flew through the air as if they had been catapulted. I was helpless as I witnessed Lady being snatched up from the ground and tossed 40 feet into the lake. To my amazement, the water opened up at the edge of the lake and something entered followed by a large splash.

My first reaction was for Lady's safety. The contact with the trash barrel re-injured my ribs and it was all I could do to get myself up off the ground. I was in a lot of pain and couldn't catch my breath. Several minutes went by and all I could do was hold onto a table to support myself. My heart was again broken, because I knew Lady must have been killed or drowned in the lake. The more I tried to move, the harder it became. I tried to call to Lady, but I couldn't fill my lungs with air. The pain continued to get worst and the next thing I knew, I began to see stars before me and I passed out.

The aroma of food filled my senses as I tried to open my eyes. It was difficult for me to focus and I could tell I was in a room that looked very familiar to me, but I couldn't place where I was. My left side hurt and the harder I tried to breathe, the more difficult it was to fill my lungs. The aroma of food cooking allowed me to realize I was back at the inn, and the same room I'd stayed in a few days earlier. It startled me when the door opened and I saw Janet walk toward me.

"Good Morning, Sweetie! How are you feeling?" She said as she sat next to me on the bed.

Seeing Janet was a wonderful sight and I tried to talk, but my ribs were so sore, I couldn't get enough air to speak. Doctor Thomas followed her in along with Betty carrying a tray of food. Janet gave me a kiss and Betty sat the food next to me on the nightstand. Doctor Thomas reached over and started examining my wounds.

"Once again, you are a lucky man," he said as he pushed lightly on my ribs and I gasped from the pain. "You have cracked two ribs and that's why you are having trouble breathing," he said as he stepped away from me.

"How did I get here?" I mumbled with the small amount of air in my lungs.

Janet grabbed my hand and said that John had found me and called Doctor Thomas. She could see I was puzzled from her answer, so she continued the explanation.

"John was working on his dock replacing some planks when he heard Lady barking from a distance," she stated. Janet said he saw me fly through the air and Lady land in the lake, because it wasn't that far from his advantage point. He jumped into his boat and drove as fast as he could to the picnic area and found me unconscious. I looked around for John, but he wasn't in the room.

"What about Lady?" I again managed to utter.

As soon as I finished speaking, the door opened and John walked through it with Lady in his arms. After seeing me, she tried to jump onto the bed. Janet stood up, grabbed her, and brought her to me so that I could rub the top of her head. Knowing she was all right brought a tear to my eye, and I really didn't care if anyone saw me cry. Janet and I both shed a tear or two and after Lady calmed down, she placed her next to me.

"John also rescued Lady from the lake," Janet said as she hugged and thanked him.

"Seeing this, made it all worth it," he stated, and everyone in the room was smiling.

The rest of the morning Janet sat with me and forced me to eat as much as I could get down. I was hungry, but it was hard to swallow the food. Doctor Thomas told Janet as long as I drank plenty of liquids, it would help to keep me from becoming dehydrated. As they departed the room, Janet thanked them all for caring for me. The last thing Betty said was to stay as long as we wanted and to get plenty of rest. I knew from staying there previously, they did not allow animals in their inn, but John told us Lady was welcome to stay as long as we remained there.

The next several days I stayed in bed with Janet by my side. When I asked her about Clair, she told me she was staying with friends. I had not seen her for a while, but I also did not want her to see me in the condition I was in. Janet also informed me that John had called her and that's how she knew I'd been hurt. She said her class was taking exams and she was able to get a substitute teacher to take her place. I knew from the tone of her voice that she wasn't going to leave me again, and I really was glad to have her there.

By the fifth day, I was feeling better and walking around with Janet's help. Betty's food tasted better and I was getting my fill of it. Janet and I were sitting on the porch with Lady talking about how beautiful the inn and view were when John sat down next to me. After asking how I was doing, he gave me my recorder. That reminded me that I still had another one located back at Lake Singletary, but I didn't mention it to anyone.

"The day I found you, I picked up this recorder along with all the other stuff you had," John said.

"What were you doing… listening to music?" Janet spoke as she grabbed the recorder and pushed the play button. "There's nothing on here!" she said and then realized it needed to be rewound back to the beginning.

Janet started rewinding the tape and I tried to get the recorder back as she laughed and said she wanted to hear what music I had on there. She was trying to be funny, but I remembered what happened the last time I replayed the sounds back at the cottage.

"No, don't play that!" I hollered at her. I could instantly see that made her mad.

"Well, you don't have to scream at me," Janet replied and tossed the recorder into my lap.

John looked at me strangely after hearing me snap at Janet. I apologized to her and started explaining why I didn't want her to play the tape. When I told them how the entity came to the cottage and somehow erased all the noise on the tape, Janet looked at me as if I was crazy. John didn't smile or say a word. He stood up and started walking into the inn.

"John, would you please sit back down?" I requested. "You know something,... don't you?" I asked.

He stood there and didn't say anything, and I could see he didn't want to talk about it. After several more attempts, he finally sat down.

"John, I need to know what you know. I need to know what is going on before someone else gets killed," I pleaded.

John stared out at the lake and his face was completely blank of emotions. Janet sat next to him and pleaded for him to tell us what was going on. John still didn't move or say a word, only stared at the lake. I asked him if whatever was out there scared him and he slowly turned his head and looked into my eyes. That's when I saw fear in his face.

"You don't want to make it angry!" he finally spoke. "We don't mess with him and he leaves us alone."

"What is he and where does he come from?" I asked, hoping I'd finally get the answers I'd been looking for.

"Leave this place and go home, ...now!" John commanded and stood up.

He pointed his finger at the lake and told us this was his home and we were no longer welcome. He wanted us to leave immediately. John went back into the inn and I could hear him telling Betty to make sure we left the premises. Janet grabbed my hand, helping me up from the rocking chair, and we went back to the room for our things. After packing our belongings into the car, I tried to pay Betty and she refused to take the money. She told us it would just be better if we left the inn. Janet thanked her for everything and we drove away feeling a little confused by John's reactions.

The picnic area was on the way and as we drove by, Lady started barking as if she could see something there. Janet slowed down for a look and I told her to move on, because I also felt something was watching us and I didn't want to endanger Janet. As we continued down the highway, Lady barked staring out of the back window of the car. Her barking got louder and she started biting at the seat as if someone was sitting beside her. Janet was startled when she felt something brush her hair. She screamed and jerked the steering wheel, and we almost ran into the ditch on the side of the road. The car stopped and I could see the back of her hair moving. Janet didn't move a muscle and she was terrified. I told her not to make any sudden movements and she indicated something was breathing on her neck.

"Janet, don't move! ...Just don't move and it will go away," I whispered, hoping I was correct.

With the previous encounters I'd had with it, I ended up injured and I was praying it would not harm her. Lady stopped barking and was on the bottom of the floor trying to hide. The movement of her hair became more intense and I could see it move from side to side as if it was sizing her up. This was the first opportunity I had to try to see it, because it had always been behind me. However, there wasn't anything there. All I could see was the hair on Janet's head moving. Looking at Janet, I saw a tear fall from her cheek and she began to whimper from the fear. At the risk of getting her hurt, I opened my door and jumped out of the car, hoping it would follow me and leave Janet alone. I got my wish, because I was struck from behind before I'd made my first step. It felt as if my back had been sliced with razors and I bent over to the ground on my knees in pain.

"Rick!" Janet screamed. "Rick! Are you all right?" she screamed as she climbed across the front seat of the car to get to me.

The sight must have been a lot worst than the pain I felt in my back, because Janet started screaming and crying. Lady was barking again and I just sat there on the ground wondering how bad I was wounded from this creature once again.

Janet pulled my shirt up over the wounds and began to treat me with one of the towels I had in the back seat of the car. I couldn't see my back, but I could tell I was bleeding from the blood-soaked towel. As Janet worked on me, a car stopped and a nurse who worked at the hospital assisted her. She was on her way home from working, saw us in distress on the side of the road and wanted to help. She asked Janet what had happened and all she told her was I had been attacked by something and we couldn't see it. The nurse paused for a second and continued treating my wounds.

"You folks ain't from around here, ...are you?" she asked, and Janet told her we were from the Charlotte area. "Then you'd better go back there," she replied as she pulled on my shirt and got back into her car without saying anything further.

"Rick, let's go home now!" Janet begged and I agreed.

The trip back home was long and we only made one stop to allow Lady to go to the bathroom and eat. Soon we pulled into our driveway and I was glad to see our home once again. Janet assisted me into the house, cleaned my wounds and wrapped me with bandages. With my ribs and now my back wrapped in bandages, I looked bad, so we decided to let Clair stay with her friends a few more days. We knew it would be difficult to explain the reasons for my injuries and besides, she was having fun staying with her friend.

Chapter 11

MARKS WERE NOT DONE BY ANY ANIMALS

Two weeks passed by and I rested, allowing myself to heal. I didn't have much of a choice, because Janet would not let me do anything but rest. When Clair came home, she was glad to see me and upset when she saw that I'd been injured. Janet and I had talked about it and decided to tell her I had been attacked by a dog instead of scaring her with the truth. The whole two weeks I was recuperating, I thought about the experiences back at the lakes. There was something strange going on and I still wanted to know what it was. Janet, I could tell, was trying to block out everything that had happened, but she knew I wouldn't let it go.

"You aren't thinking of going back there, …are you?" Janet asked one night as we sat on the deck and she caught me staring at Lake Norman.

"You know I have to, Janet," was my reply.

"The hell you do!" she snapped and stood up, walking to the rail.

Janet knew in her own mind that I would eventually go back, but she just didn't want to admit it to herself. She looked at me and told me that she was afraid of losing me. She said no story was worth losing my life over. When I agreed with her statement, she thought I was telling her that I would not pursue it any further.

"I'm going back, Janet…. I have to, because this is more than just a story," I said to her, and she appeared alarmed. "Whatever is happening has to be stopped before it kills again," I stated.

"But why do you have to stop it, Rick?" she questioned, and her voice was trembling.

"Because I have to," were my final words. I got up and went to bed.

Janet didn't say much more to me and there was some tension as we went to bed. I kissed her goodnight and there wasn't the normal response of her kissing me with emotion. She was upset and I knew that I had to appease her somehow.

The following day, I wrote down as much as I could remember in detail while Janet and Clair went shopping. I think we both needed the time apart and this gave me the chance to continue researching the bays. During my search, I ran across the name of Marsha Johnson. She was the person Doctor Thomas had originally said I needed to talk with when he first saw the wounds on my shoulder. I knew she taught at North Carolina State University, so I looked her up on the Internet. She was an Associate Professor of Zoological Medicine with her Doctor of Veterinary Medicine degree. The more I read about her, the more I thought I should contact her. When I called the number listed, it said she was gone for the summer to do research at the North Carolina Zoo in Asheboro.

That evening when Janet arrived at the house, I'd made dinner and I could tell she still wasn't pleased with me. Following dinner, I asked her to join me on the deck, because I didn't want Clair to hear our conversation. After getting her a glass of wine, we sat down and she wanted to know what I had on my mind.

"I believe I know what I need to do with the story," I said, beginning the conversation. She didn't utter a sound. "I'm going to get some professional help." She looked up at me.

Telling her about Marsha Johnson and how I wanted to meet with her made Janet feel better knowing I wasn't running back to the bays on my own. Explaining I wanted to go to the zoo and talk with her, Janet suggested that we make it a family trip, because Clair loved going to the zoo.

"While you are talking with Marsha Johnson, Clair and I can go see the animals," she said and she was smiling, so I knew I'd diverted her concerns for the moment.

Janet couldn't wait to tell Clair and when she heard about the trip, she was happy and wanted to know if her best friend, Amy, could go.

"As long as her parents don't mind, then it's okay with us," Janet said as Clair jumped up and gave each of us a kiss on the cheek.

Janet made the arrangements and I called the zoo, trying to set up a meeting with Ms. Johnson. I wasn't able to talk with her directly, but her assistant assured me I would be able to talk with her. Two days later, we picked up Amy and drove to Asheboro. Clair and Amy played games along the way and it felt good to enjoy the family atmosphere. Janet was smiling and she, too, was excited about going to the zoo. The drive was nice and only took a little over an hour. As soon as we entered the park, Clair and Amy were ready to take off on their adventure. Janet gave me a kiss good-bye and we agreed to meet later for lunch. I went to the public relations office and soon was escorted to the veterinarian's laboratory where Marsha Johnson was supposed to be.

Entering the facility, I could see many different species of animals in cages. They appeared to be separated from each other according to their species. My escort took me through a narrow space filled with snakes and that made me tense up, because I don't like snakes. Once I was bitten by a timber rattler while walking through a patch of woods during an investigation. I'd just started working for a private investigating company and they wanted me to spy on a cheating husband. He'd taken his companion to a shady motel and was about to go into the room when I thought I could get better pictures from a vantage point in the woods across from the motel. It was in the middle of the day and I didn't think I had to worry about animals. As I stepped behind a bush to focus my camera, the snake struck me just below my right knee. It never made a sound with its rattles and I did not see it until after the strike. The snakebite scared me so bad, I hollered while jumping out of the woods. The husband spotted me and quickly drove off, and I never got the evidence I was after. The snakebite ended up being a dry bite and other than a little infection, I was all right. Ever since that time, just the sight of a snake scares me.

Once we passed by the snakes, we entered a small laboratory and a woman was standing there with a mask over her face. She saw us and asked us not to come any closer. I couldn't see her, but she was short and appeared to be operating on a small lizard of some kind.

"This is a Collard Lizard and his leg was broken when a thoughtless worker dropped a rock on him while cleaning his cage," I heard her say. "He normally can reach speeds up to 16 miles per hour in the desert when he raises his tail, escaping predators while running on his back legs. But it's going to be a while before this one will run again thanks to some incompetent people around here," she said as she expressed some anger.

A few minutes later, she lifted the lizard from the table and showed me the black collar on the neck. She explained that's how it got its name. The lizard was about 10 inches long and displayed a beautiful blue and green color that made the collar very noticeable. She called out to someone in an adjacent room and gave the lizard to her, instructing her to be careful placing it in the cage.

"You must be Mr. Parker," she said as she removed the mask and reached out to shake my hand.

"Yes, and thank you for taking the time to see me," I responded.

Following the introductions, she took me to her office, saying it was quieter and we could get away from the sounds of the animals. That was the first thing I'd noticed while being escorted through the lab, was how noisy it was. Several monkeys were playing and hollering at each other, and along with the birds singing, it was loud.

"Now what can I do for you?" she asked as she poured us some coffee.

"I really don't know how to explain why I'm here, but Doctor Thomas told me about you and I need some expert help on a story I'm working on," I informed her.

"So, you are a reporter?" she said as she sat down behind her desk. "And how is Raymond Thomas doing these days?" she asked smiling.

Since she'd asked about Doctor Thomas, I began my explanation by telling her that he'd treated me for an animal attack. She wanted to know what animal had attacked me and knowing Doctor Thomas lived at Lake Waccamaw, she assumed it was a bobcat or bear. When I told her that Doctor Thomas didn't know what it was that attacked me, she looked puzzled.

"He's one of the best doctors that I've ever had the pleasure to work with," she said. "He was the one who inspired me to become a veterinarian."

She talked some more on how he'd helped her get through college and she'd do anything in the world for him. Hearing how dedicated she was to him, I figured I would try to use it to my advantage.

"Doctor Thomas is the one who told me to come see you," I said, hoping this would give me the accreditation I was looking for so she would help me, and it worked.

"Well if he sent you, then how may I assist you," she said, and I began my story.

Marsha sat there and listened while I explained how I was attacked by an anomaly. She didn't appear to be judging me as I told the story and even wrote down a few notes as I spoke. Not once did she stop me until I finished talking about the occurrence with Janet in the car.

"You're saying the animal entered your vehicle while you traveled down the road and you could not see it?" she questioned, and I shook my head to indicate it had.

"Then you are not being attacked by any animals on this earth!" she stating bluntly.

For a moment, I thought she was going to ask me to leave, thinking I was crazy, but she didn't. She asked me to remove my shirt so she could see my injuries. When I took my shirt off, she pulled out a magnifying glass and a ruler from her desk. Still sitting down, she began to examine my still visible wounds. Marsha took measurements and drew on a piece of paper how the marks looked on my back and shoulder. Before she had finished, my body was sketched and she was a good artist.

"Mr. Parker, Doctor Thomas was correct. ...These marks were not done by any animals located around here. The closest animal to these marks are ocelots and they live down in Louisiana and Texas," she stated.

I'd never heard of this animal and she told me it was part of the cat family and small in nature, only reaching 40 to 55 inches. They hunt at night and although they can climb trees, they chase their prey on the ground. Most ocelots live in South America, but a few still remain on wildlife reservations in Texas. None had even been seen in the Carolinas.

Marsha wanted to review her notes and patterns of the marks on my back. She pulled out some books and started comparing the diagram she drew of me with some in the book. Finally closing the book, she told me that no known animal created my injuries.

"Then what do you believe made them?" I asked, and she just stared across the room without replying to my question.

"I really don't know. ...I just know it wasn't from anything I've ever heard of," she finally said.

I'd told Marsha of the attack at the cottage shortly after playing the tape of the sounds from the forest, but I had not let her know I may have another tape with those sounds. Reaching in the tote bag I'd brought with me, I pulled a recorder out and showed it to her. She wanted to know if I was going to record their conversation and I informed her that I believed the entity was recorded during my last attack at the lake.

"I have not played this because I am afraid of what might happen," I told her nervously. "If it is attracted to the sounds on this tape, then I don't want to make it angry again," I said as I went to put it away.

"Rick, if what you are saying is true, then we have to investigate it further," she told me.

She went on to tell me that her specialty was clinical and applied investigations. Many times she had testified in court to her findings and was considered an expert in the field. Her interest in this was growing and I could tell she wanted to know as much about it as I did. Our conversation continued to include the possibilities of something other than earthly creatures. It surprised me to hear her talk about extraterrestrial origins.

"I've long believed that we were not alone in the universe," she said. "The galaxy is too large for us to be its only inhabitants. I thought for a long time that we shared our existence with other life forms living right here on our planet." She reached for some more books in a cabinet.

Hearing her talk this way, started to scare me a little. It was getting close to the time I was to meet the rest of the gang, so I excused myself. Marsha escorted me to the main entrance to the park and wanted me to return after lunch. As I walked away, I agreed to return and she closed the door.

Janet and the girls were waiting for me at the place we'd agreed to meet earlier. Clair was excited and couldn't wait to tell me about some of the animals they'd seen. Janet took our order and went to get the food while I listened to Clair and Amy tell me about their adventure.

"Dad, we went to Africa and saw some lions and elephants," Clair blurted out to me.

"Yeah, Mr. Parker. ...We saw some monkeys and a baboon," Amy said excitedly.

"Mom said the baboon looked like you!" Clair said, and the two girls started laughing as Janet walked up with our food.

"So, I look like the baboon...do I?" I said to Janet.

The girls again started laughing aloud, and Janet joined in the festivity by replying, "Well, it did look like you."

We sat down and ate our lunch, and Janet asked me how it went with Marsha. I did not want to say anything in front of the girls, so I told her she was interested and wanted me to return after lunch.

"No, Daddy, I want you to come with us to see the animals," Clair cried out.

After we all had finished, I agreed to go with them to the "*Cypress Swamp*" area of the park. Clair wanted to see the alligators, but was afraid to go without me. As we made our way to the alligators, Janet tried to question me as to why Marsha wanted me to return. Therefore, I let the girls walk ahead of us as I told Janet how Marsha didn't believe an animal made the marks on my back.

"If it wasn't an animal, then what the hell did do it?" she said, loud enough for the girls to hear.

Clair put her hand over her own mouth and said, "Momma said an ugly."

"We don't know and that's why she wants me to go back and see her," I replied in a softer tone.

The alligators were lying on the banks and Clair was terrified of them. She wouldn't go to the fence until I picked her up. Amy was better about it, but she held onto Janet's hand as we stood there viewing them. A large alligator was lying just below and I bent over a little to get a better look. It snapped as if it was trying to get us. There wasn't any way it could get to us, but he snapped again and appeared to get agitated that we were there.

"I want to go!" Clair screamed, followed by Amy saying she was scared.

As we made our way down the path, the alligator continued snapping and hissing at us, and this made the other alligators start snapping as well. I'd never seen alligators act so angry and Clair wouldn't let go of my neck, squeezing as hard as she could.

The next area for us to enter was the aviary section and I thought this would ease Clair's mind seeing all the beautiful birds. The first place we entered was caged in to allow the birds the ability to fly around. The moment we entered, the birds became visibly excited about something and started squawking. I told Clair it was because they were happy to see her, hoping this would make her forget about the alligators. The further in we walked, the more agitated they became. Birds were flying back and forth within the boundaries of the nets. Some flew into the nets as if they were trying to escape.

"What is going on, Rick?" I heard Janet say.

"I don't know. …They act like they are afraid of us for some reason," I replied.

"It's not us they are afraid of us, …it's you," Janet said, and she was right because the animals did not react this way earlier when I had not been with them.

We made our way out of the aviary and I was sure Clair would be traumatized by the experience and wouldn't want to see any more animals. After we stopped for an ice cream, she was ready to go to the *"Australian Walkabout"* area to see the kangaroos. This was my opportunity to head back to see Marsha Johnson, so I excused myself as I watched them walk down the path.

Walking toward the veterinarian's section took me by the Africa exhibit. Not paying much attention to my surroundings, I heard the charging of an angry lion. As I looked up, a large male lion was leaping from its vantage point on the side of a rock and heading in my direction. His roar was deafening and he hit the side of a high concrete retaining wall that separated us. There was a crowd of schoolchildren standing with their teachers and watching as he tried to climb up the wall for another attack. They screamed and started running, and I was also frozen with fear. Although the wall was between us, it was obvious he was trying to get to me. About that time someone grabbed my arm and it was Marsha.

"Come with me!" she demanded, and I didn't waste time arguing with her.

Back at her office, she started telling me that the animals could sense danger in me and that's why they were attacking. She'd gone to the security building and watched me through the cameras. On her desk was a book and she opened it to page 136. Pointing at a drawing of a creature attacking a man in the woods, she said this drawing showed folklore about an entity that had been passed down by several Indian tribes over the years. The location of the tale was Lake Waccamaw.

"No one has ever seen it, but there have been reports of it over the years," she explained. "Many investigations have been conducted and nothing has ever been seen."

Reading from several other books, Marsha told me she wanted to hear the tape. I told her I'd only allow it if it was in a closed room that was shielded from the outside. Even though we were miles away from the bays, I didn't want to take any chances. She agreed to my terms and picked up the telephone, dialing a number.

"Hi Steve, this is Marsha Johnson. Yes, I'm doing fine, but I need a favor from you," I heard her say on the phone.

Marsha talked awhile longer and even invited Steve to come visit her at the zoo. From the way she was talking, I could tell they were close friends. When she hung up the phone, she told me they had once dated in college and remained friends. Steve was a music major and composer who owned his own sound studio. He lived in Charlotte and I thought that was perfect, since I was from the area. Marsha got my telephone number and said she would contact me in a few days when to meet her and Steve. Still thinking I might scare the animals, she took me a different way out of the zoo. She had contacted Janet and they were standing at the front entrance, tired and ready to go home. I introduced Janet to Marsha and told her I'd explain everything that happened when we got home.

Chapter 12

DON'T MAKE ANY SUDDEN MOVEMENTS

Janet and I didn't say much on the way home about the strange reactions of the animals at the zoo. It was obvious they didn't like me for some reason, because after I left, the animals calmed down. Clair and Amy played all the way home with some games they'd purchased in the gift shop. I'd thought Clair had forgotten about being scared until I heard her laugh.

"Those alligators sure didn't like you, Daddy."

"Yeah, I think they wanted me for lunch," I replied, hoping to contribute to the humor.

Clair asked if she could stay at Amy's house for a while and her mother had said it was okay. So, Janet and I went home to settle in from the trip. As we unloaded our luggage, Janet started asking me why the animals acted the way they did toward me. All I could say was I had no idea and it puzzled me as well as it did her. Lady was excited to see us and the first thing Janet did was take her outside to use the bathroom. As I toted one of our bags into the house, I heard Lady start barking at the car as if something was wrong. Janet called out for her to stop barking, but she continued and acted as if something was in the car. I also called to her and she ignored me, which usually wasn't the case. Seeing Lady acting the way she was began to scare Janet, and she called for me to help her. Quickly setting the bags on the ground, I ran down the steps over to their location and grabbed Lady. She snapped at me and almost bit my hand, and Lady had never tried to bite me before.

"Do you think it's in the car again?" Janet said with her voice shaking and referring to the entity from the woods.

"I don't know. ...I can't see any signs of it being there," I said, and carefully opened the passenger's back door.

Janet started to run and I told her to be still just in case it was there. I didn't want it to attack her if she tried to run away. It seemed to react to any sudden movements and I was basing my theory on the previous attacks. It attacked when I'd moved suddenly and Lady was attacked while she ran at the picnic area. When I remained still, I could feel its presence, but it didn't attack me.

"Don't make any sudden movements no matter what you feel or see," I requested of Janet.

"I don't know if I can stand still with it breathing on my neck," she replied, but I insisted.

Lady continued her barking and when I tried to close her mouth, she bit my hand. This made me jerk my arm back and I was sure the entity would attack us, but nothing happened. Lady's attention was more toward the trunk of the car and not focused in the seating area. I gave Lady to Janet and told her to go inside the house. Janet did as I asked and I could see her through the window watching my every move. The trunk lid was opened from having already removed some luggage, so there wasn't very much remaining, other than some items Janet had bought at the zoo and my tote bag with some papers and a recorder. Carefully looking in the trunk for any signs of something other than our gear, I tossed a rock, hoping it would cause a reaction. Nothing happened and after a few more attempts, I thought to myself how stupid I must look to the neighbors and started laughing. Janet opened the door and Lady jumped from her arms and ran straight to the rear of the vehicle barking as she did before.

"What is wrong with you, Lady!" I hollered at her.

"There's nothing here!" I said as I picked her up. The only possible thing she could be barking at must have been the items Janet bought, I thought to myself.

I reached in and picked up the bag to show Lady it was all right. She didn't even look at the bag and continued barking at my tote bag.

"Are you afraid of my bag?" I said to her, and reached in the trunk to retrieve it.

Lady went crazy and bit me again, this time on the arm. I stepped away from the car. Taking her to Janet who was standing on the back porch, I went back to pick up the bag. As soon as I raised the bag, Lady bit at Janet's arm and I knew that was the cause of our problems. Janet took Lady back inside the house and I wanted to figure out what Lady was sensing. Removing the recorder from the bag and placing it in the trunk, I carried the bag with only my papers toward the house after closing the trunk lid. Entering the house, Lady was jumping, but this time she acted glad to see me and didn't bark.

"It's the recorder!" I said to Janet. "Something is on the tape that she senses, and that explains why the animals at the zoo wanted to attack me. I was carrying the bag when I met you for lunch," I said as I took Lady from Janet.

Knowing the reaction I was getting from animals, to include Lady, I was afraid to have the recorder or its tape nearby us. Even though we lived near other people, our house sat on a small hill surrounded by forest animals and a few bears had been seen over the years. I knew I had to isolate the tape somehow, so I got some aluminum foil from the kitchen cabinets. Taking the tape from the recorder, I wrapped it several times with the foil, hoping it would shield whatever was causing the animals to sense it. With the tape in the trunk of the car, I again put Lady on her leash and took her outside. This time she sniffed around and finally went to the bathroom like her normal routine. I felt better, because I purposely walked her next to our vehicle and she didn't bark.

Seeing Lady react normally again made Janet feel better, but we knew I had something very important on that tape. Janet knew now that I had to continue my investigation and even wanted to help. I wanted her to feel like a part of it, so we sat down at the table to review my notes. Janet always amazed me at how she could see things that I wasn't able to see. Just like when she helped me calculate the projection of the bays' images, she started making sense of my notes.

"You wrote down that you felt as if something was watching you," she said while placing one of my notes on the table center. "On this note you wrote down it took off through the woods in a hurry. Traveling down the road to Lake Singletary, a strong gust of wind shot across the road in front of you," she spoke aloud, still placing notes on the table, but I was not following her thought processes.

"What are you getting at, Janet?" I finally asked.

Placing the geographical maps of the lake in front of me, she asked me to show her where I was standing and in what direction the entity went as it moved away from me. I couldn't understand what that had to do with anything, but I figured I'd amuse her.

"Okay, I was about here," I said, pointing my finger on the map of Lake Singletary. "It went in this direction," I said, and with my pencil drew an arrow.

"Now do the same for the other attacks," she requested.

"The second attack I was about here and it went this way." I drew another arrow.

After I'd made drawings on the Lake Singletary maps, she told me to do the same for the cottage at White Lake when it appeared as I played the tape. Using the same map, because the two lakes were only a few miles apart, I drew the arrow of the entity's path and I dropped the pencil.

Janet picked the pencil up and used a ruler to continue the projected path. She did the same with all the other arrows and after she'd finished, we both were breathless. We knew I was only guessing, because I couldn't be sure of the exact course it may have traveled. Janet drew a circle on the map where the lines intersected and it was very close to the inn we'd stay at on Lake Waccamaw.

"They know about this!" Janet said, referring to Betty and John.

"That's why John acted the way he did and why he wanted us to leave," I said to her. "I've got to find out what is on that tape." Janet immediately said I wouldn't be going without her.

I tried to reason with her that it could be too dangerous, but she wouldn't listen to me. Thinking I could use Clair as a deterrent, Janet countered me by saying Clair wanted to go spend some time with her grandparents who lived in Myrtle Beach over the summer. She was a good debater and was the captain of the debate team in college, so I knew I wouldn't win. When Clair came home later, we asked her about going to visit her grandparents and she was ready to go. A telephone call later and the plans had been made for Janet to meet her parents at a place called, *"South of the Boarder"* on the North and South Carolina line the next day.

The remainder of the week, Janet and I enjoyed the alone time we had together at the house. There wasn't much more we could do until Marsha called with the time and place to meet. On Thursday night while we were having dinner on the deck when the phone rang. It was Marsha.

"Rick, can you meet us tomorrow around 8:30 in the morning?" I heard her ask.

"Yes, that will be fine," I replied, and she told me where to meet them.

On Friday, Janet and I stopped and had breakfast at the local restaurant in Comelius before driving to Charlotte. We sat there enjoying our coffee while talking about what could happen when I played the tape at White Lake. The wrapping of aluminum was still shielding the tape and I was glad to see it. The last thing I wanted to see were cats or dogs attacking us at the restaurant. But the meal was peaceful and we hoped the rest of the day would be the same.

The trip took us straight down Interstate 77 and south of Charlotte until we reached Woodlawn Drive. We turned north on South Blvd. until we saw a sign that read, *"Quality Sound Studio."* This was the place we were told to go and Marsha met us at the door as we entered. I was carrying the tape in my tote bag. Marsha then took us through a door to a studio where a man in his mid-forties was standing.

"Steve, this is Rick and his wife, Janet," Marsha said introducing us.

Marsha had previously explained to Steve the purpose of our visit, so he wanted to get down to business. I asked him if his studio was shielded and he told me it was soundproof and no outside noise would interfere.

"It's not outside noises I'm worried about," I said. "I'm more worried that something will hear our noises," and he looked at me puzzled.

Seeing the tape wrapped the way it was, Marsha wanted to know the reason for its appearance. Janet started by showing her the bite marks on my hand and arm that Lady gave me.

"Something's on this tape that makes animals go crazy," she said, shaking my arm. "I don't know what it is, but it scares the hell out of me," she continued to make her point.

Explaining how Lady went wild, I told them it wasn't until I'd wrapped it in aluminum that she calmed down.

"That's impossible!" Steve said, listening to my story. "A tape doesn't make sounds unless it's played through some type of player."

"Well, you explain that to my dog and the animals back at the zoo," I snapped at him.

Steve unwrapped the tape and placed it in one of his machines. He rewound it to the beginning and pressed the play button. All we could hear was the sounds of me turning the machine on and placing it on the table. I told them I was at a picnic area near Lake Waccamaw with Lady, figuring this would help set the scene for them. We could hear Lady start barking and then everything became quiet. A few moments later, loud noises of the tables flying and me hitting the trash barrel were heard followed by a distant sound of Lady yelping as she was thrown into the lake. Although it was faint, the splashing of water could be heard, and I told them it was the entity entering the lake.

Steve said he was going to replay the tape and this time, observe it on an audio wave generator that was sitting in front of him. Janet asked what the generator would do and he explained that it gave him a visual of any noises on the tape. Starting the tape, he pointed to a waveform and told us it was the normal patterns for the surrounding sounds. The generator followed the amplitude of the volume on the tape, moving up and down. It all looked Greek to me, but he understood what he was looking at.

"What is that?" I heard him saying, pointing at something. "That's not normal," he said and none of us could make out what he was looking at.

He stopped the tape and replayed it several times while marking the place the occurrences happened. From what I was listening to on the tape, it was just before I felt the presence of the entity at the picnic area. As he let the tape play, he continued marking waveforms and uttering remarks under his breath. The tape finished and he once again rewound it for replay.

"What is it that you are looking at?" Marsha queried.

"I don't know and I've never seen an audio waveform shaped like this," he said and began the tape.

Suddenly, a loud, high-pitched noise came from the speakers in the room and almost pierced our ears. His equipment was picking up the sound of something other than what was on the tape. The wall behind Steve blew inward sending him to the floor. The force was strong enough to knock Janet against a wall. Marsha and I flew several feet in the air before landing on the studio floor.

"It's him!" I managed to speak. "Don't anyone move."

The room was dark, but I thought I could see the hazy figure of something standing next to the recording equipment. With the tape still playing, knobs started flying from the console as if it were being ripped apart. Steve, seeing what was happening, jumped up from the floor, making his way to the console. I told him to stand still, but he didn't stop. Like one last burst of energy, the console exploded and the shadow of the creature attacked Steve, tossing him across the room. As with the past encounters, it quickly made its exit through the same opening in the wall and we felt a strong gust of air as it departed.

"Steve! Steve, are you all right!" Marsha screamed as she made her way through the debris to get to him.

Janet and I soon joined her as she searched for any vital signs of life in Steve. He's not breathing she said as we began CPR on him. Janet ran into the main office and called 911 for assistance. Marsha and I teamed together performing CPR. Steve wasn't responding and it felt like the EMS wasn't ever going to arrive. Finally we heard the sirens and several medical personnel entered the room and took over for us. They worked on Steve for about ten minutes and he still wasn't responding. Several of us got Steve in the ambulance and they sped off toward the hospital. Janet was bleeding from her forehead and Marsha had not realized her arm was hurt. I was sore from the fall, but didn't believe I'd injured myself. A second medical team attended to Marsha and Janet. They wanted to transport Marsha to the hospital, but she refused.

"What the hell happened here?"

"Too much rock music!" a policeman said as he scanned the room trying to make a joke of the situation.

After what we had just witnessed, none of us thought his comments were funny. Janet started to tell them what had happened, but Marsha quickly spoke up and said the console exploded while we were recording one of our songs for a new CD.

"That must have been one hell of a song," the policeman responded.

Marsha just answered, "Yes, it was."

A police detective came and took our statements as to what happened. Following Marsha's lead, we gave the same story. It was clear to Janet and I, Marsha didn't want the police to know the truth, and the more I thought about it, I also agreed. Marsha's arm was in a sling and she wanted to go to the hospital to see Steve. We drove to the hospital and were instructed where to go by the emergency room attendant. When we inquired about Steve, a doctor came out to talk with us.

"Are you family?" was his first question to us, and we told him that we were not, but we'd been with him at the studio.

"Well, I'm sorry to have to tell you that he didn't make it," the doctor said and Marsha began crying. "His ribs punctured both his lungs and there wasn't anything we could do to save him," he informed us. After telling us how sorry he felt, he went back through the door.

Marsha was understandably upset after hearing the news. We knew they had dated previously and Marsha informed us they'd started the romance again after she'd called Steve for assistance. She sat down and told us they spent the week together and the sparks they had back in college were still there between them. Hearing this made me feel even worse than I all ready felt. It was bad enough to witness his death, but now I felt responsible. Janet could see I was distraught and she knew what I was feeling inside, but it was Marsha who I wanted to console.

"Marsha, I'm so sorry," I said, grabbing her hand, and she squeezed my hand in return as to let me know she appreciated the concern. "I should have never gotten you or Steve involved. I'm feeling responsible for his death," I said to her with remorse in my voice.

Marsha looked up at me and shook my hand violently, telling me that I was not to blame for what happened.

"We knew there was something strange with the tape and Steve also knew what he was doing. None of us could have anticipated the reaction we witnessed," she stated as her grief turned into anger. "I want to find out what did this and I won't rest until we do," she boasted and headed down the hallway.

We knew the sound studio was a crime scene and it would be hard to return without being seen. So, Janet suggested that Marsha stay with us and I insisted she did as well. At first she was reluctant, but Janet can be very persuasive when she wants to be. Marsha said she had to go by Steve's apartment to get her things and then she'd be on the way. Janet asked her if she would like some company, but Marsha said she wanted to be alone and we understood.

On the way home, we stopped and picked up some steaks for later. It was getting late, but we wanted to wait for Marsha before cooking. Around 9:00 p.m., I started cooking and figured Marsha could reheat hers once she got to the house. She had our number, so we figured she would call if there was a problem. Janet and I finished our dinner around 11:00 p.m. and we still had not heard from Marsha.

"Do you think something has happened to her?" Janet questioned me as we cleaned up the dishes.

"I hope not, because I don't want to be responsible for another accident," I replied, and Janet grabbed my arm, once again explaining I had not been the cause of Steve's death.

Her encouraging words didn't make me feel any better, because I knew the tape could attract the entity and I didn't stop it from happening. It was getting after midnight when we saw the headlights of a car drive up in our yard. Lady started barking and we were glad to see Marsha step out of the car with some bags in her arms.

"I'm sorry I'm so late," she said as she entered our residence. "I made a stop by the studio on the way here," she told us.

She was hungry and Janet warmed the leftover food while I showed her to one of the guest rooms. Marsha was dirty and wanted to clean up before sitting down to eat. Janet placed the food on the table and Marsha thanked us as she began to eat.

"Thank you so much for your hospitality and letting me stay here," she spoke as she chewed on her steak. "This steak is wonderful and I'm starved!" she boosted.

We wanted to know what happened when she went to the studio, so she reached in her pocket and pulled out pieces of a cassette tape. She explained that was all that was left of my tape. Saying she found a key to the studio in Steve's apartment, she entered the premises after parking her car so it was out of sight in case someone came by.

"It was difficult seeing with only a flashlight, but I was amazed how much damaged was done to the console," she indicated. "Standing in the room, I thought I felt Steve's spirit was there with me and I talked to him for a while," she said as tears fell from her eyes. Suddenly, she stopped eating. "I really didn't know how much I cared for him until this happened." Janet tried to console her by giving Marsha a hug.

While pointing at the tape on the table, Marsha managed to gain her composure and told us how all the equipment had been destroyed. "That creature sure is covering up its tracks," she stated, and that's when I realized what was happening as well.

It knew somehow there was evidence of its existence on the tape and it was trying to destroy it. When I played the tape at the cottage, it appeared. Now, it had shown up at the studio. Only this time it had killed someone in the process. Marsha, Janet and I talked until 3:00 a.m. about the creature and what information I had.

"What is it that Steve was seeing on the tape?" Janet asked, and none of us could answer her question.

"The strange waveforms are the keys to its identity," I suggested and Marsha agreed.

Marsha said she wanted to get more recordings and that would mean going back to the bays. Janet was totally against the idea, having seen what it did to Steve. But Marsha was as determined to do it as I was, and Janet knew she would not be able to stop us from going.

"I'm against this whole idea, but if we must go, then I suggest we take a different approach instead of entering the creature's domain," Janet said to us.

"What are you referring to?" I queried.

"Instead of placing a recorder somewhere in the woods and endangering ourselves, why don't we get a long range microphone like you have used before on some of your investigations," she replied.

"I don't know why I hadn't thought of that before," I chimed in, and agreed that it might provide us a safe distance to record.

Janet smiled at us, because she knew she'd provided me some answers to the investigation on how to conduct the search. I was proud of her, but I didn't want to make her head swell up any bigger than it was.

"So, you are the one who is the investigator?" Marsha said, looking at me and smiling.

"Maybe you two need to change jobs," she said as both the ladies got a big laugh from her comments.

I didn't find her remarks funny, but I went along with the joke knowing Marsha's loss. Everyone was getting tired and it had been a long day, so we went to bed.

Marsha went home the next morning and we agreed to make plans to go to the lakes the following weekend. We all wanted to attend Steve's funeral and it was very difficult facing his family. Fortunately for us, no one knew what had really happened at the studio but us. Steve's mother knew Marsha, and she apologized to us for the studio exploding.

"I told Steve on more than one occasion to clean that place up, but he wouldn't listen," she said to us almost in tears. "Marsha, I've always loved you and I'm so sorry it didn't work out between you and Steve," she said while hugging her.

Marsha didn't say anything to his mother about spending the week with Steve. She later told us that she didn't want to tarnish Steve's reputation in his mother's eyes. We understood and thought it was wonderful how she protected him. Following the funeral, Steve's mother invited us back to her house along with the family. Janet and I felt uncomfortable with it since we had only met him once, so we opted not to go, telling Marsha she could stay with us when she finished visiting. Marsha thanked us, but said she needed to go home and would call us later.

Chapter 13

WE HEARD A LOUD SCREAM

The next two weeks, Janet and I visited several stores in Charlotte and picked up some surveillance equipment. One of the places we went to, I'd used before and they didn't question my reasons for wanting the gear. The main store manager, Bill, had assisted me several times in the past. He picked out a long pointed microphone and told me it could hear mosquitoes making love at 1,000 yards away. He'd assumed I was chasing a cheating wife or husband, and that's why he made the comment.

"Now this is the top of the line stuff," he said, picking up an infrared heat sensor. "You'll be able to watch them do their thing through a solid wall," he laughed while winking at me as if I was going to watch something dirty.

After a few lessons on how to use the equipment, Janet and I left the place. We'd spent over $10,000, but we knew if we were able to capture the entity on tape and video, then it was worth the investment.

That evening after we finished our dinner, we thought we would play with the equipment to make sure we knew how to use it properly. It was getting late by the time we had set it all up on the deck and with the cover of the night, we knew the neighbors would not be able to see what we were up to. Janet felt uncomfortable seeing that we were about to spy on the house located just across the bay from us. The distance was about 1,000 yards away and I thought it would test the equipment's capabilities. With Janet's assistance, we pointed the camera and microphone at the darkened house while tuning in the frequencies for the best quality. It wasn't long before we began to hear someone talking.

"What do you mean you didn't get it?" was the sound of a man's voice talking. "I told you last week to pick it up and once again all you did was sit on your lazy ass!" came this demanding tone through the headsets.

Janet and I could tell from the anger in his voice, he wasn't happy. Using the camera, I was able to focus in on a man somewhere in his mid-thirties pointing his finger at a woman sitting at the kitchen table. She was visibly upset and crying. Through the headphones, we could hear him continue to yell at her, and all she would say was that she was sorry for not picking up the item he wanted.

"That must be a very important package," Janet said looking at me and smiling, and I shook my head in agreement.

About that time, we heard a loud scream from the woman getting slapped by the man. The hit was so hard it knocked her to the floor. She pleaded for him to stop hitting her, but he struck her repeatedly with his fist. Watching the video on the camera, she was getting battered pretty badly.

"I'm going to call 911!" Janet said as she jumped up for the telephone.

"What are you going to tell them, that …we are spying on our neighbors?" I said as she dialed the numbers.

"I'll think of something…. Yes, I want to report a domestic disturbance," she said to the operator. "My husband and I are sitting on our deck and we can hear the screams of a woman being beaten," she replied.

The operator took down some more information and I continued watching the lady receive a beating from this man. For a second, I almost started to go over to the house to intervene. Just as I was about to take off running, the man stopped his attack. I was amazed at how well I could make out the woman lying on the floor. She was bleeding from her forehead and I assumed it was from the beating she'd received. Within a few minutes, we heard the sounds of police sirens coming down the road. The man, upon hearing the approaching sirens, ran out the front door to a car in the driveway. As he was trying to back out, a police car blocked his exit. A pursuit followed and after a short chase, he was captured. Janet and I watched the whole event with the infrared camera and were able to track the fleeing man through the woods surrounding the place. It wasn't long before a rescue squad showed up and transported the woman to the hospital.

There was a sense of excitement knowing we'd been able to watch the events of the evening. At first we felt we had invaded their privacy, but knowing we had helped the woman made us feel better. The equipment functioned properly, so we dismantled it and got ready to go to bed when the doorbell rang. It was the police.

"Good evening folks. …We're sorry to disturb you at this hour, but I understand you were the ones who called 911," stated the officer.

"Yes, we did officer," I replied.

"Well, we wanted to thank you, because this man was on our top 10 wanted list for the State of North Carolina," he said. "Yeah, we have been searching for him for months and he's been able to evade us up until now."

"What was he wanted for, may I ask?"

"He was wanted for espionage, terrorist threats, bomb attacks, and murder," said the officer. "This guy is a bad mother-f... Oh, I'm sorry ma'am," he said, seeing Janet walk up behind me.

Janet didn't like hearing bad language, but she told him that she understood after hearing all the charges against him. We were glad he'd been caught and wanted to know how the lady was doing after seeing how badly she'd been beaten up. He informed us that she was taken to the hospital and her injuries appeared to be severe.

"She is his girlfriend and accomplice, and she will be charged as well," he said as he turned and walked back to his vehicle.

The following morning, Janet and I talked over breakfast about how well the equipment worked. We reviewed the surveillance tape we'd recorded and I was surprised by the quality of it. Bill had been correct, because we could see the images of the man and woman through the walls of the house. When they were standing in plain view through the window, we could see them clearly. As they walked behind an obstruction, the images were infrared, but very visible.

Several days passed by and we had not heard from Marsha Johnson, so Janet and I decided to go to White Lake for a little investigation of our own. We were not able to get the same cottage that we normally stayed in, so the real estate agent told us about another place directly on the lake. The place was smaller, but the view was nice and it had its own private pier. We were also able to use the speedboat tied next to the dock. So after we'd settled in, Janet and I took a ride in the boat. It was getting late in the day and the sun was setting, which made the lake look beautiful. Most of the other boaters that had been on the lake had retired for the night, so there was only a few boats out as we departed on our journey. Janet and I stopped in the middle and enjoyed the tranquility of the lake. Lights from cottages and other sources glittered in the background creating a perfect romantic setting. Janet laid her head in my arms and we stared at the bright stars in the night sky.

"Look! Did you see that?" Janet asked me.

"See what?" I inquired.

"It was a shooting star. ...There's another one," she said pointing up.

As I looked quickly in the direction she was pointing to, I saw the trail of the shooting star streaking past the horizon. Within the next 10 minutes, several other shooting stars shot across the dark sky. Janet loved watching them and as she laid in my arms, I was gently stroking her face with my fingers. The more I brushed lightly against her ear, the more excited she became. It wasn't long before she pulled my head down she kissed me. Moving herself to a better position, she started kissing me passionately. The boat was rocking slightly and the only thing we could hear were the sounds of the waves in the lake and the screams coming from the amusement park. Looking around for others that might be near, I didn't see anyone. Janet and I felt comfortable that we were alone and the next thing I knew, we were making love. Just as we'd finished and were lying in each other's arms, a loud noise came from the lake not far away. It sounded like a giant air bubble had been released from the bottom of the lake. The turbulence from the waves rocked the boat violently. The sudden noise scared us, so we didn't move. The lake again became quiet and there was an eerie feeling that came over us as if we were not alone. I whispered to Janet not to move no matter what happened, and she nodded her head as if she understood my request.

The boat had settled back in the water and there was a slight pull on the right side as if someone or something was climbing in. Janet was still in my arms and I felt her tense up knowing something could be behind her. Looking in her direction, I saw a hazy figure. I couldn't make out what it was, but I definitely could see something was there. It almost seemed to be scanning Janet's body and I could feel her flinch as it moved across some areas of her naked body. Janet's head was resting on my shoulder and I suddenly felt her hair fly on my face from a puff of hot air. Janet's fingers sunk into my side and I thought I would be the one who moved, but I stayed perfectly still while fighting the pain of her fingernails. As quickly as it appeared, it left us and jumped into the water next to the boat. There was a loud sound of a splash that sent water flying into the boat and soaking us. Janet finally screamed and jumped from my arms.

"Was that it?" she said, still shaken.

"I believe so," I replied and suggested we return to the dock.

We quickly put on our clothes and headed toward the lights in the background that I knew would take us close to the pier. Along the way, we saw another boat not far from us and there wasn't anyone on it. Janet wanted to continue to the pier, but I made a quick detour to investigate. Using a small flashlight we'd brought with us, I shined it inside the boat. There wasn't any evidence that someone had been on the boat, so we assumed it must have come loose and drifted out onto the lake. We tied a rope to the bow and towed it to the dock, thinking we would try to locate the owner the following morning. Janet and I were still a little shaken from our experience on the lake and went straight to bed without discussing it further.

"Bang!"

"Bang!"

"Bang!"

"What's that?" Janet screamed at me, and I could see the morning sun had barely risen.

"Someone's at the door," I replied, and heard the loud banging of someone still pounding on the front door.

Quickly putting on some pants, I made my way to the door. When I opened the door, two police officers were standing there requesting to enter the cottage. As I slowly opened the door, they pushed their way in as if they were looking for something or someone.

"What's going on here?" I demanded to one of them.

"Just stand still, sir, and don't move," he replied while the other barged into the bedroom where Janet was.

"Sorry, ma'am," he hollered and asked if anyone else was in there with her. She replied that she was alone.

The officers searched the remainder of the cottage with caution and one hand on their revolvers. Janet came into the living room area and I, again, asked them what they were looking for.

"There's a boat tied up on your dock and we are looking for the two kids that were in it last night," one finally replied. "Do you know anything about how that boat got tied to your pier?" the other quickly questioned.

I explained how Janet and I had been riding on the lake the night before and found the boat drifting on the lake. Telling them we did not see anything unusual, we towed it to our dock in hopes of finding the owners during the day. The officers seemed to believe our story and calmed down a little. Janet asked them what had happened.

"All we know is two teenagers, one male about 16 and one female, 15, left around eight last night from their premises," the taller officer spoke. "They have not returned home and their parents are upset."

"Oh, My God!" Janet sighed. "I hope they are all right!"

The officers apologized for their interruption and we told them we understood and if there was anything that we could do to help, just let us know. They said they would need us to help if they had to search the lake. It was obvious they felt it was a drowning by the way they indicated the need to drag the lake or have divers called in.

After the officers left, Janet and I sat at the kitchen table drinking a cup of coffee and eating some donuts. She looked at me and a tear was coming from her cheek.

"Do you think it got them last night?" she said through her tearful voice.

"I don't know, and there wasn't any evidence of a struggle," I responded. "Maybe they ran off and just haven't come home," I said as if I was trying to convince myself.

"I hope so," Janet said.

The rest of the morning, we talked about our experience. It was the first time I'd heard of something mysterious happening at White Lake. It was all the surrounding lakes that had disappearances and strange things occurring. Other than the entity showing up when I played the tape, there were no other occurrences. The key is still either Lake Waccamaw or Lake Singletary, I insisted to Janet as we discussed what our next move would be. Because Lake Singletary was closer and we'd both had experiences there, we agreed to set up the equipment that evening to monitor for unusual sounds. The activity around the lake the rest of the day was centered on the search for the two missing teenagers. Janet and I joined in the effort on the lake for the search. The police seemed to accept our help and directed us where to search. All day we searched along with over 100 other boats combing the lake. We had to be extra careful, because there were divers in the lake looking on the bottom. The normal clear waters of the lake became silty from all the boat traffic, and the police called off the search.

Janet felt more grief because the teenagers had not been found and wanted to go to the police station to tell them what we'd seen the night they disappeared. I was against telling them anything, thinking they would believe we were either involved or crazy. But she was once again persistent and we headed down to the station.

Entering the front door, I saw Deputy Jack Wilson walking down the hallway. Upon seeing me, he called us over to him and wanted to know why we were there. The last time I was at the station, he warned me not to return to the area and he didn't appear happy to see me again.

"Mr. Parker, I see you didn't listen to my request the last time we spoke," he said to me, and Janet was puzzled by his words.

"Deputy Wilson, we'd like to make a report on something that happened to us on White Lake," Janet spoke up to draw his attention away from me.

He first looked around at the other officers in the building and then asked us to follow him. Janet smiled at me as if she'd gotten away with something, but I knew the deputy wasn't happy to see us. We followed him to the same interrogation room that I'd been taken to previously. I knew he didn't want anyone to hear our conversation and this was the reason he had taken us there.

"Okay, what is your complaint about?" he began the conversation looking at Janet.

His demeanor was totally different from the last time we spoke. Before, I could tell he knew more than he let on, but this time he was all business. There weren't any forms to fill out and he wasn't prepared to take notes. Since Janet had not met him before, she told him that she was my wife and we were on a romantic getaway.

"I always loved going to White Lake as a young girl and I wanted to spend some quality time with my husband," she told him. I knew she was trying not to let on the real reason for our visit, because she had never been to the lake as a young girl.

Okay, ma'am, I get the picture. ...How then, may I help you?" Deputy Wilson replied.

Janet told him about our romantic cruise on the lake, as she described it, and for a moment, I thought she was going to reveal more information than I wanted him to know. She stopped short by telling him that we were stargazing when we heard the sound of the water splashing and something coming on our boat. Deputy Wilson didn't blink an eye while hearing her describe how the entity stood over her and she could feel its hot breath on her skin. As she continued her statement, he seemed as if he wasn't interested in her story and Janet soon picked up on his disinterest.

"Are you hearing me, Deputy?" Janet screamed at him. I just knew this would anger him.

"I hear you just fine, Mrs. Parker. Do you realize how ridiculous this sounds?" he snapped back at Janet, but she didn't make a sound.

"Okay, you were right. ...Let's go," she said to me and stood up to leave the room.

"Please sit back down, Janet," the deputy requested, and this time he was being very polite in his request.

His mannerism had completely changed and he looked at me, and again stated he did not want me to come back. I asked him why he was so upset and he said he wasn't, and pointed at a small object sitting on a table in the corner of the room. I knew he was telling me it was a listening device. His back was turned away from the two-way mirror and he tried to shield his gestures. He started asking some generic questions and I knew it was for the benefit of anyone else that might be watching. After a few more questions, he let us go. Deputy Wilson escorted us past the Duty Station and out the door, all the time pretending to act concerned. As he opened the door for us to leave, he whispered into my ear that he would contact us later and closed the door behind us. Walking away from the building, I looked back in and I could see him making gestures as if we were crazy and laughing.

The other officers were laughing as well, but I didn't get angry, because I felt he was trying to defuse the situation. It was getting late and Janet and I wanted to set up our equipment near Lake Singletary, so we left the station. She was still upset with how she was treated and I explained how I felt we were watched while in the room. She seemed to understand and we headed toward the lake.

Approaching the lake, I didn't want to stop on the side of the road and be seen by passing vehicles, so I turned down the entrance to the ranger's station, but and the chain was up. I figured they had gone home for the evening.

"This is perfect," I said as I removed some of the gear from the back of the car. "I'll set it up here." I placed the camera on a tripod next to the woods.

Janet was nervous and felt uncomfortable, but she assisted on getting the sound equipment going. Once we had it running, she wanted to leave it and come back later. I wanted to stay, because I didn't want to leave $10,000.00 worth of stuff unattended. We argued for about 15 minutes and I finally told her that she could leave me there and come back later.

"You're crazy if you think I'm going to leave you all alone in these woods," Janet said in a loud voice, and I tried to tell her to keep her noise level down.

I had on a set of earphones and I suddenly heard a strange noise coming from deep in the woods. I quickly stuck my hand over Janet's month and motioned for her to put on the extra headphones. As she put hers on, I looked into the camera for any indication that something was out there. Scanning from side to side, I stopped when a flash of something appeared in the distance. The sounds of the forest were again gone and we could make out a high-pitched noise coming from the same direction as the object. I managed to focus on it using the infrared settings on the camera. For the first time, I could see plainly a figure of something near the lake. Again, I cautioned Janet not to move or make a sound of any kind and she understood. The figure moved slowly back and forth next to the lake as if it was working on something, but I couldn't tell what it was doing. Then with a quick dash, it jumped up into the air and leaped into the lake. Within a few minutes, the forest sounds returned and we packed up our gear.

Knowing what had happened the last time any tapes were played of the recorded sounds, I wasn't about to review any of the evidence. Janet wanted to see the video, but I was afraid it too, could provoke the creature. We had been so excited about the sightings, we had forgotten to eat anything. So, we drove to the restaurant and it was closed. We had not realized how late it was, so we settled for some items from a local convenience store. Janet and I were happy that we had been successful in recording the entity and looked forward to more surveillance. Driving up to our cottage, we noticed a strange vehicle sitting in front of it. As soon as we stopped, Deputy Wilson stepped out of the car.

"Sorry to bother you folk this late at night," he spoke to us, and Janet grabbed my arm. "May we come in and talk with you for a minute?" he said, and Marsha Johnson got out of the other side of the vehicle.

"Hello Janet, …Rick," Marsha said, coming around the front of the car. "I can see you are surprised to see me here."

"No, I'm not surprised to see you, …I'm surprised to see you with him," I said, pointing at Deputy Wilson.

"Well invite us in and I'll explain," she replied and we went inside the cottage.

Once inside, Janet made a pot of coffee for everyone. Marsha started off by saying Jack Wilson was an undercover agent working for AEIO. I'd never heard of that organization and wanted to know a little more about it.

"It stands for, Advanced Extraterrestrial Intelligence Organization," Jack replied to my question.

Sipping on his coffee, Jack explained he was undercover as a deputy to gather information for the agency. When I asked him what kind of information, he told me it had to do with the strange occurrences we'd seen.

"Why are you undercover and how come this is so secretive?" I asked him.

He said his organization had been monitoring the area for many years and it had taken him 10 years to get infiltrated into the local police. I still didn't understand his reasoning and he began telling us how his organization came about.

"With this information, you both will be held responsible and will be prosecuted to the full limits of the United States Government if any information is leaked to the press," he stated with a harassed tone.

After he swore Janet and me to secrecy, he gave us more details. The AEIO was established in 1947 by President Truman to monitor the newly formed National Security Council. The NSC function was to coordinate policy recommendations for the different branches of the government, military and intelligence communities into a coherent set of recommendations that presidents can choose. President Truman didn't trust some of the appointed members and felt they were creating clandestine organizations of their own based on separate policies and agendas. These members were called the "Twelve Wise Men" and they were the key members of the NSC. It was named the "Twelve Wise Men" because of the twelve different organizations they control to include the Council on Foreign Relations and CIA.

These groups of men were very powerful, and President Truman wanted to make sure they were monitored to ensure no one person could gain more power than the other. He wanted to prevent an Adolf Hitler uprising in the United States. Truman understood how Hitler rose to power in Germany and it was his wishes to prevent that from ever happening in our country.

The AEIO provided him intelligence about all the organizations and only answered to the president. Over the years, the organization started tracking other agencies whose interest was extraterrestrial. Jack rambled on for hours while we drank another pot of coffee and listened to his story. He even told us how President Eisenhower had signed a secret treaty in 1954 between him and a race of large-nosed *Gray Aliens* that had been orbiting the Earth and landed at Holloman Air Force Base. He said this race originated from a planet around a red star in the Constellation of Orion and called them, *"Betelgeuse."* Hearing this made Janet and I look at each other as if this guy was a little off his rocker. I couldn't help from asking him what kind of treaty was signed.

"Col. Phillip Corso, who served in Eisenhower's National Security Council, said the aliens wanted us to surrender," Jack said and told us what the treaty stated. "We had negotiated a kind of surrender with them as long as we wouldn't fight them. They dictated the terms, because they knew what we feared most was disclosure of them. The world would not be able to handle the widespread panic that would surely follow," he said.

"Okay, what has all of this got to do with us?" I finally asked.

"Unfortunately, you have discovered one of the aliens who lives here on Earth and monitors the treaty," he replied, and I almost dropped the coffee cup in my hand.

"What do you mean, …monitors the treaty?" I quickly responded.

Jack said there were many of their kind placed on Earth to monitor the treaty that President Eisenhower signed. One such monitor is based out of Lake Singletary and that's why it's a national park. All the ones in the United States are on national parks so that we can keep them hidden from the public. The problem is the development of the land surrounding the parks is bringing people closer to the aliens and they are feeling threatened. He told us that he was working undercover in the police department to watch for any strange reports like the one we made.

"Consider yourselves lucky," he stated. "Most of the time it takes care of the problem on its own," and I knew he was referring to the missing people.

"What is your involvement?" I questioned Marsha.

"After Steve's death, I began my own investigation and made several telephone calls to some of my colleagues that specialized in paranormal sightings. Witnessing what happened to Steve, I believed it to be an anomaly of some kind. Doctor Gordon Howell, a paranormal investigator, gave a lecture at a conference I once attended on the paranormal anomalies. He's spent most of his life investigating them, so I contacted him," she further stated.

Marsha said she met with him at the University of Virginia where he was teaching. They spent several hours together and she described how Steve had been killed by the entity in the sound studio. He told her he'd never seen any anomaly harm anyone directly over the years. Usually the harm came to people who were trying to escape.

"It was during this meeting that one of our agents was monitoring Doctor Howell's house and over heard Marsha tell of the events at the studio," said Jack. "We knew from the Charlotte police report that it was a Betelgeuse alien, ...we just didn't know why it attacked the studio."

Marsha told us that once she returned to her home, Jack contacted her. He was already having Janet and I followed, and it was he who insisted Marsha come with him to visit us. Marsha looked at me and told me she wasn't too sure what Jack wanted, but she didn't have much of a choice. Jack was looking at me as she talked and Marsha gave me a wink. I knew she was trying to tell me something.

"Okay, Jack, now that you have us all together, ...what is it you want from us?" I asked.

"It's really pretty simple," he said in a smirked tone. "We can't afford to expose our alien friends, because the world would not be able to handle knowing beings from another galaxy were living on our planet. It's my job to protect them," he stated.

"Well who's protecting us from them?" I snapped back, and his demeanor changed.

He didn't appreciate my question and seemed aggravated. Reaching behind his back, he pulled out a revolver and pointed it at Janet. For a few seconds, he stood there and didn't say a word. He just stared at her and smiled. Marsha begged for him not to shoot Janet and he still smiled while focused on Janet.

"Jack! Don't do this!" Marsha screamed. He turned the gun in her direction and I knew he was going to shoot.

Seizing the opportunity, I snatched up a large figurine of Jesus that was sitting on the counter and hurled it at Jack, striking him in the back of his head. He fell to the floor from the impact and pieces of the shattered figure flew everywhere. Janet and Marsha jumped up and ran over to each other as I grabbed Jack's gun, which was lying next to him.

"Oh God, did you kill him?" Janet said as I checked for vital signs.

"No, he's still breathing," I replied. "All I can say is, thank you, Jesus." I picked up a large piece of the figurine of Jesus' face looking upward.

From the shed outside, I found some rope and tied Jack's hands behind his back. Janet and Marsha attended to the wound on the back of his head because he was bleeding. They both were concerned what we were going to do with him once he woke up. I told them we couldn't call the police, because they were also involved. As we continued discussing the situation, Jack started groaning and moving his feet. It wasn't much longer before he opened his eyes and tried to sit up. We lifted him from the floor and placed him in a chair.

"Okay, what now?" Jack mumbled.

"I say we shoot him!" Marsha spoke, and it surprised Janet and me.

"Marsha, we can't do that!" Janet responded.

Marsha didn't like the fact that he was going to shoot her and she wanted to repay him, but I stated we couldn't commit murder. She calmed down after a few more exchanges and during the discussion, Jack smiled at her, making Marsha even angrier.

"Maybe we can use him to our advantage," I said, and they wanted to know what I was talking about.

I told them our mission from the beginning was to get evidence of the entity, so we could use Jack as bait. Janet didn't comprehend what I was suggesting, but Marsha knew.

"Yes, let's take him out there and see if it will make contact while we record everything from a safe distance," Marsha said.

Janet didn't like what she was hearing, but she didn't try to stop us either. She knew Marsha and I would go ahead with the plan, but cautioned us about being careful. Jack, hearing our plans, laughed and said it would never work, and we'd end up dead as a result. The more we made our plans, the more he became vocal.

"It knows that I'm going to protect it and you will be the ones it goes after," he said, laughing aloud again. "Besides, when I don't report in soon, they will be looking for me."

"Shut him up!" I yelled, and Marsha tied a towel around his mouth.

We knew that Jack could be right and others may be out searching for him, so we agreed we needed to move quickly. It was still late and we knew it would be dangerous in the woods at night, but we were willing to take the risk. Having been there several times previously, I suggested we go to the ranger's station to set up the equipment. For whatever reason, the station seemed to be a safe haven from the alien. I assumed it was part of the agreement treaty.

Jack tried to struggle with us as we placed him in the back seat of his

car. Marsha drove and I sat in the back seat with the gun pointed just in case
he tried something. I wanted Janet to stay at the cottage, but she would have
nothing to do with that idea. She wasn't going to let us go without her, so
she climbed in the front seat along with Marsha. The closer we got to Lake
Singletary, the more nervous Jack became. Marsha turned off Highway 53
into the park entrance. The chain was stretched across the road and we were
sure no one was around. I cut the chain with a hacksaw and we made our
way to the station.

The stillness of the night was very eerie and there was a new moon,
so we were in total darkness. Hoping my theory that we were safe was true,
Janet and Marsha set up the microphone while I placed the camera and
recorder in position. Once everything was operational, I did a scan of the
area for any signs of the alien. Hearing the forest noises, I felt it wasn't
around at that moment.

Janet made a plea to us not to use Jack as bait, but Marsha and I
grabbed his arms and escorted him to the edge of the lake just beyond the
park boundaries. There was a large pine tree next to the lake that we tied
Jack to and I made sure he was securely attached. As we left him, Marsha
pulled the towel from around his mouth and he started screaming as loud as
he could for help. We knew this would attract attention and we quickly ran
back to the ranger's station to monitor the equipment.

"Get back here and let me go!" Jack hollered. "Don't leave me here,
you son-of-a-bitch!" he screamed at me.

"Something's happening!" Janet said under her breath, and we looked
at the infrared screen on the camera.

The water from the lake started bubbling as if a submarine was sur-
facing, then the noises from the forest stopped in our headphones. All we
could hear was what sounded like boiling water just down from Jack and
about 40 feet into the lake. Suddenly, we saw the water open up and a quick
flash of something jumping out. I turned the camera toward Jack and there
was the image of an odd-shaped creature standing behind Jack as if he was
trying to figure out why he was there. The alien looked to be almost seven
feet tall and it was hard to see any distinguishing features, because it looked
fuzzy through our lens. Its head was rather large and had an hourglass shape
about it.

Through the camera's lens, we could see Jack's image and he wasn't
moving. Listening to the sounds in our headsets, there was a high-pitched
whining noise that varied in intensity and almost hurt our ears.

"Don't hurt me!" Jack yelled at the creature, and for a second it
moved back away from him. "I tried to stop them," he said, pleading at the
creature. "Get away from me!" he again screamed.

A loud shrilling noise came through the microphone that made all of us pull off our headsets. And then we heard Jack scream loud enough for us to hear, and we saw him fly away from his position next to the tree toward the lake. Janet screamed, seeing him ripped from the tree. The alien stopped and suddenly darted in our direction, and I knew we were next on its hit list. But as I'd predicted, it stopped short of the station right on the edge of the lake and I moved the camera slowly toward it. Watching the screen on the camera, it seemed to be studying us as if it knew we were not the normal people that inhabited the station. But it never came any closer and no one moved as we gazed in amazement while studying it as well. Finally, it took off quickly and the water opened up, allowing it to disappear in the lake.

"Did you get all of that?" Marsha questioned very quietly.

"I think so," I replied. We gathered up our equipment and drove back to the cottage.

None of us had realized what time it was and just before arriving at the cottage, the sunlight peered across the sky and we knew it was close to daybreak. It had been a long night and we understood it wasn't over, because we had to get rid of Jack's car. I dropped Janet and Marsha off and told them to meet me at a shopping center in the nearby town of Elizabeth-town. This would allow me to exit the vehicle in a busy area and not draw any attention to myself. So, shortly after I parked the car, they picked me up and we headed home to get some rest. Everyone was exhausted and wanted to get some sleep.

Arriving at the cottage, something didn't look right to me. I couldn't put my finger on it, but something was different. Janet opened the door to the place and she jumped back and screamed. Seeing her jump, I ran to the door and saw the inside of the place was destroyed. It was obvious that someone had been inside, because stuff was tossed everywhere. Our clothes were on the floor, having been removed from the closets and drawers. We gathered up what we could and left, thinking whoever did this might come back. Leaving the premises, we weren't too sure where to go, so Marsha suggested we head toward Lake Waccamaw. She said Doctor Thomas would put us up, because they were close friends.

"I can't go back there," I said to her, telling how he'd told me to leave the last time I was there.

"It's okay, trust me. ...He will help us," she insisted, and we pointed the car in that direction.

Chapter 14

I TRIED TO WARN YOU THE LAST TIME

The ride to Lake Waccamaw seemed to take forever. We had to drive by Lake Singletary and it gave all of us an eerie feeling knowing a few hours earlier we'd witnessed the death of Jack Wilson. There was also some anxiety among us that the alien could possibly attack us knowing we had seen it. However, we made it by the lake and stopped once to get something to eat.

Marsha gave directions to Doctor Thomas's house and I noticed it wasn't very far from the inn Janet and I had stayed at previously. We knew it was early in the morning, but Marsha had called him when we'd stopped to eat, so he was expecting us. Seeing him standing on his porch as we drove up made me a little nervous, and I wasn't sure he'd welcome us warmly.

"Raymond, how are you doing?" Marsha said as she got out of the car and made her way toward the house.

"Marsha, I couldn't be better and it is so good to see you again," he replied.

"I believe you already know Rick and Janet Parker," Marsha said while pointing in our direction.

"Sure do. You folks come on in," he spoke in a friendly manner.

There was a sense of relief seeing him act so friendly and Janet smiled, thanking him for his hospitality. Doctor Thomas led us to his kitchen area where he had fixed a fresh pot of coffee and invited us to sit at the table. He and Marsha continued hugging each other and I could see the closeness she'd talked about was sincere from the way they acted. Once we all sat down, he offered us some blueberry muffins and said they came from John and Betty's inn.

"That Betty can make the best muffins around here," he said while passing the platter over to Marsha.

"Yes, she is a great cook," I replied and he smiled.

"Okay, tell me what all this is about," Doctor Thomas said, looking at Marsha.

Marsha started explaining the situation to him and how Jack Wilson more or less forced her from her home and came close to killing us. He remained calm and didn't appear to be shocked from the news. Continuing, she told him how we had used him as bait to lure the alien from Lake Singletary. This got a reaction from him and he wanted to know what happened.

"It appeared to try to communicate with Jack and then all of a sudden, it ripped him from the tree and killed him," Marsha said. "The alien tried to attack us, but stopped short when it reached the boundaries of the ranger's station."

Doctor Thomas wanted to know more about Jack, and Marsha told him that Jack said he belonged to an organization called Advanced Extraterrestrial Intelligence. He said he'd never heard of that organization and truly suspected it was a front for something else. Hearing him say this confused Marsha and she wanted further clarification.

"You folks are messing around in an area you don't need to be in," he said, and this time he wasn't smiling.

"I tried to warn you the last time you were here and you didn't listen," he said while pointing at me.

I explained to him what my real purpose was for coming to the lake and when he heard me say I was an investigator, he once again became angry towards me. He sternly informed me this was one investigation I needed to let go, because it involved things I wouldn't understand or could prove.

"Oh, I can prove it, because I have video and a sound recording of it communicating to Jack Wilson," I replied in a forceful manner.

He didn't say a word, only stared at me as if I had asked him to step outside to fight. Marsha touched him on his shoulder and asked him for help.

"Raymond, we came to you for help because we know this involves National Security issues and there's no one else I trust with this information," Marsha pleaded.

Doctor Thomas just sat there for a few seconds and finally agreed to assist in the investigation. He said he didn't want us running around scaring people with our alien story, because the locals already seemed spooked. The disappearances over the years had led to stories of mysterious monsters coming from the bottom of the lakes and snatching people. His mannerism seemed to change and he was more cooperative to Janet and me.

We sat there for a couple of hours telling him everything that had happened, and Marsha's eyes watered up when she talked about Steve. When she told him she had visited Doctor Howell, the paranormal investigator, he seemed to get upset again. He told Marsha that Howell was a nutcase and she didn't need to communicate with him. When asked why, all he said was, "He's a ghost chaser and a fruitcake." By midmorning everyone was tired and we went to the extra bedrooms located upstairs in his two-story house. Doctor Thomas told us he used to live upstairs when his wife was alive, but moved downstairs after she died. He said there were four separate bedrooms, so Janet and I chose the one facing Lake Waccamaw for the view. Marsha stayed across the hall from us and it wasn't long before we all went to sleep.

Janet and I were wakened up by the sound of someone knocking on our door. Looking at my watch, it was 5:00 p.m. and there was an aroma of food in the air. At the door was Marsha and she insisted we come downstairs to join them for dinner. It didn't take us long to get dressed and as we entered the dinning room area, there was Betty and John Mallard sitting at the table.

"Well it's good to see you again," John spoke followed by Betty.

"Look what Betty's prepared for us," Marsha said, smiling and inviting us to sit down.

After saying our hellos, we took our places at the table. Betty had fixed southern fried chicken and mashed potatoes with cornbread. Everything looked and smelled delicious, so we helped ourselves to the fine meal before us. Betty reached in her purse and tossed an envelope at me. Inside were the pictures of the wounds on my back she had taken when I'd been injured. Janet gasped when she saw the damage done to me. The scars were still there, but she had not seen how it looked after I'd been attacked.

"Ray tells me you are back looking for the monster again," John said as we looked through the pictures. "I told you to leave him alone and he will leave you alone," he said in a strange way. "Now I heard you have made it mad and all of us may be in danger!" There was almost a sense of fear in his words.

"John, they think it's an alien from outer space!" Doctor Thomas said, and they all started laughing at his remark.

I have to admit, it sounded like we were a little crazy, but I didn't believe it was any worse than John's monster story. So, I wanted to hear him tell why he thought there was a monster in the lake. Hearing my request, Betty grabbed John's arm and asked him not to say anymore, but he said to her we needed to know the truth.

His story started with his grandparents and it had been passed down through the generations. He told us how his grandfather first saw the monster one night on the edge of the lake working on something. He couldn't see what it was working on, but he knew it was doing something.

"Some youngsters in a boat rowed up close to the monster and it took them to the deep, and they were never heard from again," he stated.

His father told him stories similar to that and he also stated he'd seen strange things at night. I questioned him if he had ever visibly seen the monster and he told me no.

"So, what makes your story believable and not mine?" I questioned, and his reply was that others in the community had stories of their own to tell.

We listened to more of his stories and they sounded more like folklore than fact to me. After dinner, the ladies cleaned the dishes while John, Raymond and I sat on the porch, which had a wonderful view of the lake. The sun was setting and it was as beautiful watching it at the doctor's house as it was at the inn. It wasn't long before the ladies joined us and Janet asked me to walk with her to the long pier jetting out on the lake. I wanted to stay and talk more about the alien, but she insisted that I go with her, so I did. Once on the dock, I asked her what was wrong and why she needed to get me away from the house.

"While cleaning the dishes, Betty told us that we were in danger," Janet said and she was upset.

"So, John said the same thing during dinner," I replied in a puzzled tone.

"She told us not to say anything to John or Doctor Thomas, but she knew something was out there and it wasn't a monster like the one John talked about. Rick, she is terrified and begged for us to leave, because she believes our explanation could be correct and if we continue our investigation, we all may die." Now she had fear in her voice.

Janet had a tremble in her voice and the once strong and adventurous person that began the quest was now showing signs of wanting to give it all up and go home. We talked a little longer and I tried to make her understand that I couldn't stop, because this was more than just a disappearance story. This was perhaps the most important discovery in the world's history.

"Janet, if there is an alien living here among us, we need to know why it's here and why it is attacking people," I said to her.

My determination would not allow me to walk away and leave it alone. It wasn't much longer before we heard Marsha yelling at us to rejoin them, so we headed back to the porch. Betty had placed some cookies she'd baked on a table for everyone to enjoy. As we sat down, she looked at me and I could see a sense of fear in her eyes. Trying to make her feel more at ease, I winked at her and smiled, but she didn't return one back to me.

"Raymond's going to help us survey the area tomorrow," Marsha said as we grabbed for a cookie. "He's told us about some spots for us to go where he has noticed unusual activity." We all agreed to enjoy the peaceful evening and start in the morning.

The morning seemed to come quickly and the sun had barely risen in the sky when Marsha was banging on our door ready to begin the day. She told us later, she had always been an early riser and she had prepared sandwiches with some of Betty's cookies just in case we didn't have time to stop and eat later. Janet wasn't feeling very well and I suggested she stay at the house, if it was all right with Doctor Thomas. He examined her and said he felt she was feeling the effects of the stress of events during the last couple of weeks. He suggested she stay, enjoy his house and get some rest. She didn't want to stay and insisted on going, but he gave her some pills to relax her and they started taking affect as we finished our last minute preparations. She gave me a kiss and told me to be careful, then went back to the room to lie down.

"She'll be fine, Rick," Doctor Thomas said as we jumped into the car. "I gave her some sleeping pills and she'll be resting most of the day."

Doctor Thomas took us down a back road that traveled around Lake Waccamaw. He said only the local people used this road and on several occasions, he had seen strange things while traveling to visit patients. Marsha asked him what kind of strange things he had seen.

"Something different than normal," was all he said.

She didn't probe him any further and we continued down the road until turned off onto a small road that led to the lake. We could see the lake once we turned, and there was nothing but trees everywhere and no signs of civilization.

"Stop right there!" he commanded while pointing at a small opening next to the lake. "I used to fish here when I was a little boy and many times I saw the large bubbles coming from the lake over there." He was pointing about 50 yards to the right of us.

Marsha assisted me with the equipment and it wasn't long before everything was set up. After a quick test, I turned on the recorder and pointed the microphone in the general direction Doctor Thomas had pointed. The only sounds we heard were the normal noises of the forest. I could hear the rippling of the water, but I knew it was the gentle breeze across the lake creating the sounds. We continued monitoring, all the while hearing Doctor Thomas discounting John's monster story and our theory an alien was living in the lake.

"These folklores attract tourists just like you," he stated at one point. "People disappear in lakes all the time and are never found, and that just adds to the mystery."

"What about the wounds that you examined on my shoulder and side? Was that folklore?" I said to him and he smiled at me.

Still smiling, he said I had more than likely gotten scared and during my fall to the ground, fell on some limbs or brushes. He stated the area was dense with grass, leaves and dead limbs, which probably caused my injuries.

"Most of the injuries I have treated over the years came from people falling on such debris," he stated while kicking at some underbrush.

"Maybe so, Doc, but I've got the alien on tape, remember?" and I repeated the events at the ranger's station.

He stopped his conversation and suggested we move on. Marsha and I agreed and packed all the gear into the car. His jubilant ways had turned serious and once again we followed his instructions to another location. We only set up the microphone this time and Doctor Thomas sat in the car without saying much. Marsha tried talking with him and he would not talk to her either. Several more stops and the same results, so Marsha and I were ready to stop for the day.

"Okay, let's make one more stop before we head back to the house," Doctor Thomas requested and we agreed to go.

He took us to Indian Mounds, the place I visited the last time I stayed at the inn. When I questioned him why we were there, he just indicated for us to follow him. Parking next to the tourist area, he walked straight to the mound and pointed directly at it.

"This is what I'm talking about," he said. "The Indians believe this to be Holy Ground, because nothing will grow here," he said, reaching for the bare soil. "The ground is saturated with acid soil, so nothing will grow. But with a little lime, they could produce some fine tomatoes," he said, finally smiling again.

The point he was trying to make was the Indians used the mound to attract tourists and it was a way to make money for them. He informed us of several places around the area that had acid soil and wouldn't grow anything. One of the areas is called, "*Devil's Tramping Ground*" located not far from Lake Waccamaw near the small town of Siler City. It is a perfect circle that is exactly forty feet in diameter and no plants or trees will grow within the circle. The first settlers to the area thought it came from the Indians holding their tribal ceremonies there, but the circle remained long after the Indians were gone.

"There were people like you suggesting the ground was sterile because aliens had landed there," he said and started laughing at me. "The truth is, the ground has a high level of salt in the soil and salt is the key ingredient of weed killer," he said as if making his point once again.

"Raymond, what we witnessed was not a figment of our imaginations," Marsha snapped, and I could see she was upset with him.

Doctor Thomas stopped laughing and looked at Marsha, grabbing her arm. He told her what we saw was more than likely a phenomenon similar to swamp gas. Continuing, he tried to tell us how southeastern North Carolina was known for ghosts that turned out to be nothing more than swamp gas.

"Yeah, when I was younger, we'd travel to Maco just south of Wilmington to go see the *Maco* light. It was said this was the beheaded body of Joe Baldwin, a conductor for the railroad, and he still appears on warm summer nights searching for his severed head. As a young boy, I was terrified seeing the small light down a dark railroad track grow to the size of a lantern they said he was carrying at the time of his death," he stated.

"Stop! This is not a ghost story and we know what we saw," Marsha said, interrupting him.

The tension between them was getting higher, so I suggested since it was getting late in the day, we head back to his house. The trip back was quiet. As I pulled into the driveway of the house, Janet was standing on the porch waiting for us to return. Knowing her the way I do, I could see she was distraught about something. Marsha and Doctor Thomas went inside the house and Janet escorted me to the pier. Along the path I tried to ask her what was the matter, but she would not say anything and squeezed my hand every time I asked.

"What's the matter, Janet?" I finally questioned as we stepped onto the dock.

"Doctor Thomas has a basement in his house," she mentioned.

"So, a lot of houses have basements," was my reply.

"Rick, I went down in his basement while you were gone and I was horrified by what I saw," she said, her hand was shaking. I asked her to explain.

Her voice was mumbled and I could see a genuine sense of fear in her eyes as she told me what she'd seen. She explained how the stairs led to a large room under the house, and there were many skeletons hanging from the walls and ceiling. I suggested he was a doctor, so it wouldn't be uncommon for him to have human skeletons.

"Rick, they're not human skeletons," she said, and I indicated that maybe it was different types of animals from the region.

"Rick!" she hollered, "what I saw wasn't any animal on this Earth," she replied and squeezed my hand, sinking her fingernails in and drawing blood.

At first I tried to reason with her that maybe she was hallucinating from the pills that the doctor had given her and this angered her. She pulled her hands away from me and told me what she saw was real. It was then that I realized I was acting the same way that Doctor Thomas treated us earlier, and Janet wasn't one to make up stories. Therefore, I questioned her on what else she saw in the room.

"It's more than just a room. I believe it's a laboratory where he is conducting experiments," she stated. "There's a large table in the middle of the room with straps to hold someone on and as I looked closer at the straps, I could see fresh scratches on them," she said while staring out at the lake. "I saw the same clothing that Jack Wilson was wearing the night he was killed," she said and hugged me.

Hearing Janet tell of the room made me fear for her life as well as Marsha and myself. I couldn't understand what type of experiments he would be doing or why he would be doing them in the first place. The puzzle was getting more complicated, but foremost in my mind at that point was getting everyone out of there.

"Are you two coming to dinner?" we heard coming from Marsha standing on the porch yelling at us.

I waved at her and told Janet to pack our things up after we ate, because we were leaving as soon as possible. She wanted to know how we were going to explain leaving and I told her I'd think of something. Getting Marsha to go would be a little more difficult, because I didn't want to mention what Janet had seen around Doctor Thomas.

The tension was still high between Marsha and the doctor as we walked into the dining room area. Betty and John were both sitting at the table and I was surprised to see them, because I had not seen their vehicle on the way to the house. Even their demeanor wasn't the same as they had previously acted, and I assumed it was because Marsha and Doctor Thomas weren't speaking.

"Hello, I didn't know you folks were here," I said to Betty and John, trying to make conversation.

"Why, you don't want us here?" John harshly replied.

"No, I'm glad you are here. I just didn't see your car," I said and sat down as John gave me strange looks.

During the meal it was very stressful for us and several times I looked at Betty. She was almost crying. Her tears were ones of fear and not sadness and I knew we had to leave that place. Several more minutes passed and still no one spoke. Still trying to break the tension, I commented to Betty on how good the meal was she'd prepared and she just nodded her head to say thank you.

"We are going back home tonight," I blurted out and everyone stared at me. "I think we have investigated this hoax long enough."

John and Doctor Thomas grinned at each other as if they'd won a battle. John said he thought it was a good idea for us to leave and Doctor Thomas shook his head as to say yes. Marsha looked at me strangely, but didn't protest. She too, understood something was wrong and was ready to leave.

Following dinner, the women asked to help clean up and John wouldn't allow them in the kitchen area, saying Betty would take care of it. He suggested we leave as soon as we were packed. Following his request, we loaded up our things and started down the road as if we were making our escape. I found it odd when Doctor Thomas gave Marsha a hug and told her to come back and visit him sometime. He didn't make Janet and me the same offer, and neither did John. We weren't sure where we were headed, but we said our goodbyes and departed.

"Okay, Rick, what's going on and why the hurry to leave?" Marsha asked as we turned onto the main highway.

I asked Janet to explain to Marsha what she had seen in the basement while we were out with Doctor Thomas. Marsha was apprehensive at first, trying to justify all the skeletons in the same manner I did when Janet first told me. However, I quickly informed her that Janet wasn't imagining what she saw. She wanted to know more about what the skeletons looked like and Janet was still visibly shaken trying to describe them.

The ones I saw hanging from the wall looked to be at least seven feet tall," Janet started out saying. "Their skulls were large and the eye sockets oval and elongated."

"They appeared to be human in shape, but different," she finished saying.

The more Janet described the skeletons, the more it sounded like the same entity we saw and recorded at the ranger's station. What confused Marsha and myself, was when Janet said she saw some clothing resembling what Jack Wilson wore the night he was attacked. Marsha surmised Doctor Thomas must have found the clothing floating in the lake and that's why he had them. It was easy to explain the clothes, but the skeletons were a different matter.

It was getting late and our travels took us by Lake Singletary. I suggested we stop for a quick listen on the microphone to see if we could pick up anything. Janet was dead set against that idea and wanted to continue heading home. Marsha was tired, but agreed to setting the equipment up for a quick listen. Knowing the ranger's station seemed to be a safe haven, I pulled down the dark dirt road that I'd driven before. The chain was not up as it had been in the past, and this made me wonder whether or not someone would be at the station. Pulling up to the first cabin, everything looked dark and I felt everyone had gone home for the evening. Marsha and I set the equipment up to include the video camera while Janet sat in the car. She felt uncomfortable and still wasn't feeling well, so I asked her to wait in the car.

Marsha had just finished with the microphone and I was almost done tuning the camera when I heard Janet scream. Quickly turning to see what was wrong, the vehicle was rocking side to side as if something was trying to turn it over. Because of the darkness, I couldn't see what it was, so I used the camera, hoping to see what was attacking Janet. As soon as I turned the camera in her direction, I could see it was the same creature we'd seen the last time we were there. Marsha also turned the microphone toward it and I heard her scream loudly. Still viewing through the camera, it stopped shaking the car and stood up looking in our direction. The camera was focused and I could clearly make out all the alien's features. For a second it stared at me and then turned its attention toward Marsha. Suddenly it flew in our direction and I heard Marsha give a blood-curdling scream as she disappeared into the lake with the alien. The equipment went flying through the air falling short of the lake. I called to Marsha and there weren't any signs of her. Janet hollered from the car for us to leave and I gathered up the gear as fast as I could and threw it into the trunk. A few minutes later, we took off traveling down the dirt road exiting the park. Janet was crying and I was shaking as well.

"I feel so sorry for Marsha!" Janet sobbed.

"I told you not to stop. ...I told you not to stop!" she again cried at me and this made me feel even worse than I all ready felt.

We drove past White Lake to Elizabethtown located about twenty miles from Lake Singletary. Still upset from the events, I stopped at a local motel and indicated to Janet that we needed to get some rest. She wanted to go home, but I convinced her we needed to stop. Neither one of us could say much to each other as we settled into the room. Janet took a shower while I tried to jot down some notes. When she'd finished her shower and walked back into the room, she slapped me as hard as she could in my face.

"Do you know how close you came to getting all of us killed?" she yelled at me. "I would never forgive you for that!" she said and went straight to bed.

The slap was hard enough that it left a red mark on the right side of my face. For a second, it stunned me and I wasn't sure I'd heard all of what she said to me. But one thing I did understand was she wasn't very happy with me.

Janet cried as she lay in the bed and I continued my notes. It wasn't long before she had cried herself to sleep and I was glad she was getting some rest. There had to be a pattern to what was happening, but I just could not find it. I'd witnessed the alien or monster attack two people, and was even attacked myself. Searching through my research, I wanted to find anything that made sense to me. The more I studied the notes, the more it pointed me back to Doctor Thomas. Hearing Janet describe the laboratory in his basement made me realize I had to investigate it myself. So, I wrote Janet a note telling her not to worry about me, but I had gone out to get something to eat.

"I'll bring you back something and I love you," I wrote in the note and quietly left the room.

Chapter 15

IT WILL BE OVER BEFORE YOU KNOW IT

My intentions were to set up the equipment within a safe distance close to Doctor Thomas's house to monitor any unusual activity. Approaching his driveway, I pulled off the road and parked my car. I tried to hide it behind an abandoned store located about 500 yards from his entrance. It was completely dark which made my trek down the driveway harder for me to follow. I was afraid to use my flashlight, but several times I had to because I couldn't find my way. Before long, I was close enough to set up my gear. There was a large bush I felt would provide me some cover and still allow me the ability to scan the area, so I went into action.

It was after midnight and I was surprised to see some lights on in the doctor's house. Viewing through the infrared camera and listening in the headphones, there was activity going on inside. From the muffled sounds I was hearing, it appeared the noise source was in his basement. As good as the equipment was, I couldn't make out the source. Using the camera, I could see an image of someone walking around in his kitchen area and disappear as if they were walking down a flight of stairs. Leaving the camera on and recording, I moved closer to the house, trying not to be detected. I wanted get a better understanding of the sounds being picked up through the microphones. I was almost next to the house when I heard the voice of a woman and she seemed to be pleading for her life. At first, I couldn't make out who it was, but soon I realized, it was Marsha.

"How can that be?" I said to myself and not believing what was coming through the headsets. "She was killed by the alien," I again reasoned.

"Please don't do this," I clearly heard Marsha scream.

"Just relax and it will be over before you know it," was the reply coming from Doctor Thomas, and I knew he was conducting some type of experiment on her.

Knowing Marsha was in danger, I entered the house through the back door that was open, making my way into the kitchen area. Looking for some sort of weapon, I spotted a large poker similar to the ones used to stoke fires in a fireplace, sitting against the wall. There were other sounds coming from the door leading into the basement area. It sounded like high-pitched motors running and drills that a dentist would use.

Pushing slowly on the door, I made my first step down the stairs ready to swing if required. Marsha continued begging for Doctor Thomas to stop, and I was hoping he was too occupied to notice me coming down the steps. Because of the layout of the room, it was difficult for me to see as I continued my way down the stairs. I tried to bend my head down below the flooring to get a better look and there was Marsha strapped to a table. It was still hard for me to believe I was looking at her, but there she was. There were a couple of tubes running into her arm and she had a terrified look on her face as if she was about to die.

Seeing Marsha made me jump the rest of the way down the steps to the floor ready to defend myself against any attacks. But to my surprise, I didn't see anyone around the room. Just a few minutes earlier, I heard Doctor Thomas talking, so where did he go?

"Rick, help me!" Marsha yelled at me and I hurried over to her.

"Quick, pull out the IVs," she screamed and I removed them from her arm as a blue liquid flowed from the tubes to the floor.

As I was unbuckling the straps to release Marsha, she screamed. Quickly turning my head, I saw John Mallard and he was about to hit me with a hammer. As he swung the hammer, I darted to my left causing him to barely miss the top of my head. He swung again almost hitting my ribs, but I managed to avoid the attack by jumping out of the way. Moving back to the table, I picked up the poker from where I had placed it while helping Marsha and with one swing, struck him on the left side of his head. The blow sent him falling to the floor and the back of his head struck the end of the table knocking him unconscious. Marsha managed to unbuckle herself and tried to stand up off the table, but she was too weak to stand on her own.

"Where is Doctor Thomas?" I questioned her.

"I don't know, but we need to get out of here as fast as we can," she insisted.

Marsha was a petite woman and I was glad at that moment, because I had to carry her up the stairs. So, with her in my arms, we started up the steps to make our exit. We'd just made it into the kitchen area when we spotted Betty standing next to the kitchen table and she was pointing a pistol at us. With Marsha in my arms, I froze, staring down the barrel of a gun.

"Betty, please don't stop us?" I pleaded and she didn't reply.

"Marsha needs help and I want to get her out of here," I said, hoping she'd let us by.

About that time, I heard the gun fire and I was sure I'd been shot, but I didn't feel anything. She fired another round and this time I could see she was shooting behind me. As I turned with Marsha, John fell to the floor next to us and it was obvious he'd been shot in the head by Betty. When I looked back at her, she was crying and had lowered the gun.

"I can't allow them to do this anymore," she cried openly.

"Do what anymore?" I asked, but she appeared to be in shock.

"No more —will I help them," she yelled, quickly raising the pistol up to her chin and pulled the trigger.

Marsha screamed out Betty's name as we watched her limp body fall. There wasn't anything I could do to prevent her from shooting herself, but I felt helpless watching her pull the trigger.

"Let's get out of here, now!" I said to Marsha.

Knowing the danger we were in, I picked up the pistol and placed it in my back pocket. The only weapon I'd had was that poker and I felt we might need a better choice of weapons. Marsha was still weak, but wanted to walk, so I grabbed her arm as we made our way back to where I'd left the recorder and the camera. Quickly picking everything up, we made it to the car hidden behind the store. Marsha was acting strangely and I could tell she needed help. The only problem was, I didn't think I could take her to the hospital because they would turn us in to the local authorities. At the risk of losing her, we returned to the motel. Along the way, I stopped and got water for Marsha because she complained she was thirsty. The more she drank, the sicker she became.

The lights were on in the room as I fumbled with the key to the door. Barely inserting the key, the door flew open and Janet was standing there not appearing very happy to see me. She hadn't seen Marsha, because she was out of her vision standing in the hallway.

"Just where the hell have you been?" she hollered at me, and I was sure she would wake up everyone in the motel.

Marsha stepped from around the door and Janet screamed again seeing her. I explained to Janet she was sick and needed to lie down, so with her assistance, we placed Marsha on the bed. The color on Marsha's face was a pale white and her eyes were rolling back and forth.

"She needs to get to the hospital," Janet said to me.

"I know, baby, but you know we can't take that chance."

Janet got a cold towel and wiped the top of Marsha's head. She was running a fever and Janet knew we had to get it down so she wouldn't go into convulsions. For the rest of the night, Janet attended to Marsha. Taking the risk of getting caught, I went to a drug store to purchase a thermometer and medicine for her fever. Marsha's temperature reached 105 degrees at one time and we placed her in the tub, pouring ice cubes over her until it broke. Other than getting something to eat, we never left the room. Finally on the third day, she opened her eyes and smiled at us.

"How are you feeling?" Janet asked. She was still weak from the experience, but managed to say she was fine.

Knowing Marsha didn't need to be moved anytime soon, I went to the front office of the motel to make arrangements to stay a couple more days. Sitting on the table in the lobby was the local daily newspaper. On the front page was John and Betty's picture with the headline: "*Local Woman Kills Husband and Then Herself.*" The manager of the motel saw me reading the paper.

"It's a shame what happened to them folks," he stated. "I've known John and Betty for a long time, and I never thought Betty was capable of doing something like that," he said as I signed the registration card to stay two more days.

Purchasing a paper, I returned to the room and showed Janet and Marsha. I'd explained to Janet what had happened that night and seeing the paper upset her even more. Marsha wept while reading the details of the article and I could see she was thinking of the events that happened to her as well.

"Marsha, how did you survive the attack?" Janet asked her.

"I don't know," was her response. "We were standing there looking at the car shaking and the next thing I knew, I was strapped to a table and Raymond was standing over me."

"What was he doing to you?" I questioned.

"Again, I don't know. ...He said that I would be like him soon and that's all he told me," she said while tearing up.

Everyone was getting hungry, so I went and got us some food while Janet and Marsha remained in the room. Returning, I noticed they both had been crying and I wanted to know why. Janet looked at me and said Marsha had a vision of something terrifying. Still not understanding, she told me Marsha could feel the presence of Doctor Raymond and felt he would soon be coming for her.

"He knows where I'm at!" Marsha cried out and I could see she was terrified.

I tired to talk calmly to her, saying there was no way he could find us because I'd used an alias name when I registered. She continued telling us that he knew she was there and it wouldn't be long before he'd take her again. This time I questioned her as to why she thought he could locate her, and she said it had something to do with the liquid he was injecting into her.

"What was that stuff?" I asked.

"I don't know," she replied.

For the rest of the afternoon, we tried to assure her everything would be all right, but nothing we did seemed to help. Every time she heard a noise outside the room, she jumped thinking Doctor Thomas was coming through the door. As night fell, I knew we needed to eat again and I suggested we all go to a restaurant not far from where we were staying. Marsha was frightened to leave the room, but Janet convinced her it would do us all good.

Marsha was still very weak and we had to assist her into the restaurant. The place was almost full and there was only one table available, so the host escorted us through the dining area to be seated. Several people stared at us and this made me feel uncomfortable. One man wouldn't take his eyes off Marsha and I was about to say something to him when Janet stopped me, seeing what I was about to do. As we were eating our meal, two deputies walked in and headed in our direction.

"Excuse me Sir, but is your name Richard Parker?" one of the deputies asked standing next to me.

"Yes, it is officer. Is there something wrong?" was my reply and he said he wanted to ask me a few questions.

When I indicated to the officer it was all right, he asked me to go outside to his vehicle. This made me suspicious, but I agreed against Janet's wishes. As I stood up from the table, I told Marsha and Janet to finish their dinner and I'd be returning soon.

Once we were outside the restaurant, one of the officers grabbed my arm and threw me on the top of a parked car. He pulled both my arms behind me and put handcuffs on me. I tried to ask why they were being so violent and the other officer told me to be quiet if I knew what was good for me. They threw me in the back of the car and carried me to the police station. At the station, I was led into the same room I'd been placed in twice previously. It wasn't long before the door opened and Deputy Hawthorne walked into the room and sat down in front of me.

"Remember me, Mr. Parker?" he asked. "I was the one who found you in the woods by Lake Singletary several weeks ago," he again said, and I nodded my head to let him know I remembered.

"Thank you again for coming to my aid. ...Why am I here?" I questioned the deputy.

He started off by telling me that he'd been searching for me and thought I might know more about what happened to Jack Wilson. When he mentioned his name, I know I tensed up, but I tried to remain calm. He said his car had been found in a parking lot at a nearby shopping center and he had not been heard from for several days. Looking straight into my eyes, he said I was the last one who may have seen him, because he knew Jack was with me the night he'd disappeared. The questioning went on for another hour and I continued telling him that I didn't know what had happened to him. Finally, after being drilled with more questions, I told them to either arrest me or let me go, hoping this would prove to be a good bluff. It worked, because he stood up and said I was free to go, but he might want to ask more questions later.

The same two officers that came to the restaurant took me back and when we got there, the place was closed. Janet and Marsha were gone, so I figured they must have gone back to the motel. I asked the officers to take me there. At first they complained that it wasn't their job to taxi me all over town, but gave in. When we pulled up, I saw our car and I was sure the ladies were fine, so I thanked the officers and went to the room. First knocking on the door, I inserted my key and entered the room to find it empty. Janet's purse was sitting on the bed and that wasn't like her to go off and leave it. Although it was late, I thought they might have gone to the pool area since it was a nice night, so I made my way to the other side of the motel where it was located. No one was at the pool and I searched every place I could. They weren't anywhere around and I started remembering that Marsha had said she felt Doctor Thomas was coming for her.

"My God, he's taken them," I said to myself and ran back to the room.

The gun I'd taken earlier from the doctor's house was still where I had placed it between some towels in the bathroom. It was loaded and I rushed to the car, hoping I could get there in time to save my wife and Marsha. Driving as fast as I could, it took me about an hour to get to Lake Waccamaw. This time I didn't stop short of his driveway, I turned in and headed to his house. Just before reaching the end, I turned off the lights and engine. Immediately, I knew something was happening at his place. The lights were on and someone was walking around, because I could see their silhouette through the window.

As much as I wanted to rush the house, I knew I had to know what I was facing or I'd be putting Janet and Marsha at more risk. I wasn't positive they were in there, but my gut feelings told me they were. Trying to get a better understanding, I turned on the microphone hoping to hear voices.

"Now you won't escape me this time, Marsha!" I heard and I knew at least one of them were there. "Once I'm done with her, then we'll be next," said a man's voice and I assumed it was Doctor Thomas.

Knowing I didn't have very much time, I tried to enter the house through the back door. This time it was locked, so I attempted to enter through the rest of the doors and they all were locked as well. Looking through a window, I saw two men walking around inside. Neither one was Doctor Thomas, so I figured he was downstairs with the girls. My only chance to save them meant I had to catch the men by surprise, but I didn't know how that was going to happen.

Running around to the opposite side of the house, I saw a window on the second floor that looked like a good entrance. I had to climb up on the back porch section to get to the window, and that was where the two men were located inside the house. So, as quietly as I could, I made my way to the top and almost slipped as I pulled myself up on the roof. The window was locked, but I knew I had to get inside, so I used my elbow to break the windowpane. With the gun in my hand, I climbed in through the window, expecting to see someone come into the room. No one entered as I stood there in what I assumed was Doctor Thomas's bedroom. The odd thing about the room was that it looked like no one had slept in the bed for years. Only having the benefit of a security light from the yard, I could see nothing had been moved in this room for a long time.

The door was locked, but I was able to unlock it and exit into the hallway. The stairs were just to my right and I began carefully walking down one step at a time. Suddenly, I heard Janet scream and I rushed to the bottom. One of the men, who had been sitting in the kitchen, ran in the area I was at and I recognized it was one of the officers who had taken me to the police station. He pulled his gun and it was obvious he was going to shoot me, but I fired first, hitting him in the chest area. Suddenly, I heard a shot and the bullet brushed by my head hitting the doorframe. Reactively, I turned and fired hitting the second officer in his shoulder, causing him to drop his gun. The two men needed medical aid, but my concern was for Janet and Marsha. Without any regard for myself, I ran down the stairs to the basement, ready to shoot anyone who got in my way.

Janet saw me and screamed for me to watch out, as I looked toward the table that Marsha was strapped securely on. Doctor Thomas was standing over her and I hollered for him to move away, but he didn't move.

"Get away from her!" I yelled at him, but he continued turning the dial on some equipment attached to her arm.

"Step away or I'll shoot!" I again barked at him.

Doctor Thomas stopped, smiled at me and made one last turn of the dial. Marsha screamed as if she was in pain, so I pulled the trigger. At that moment, he flew back from the impact of the bullet hitting his chest and I knew I'd killed him. Instead of falling, he smiled at me and disappeared into thin air. Suddenly, I was knocked to the floor from a strong force hitting me and the wall behind me opened up. It felt like the air was being sucked out of the room as he passed into the opening and the wall shut behind him.

"Are you all right, Janet?" I said, quickly jumping up and running to her, as she was still tied up in a chair.

"I'm fine," she replied, and hugged me as I freed her.

We clung to each other and I told her how much it scared me thinking she may have been killed. She indicated the same to me and we turned to assist Marsha. She still had the tubes inserted in her arm and something was happening to her. Her body began to shake and a bluish fluid started coming out her nose and ears. It looked like the same liquid I'd seen the last time I pulled the tubes from her arm. The shaking became more violent and she opened her eyes.

"Ki...ki...me," we heard her say, but couldn't understand her words.

"Ki... Kil... Kill Me!" she finally spoke and we knew this time what she wanted.

"No Marsha, we can't do that to you!" Janet said and started unbuckling the straps.

"I don't want to be like him!" she screamed and then without warning, the straps went limp and Marsha was gone.

The wall opened once again and we felt the rush of wind push by us, but this time it didn't do any harm as it exited the room through the opening. As previously, the opening closed and the room felt empty as if we were the only ones around.

Grabbing Janet's hand, I led her to the stairs and she began weeping. We both knew Marsha was gone this time and there wasn't anything we could do to bring her back. Knowing it was the doctor's laboratory, I wanted to destroy it before leaving. Seeing a box of matches sitting on a shelf, I started a fire using some paper I'd found. Janet hollered for us to leave and started up the stairs. She had only taken one step and I heard her scream again.

"So, you want to burn the place down!" I heard coming from the officer I'd shot in the shoulder. "You'll burn with it!" he shouted and slammed the door.

The fire was already beginning to rage and I knew I couldn't put it out. I tried to get the door open, but he had secured it tightly and I knew we couldn't get through it. The smoke was filling the room and the heat was also intensifying.

"Rick, the wall!" Janet screamed at me and I knew what she was referring to.

Doctor Thomas and Janet had gone through an opening in the wall, so it was our only hope of escape. Fighting through the smoke and trying to protect ourselves the best we could, we made our way to the spot where the wall had opened. Using a hammer I found lying on a table, I started beating on the wall. Soon I had punched a hole and could see only the outer wall. It looked as if we were trapped and about to die when Janet suggested I move to my right a couple of feet and try it again. On the first hit of the hammer, I went through and saw a tunnel. Air began to push into the room and it flamed the fire even more. After several more strikes, I ripped the remaining wall open enough to allow us to enter.

I was the first to go into the tunnel and once inside, pulled Janet to me just before some of the flammable liquid exploded and filled the room with flames. There wasn't any light in the tunnel, but we knew that was our only choice. Leading the way, I felt the sides of the walls and carefully stepped, hoping not to fall into a deep hole. We didn't know where it led and what might be waiting on the other end. Obviously, Doctor Thomas, and now Marsha, could be there ready to attack.

We traveled for a long time and it felt as if we'd walked miles, but it was hard to tell, because there wasn't any sense of how far we'd gone inside this completely dark hole in the ground. The one thing we could tell was the tunnel appeared to be wet. Several times we stepped into a pool of cold water. Exhaustion was beginning to set in and Janet wanted to stop, but I wouldn't let her.

"Rick, I can't go any further!" she begged.

"Baby, we can't stop and you know that, so hang onto me and we'll make it," I told her as I kissed her lips in the dark.

We pushed our way further into the tunnel and I pulled on Janet as much as I could. I was getting exhausted as well, but I wouldn't let Janet know. Just when I was about to give in and stop, ahead was a glimmer of light. It seemed as if it was a mile away, but I knew there was some hope, and seeing it gave Janet some encouragement to continue as well.

The dimensions of the tunnel were not big and we soon reached the source of our journey. Because we had been in total darkness for so long, it took a while for me to be able to see in the brighter environment. As soon as my eyes were able to focus, I saw we were in some kind of building, but I didn't know where. The sun was shining, so I knew we had been in the tunnel for more than six hours. With little strength left, we pushed on the partially opened door and exited the tunnel. We were standing in what appeared to be a storage building of some kind, because there were tools and garden equipment all around us. We could hear some activity outside the building, but I was still leery that Doctor Thomas or what emulated him, was around. Carefully and as quietly as we could move through the loaded room of gear, I took a look through the window.

"We're in the Indian village," I whispered to Janet. "I can see the stores and Indian Mound about 500 yards to the left."

There weren't any signs of Doctor Thomas or Marsha anywhere I looked. Janet and I sat down for a much needed rest and before we knew it, we fell asleep. Finally stopping after the long night's journey was more than either one of us could endure, and it did not take long once our eyes closed.

"Mister, Mister, are you all right?" was the next thing I heard.

"Ma'am, what happened to you?" we heard coming from an older man's voice.

Opening my eyes, I saw the same old Indian man I had seen carving animals out of wood the first time I visited the village. He asked us again how we were doing and I told him we were tired because we'd gotten lost during the night wandering through the woods.

"You don't want to get lost in these woods," the old man said and reached down to help Janet up off the ground. "You come with me," he insisted and still holding onto Janet's arm, he helped her through the front door.

The man walked us past the village to the place where I'd seen all the carved animals he said no longer lived at the lake. Once inside the building, he opened a door leading us to another section. He lived there and I was surprised to see how big this part of the place was. He had converted the front porch of his house into the display area where all the carvings were located.

"You rest here after you eat," he again insisted and started fixing us some food.

I started to decline his offer, but Janet looked like she couldn't go any further and we both were hungry. Not one time while he was preparing the meal did he ask any questions. He fed us and then suggested we get some sleep, and he closed the door as he exited the room. Taking advantage of his hospitality, we once again went to sleep.

Chapter 16

SOMETHING INSIDE THE HOLE

"You look good for dead folks," the old man spoke as we awoke to the aroma of food cooking.

Janet and I were puzzled by his comments and I asked him what he was talking about. He explained how the local news reported two officers and a couple were killed in a raging fire at Doctor Thomas's place three days earlier.

"According to the doc, the officers died while protecting him from a man and woman who'd broken into his house," he stated from a newspaper. "From the looks of you two, I have to say you must be the man and woman in question." He'd seen the affects of the black soot from the fire was still on our clothes and faces.

What caught my attention was when he said it had happened three days earlier. When I questioned him, he explained we'd slept for 24 hours and we had no idea we'd been there that long. Janet apologized and asked why he had not turned us over to the authorities. His answer was that he always felt something wrong went on over at Doctor Thomas's place and we didn't look like the kind of folks who would do harm to anyone. Janet and I stared at each other, because we knew I'd shot the officers in self-defense.

"My name is, George Blackwater," he said, introducing himself.

Again, we thanked him for assisting us and he wanted to know what happened inside of the doctor's place the night we were there. His interest in the details surprised me, but I told him everything, knowing this could possibly come back and haunt us if the authorities caught us. George seemed very interested in the laboratory in the doctor's basement.

"Did you see what the fluid looked like he was injecting into your friend, Marsha," he questioned.

The best I could remember was that it was a bluish color and Janet confirmed it. Janet informed him while she was tied up, the doctor mixed several things together to come up with the final solution. She continued saying Doctor Thomas stored several bottles of liquids inside a cabinet in the basement, along with notes he read from while mixing the formula.

"What I do remember seeing were the words, *Project Stealth* on one of the notebooks in the cabinet," Janet said and George seemed even more attentive.

George questioned us more on how Marsha and Doctor Thomas vanished in plain view, and I explained what we'd witnessed. He said we were lucky to be alive and we agreed. This was when I let him know I'd recorded the entity and could prove its existence. The only problem was, the equipment was in the truck of our car at the doctor's place. He agreed it would be difficult to retrieve, but not impossible if the vehicle was still there.

Doctor Thomas's house was completely burned to the ground and there was very little evidence left, he explained to us. Most of the investigation by the local authorities was finished and he thought he should be able to get in and out without being detected. He said when it was dark later he would go to the doctor's house for the gear. I suggested that I go with him, but he was right by saying everyone was looking for us in connection with the murders. Janet and I felt like prisoners in his place, but safe for the time being.

As darkness fell on the lake, George got in his canoe and took off toward the doctor's place. He said it would take him about 30 minutes to get there and the lake would allow him to sneak in and out easier. My concern was the lake and the dangers that lay inside of it, but he told us not to be worried, because the lake was his friend. Friend or not, I still feared for his life.

Watching George disappear in the darkness of the night made Janet and I wonder why he was being so kind to us and why he had not turned us in. He seemed genuine with his wiliness to help us, but we couldn't help but think there was another motive. The time passed by and we stared at the lake for any signs of him returning. Finally, after three hours had passed since he began his journey, in the distance we saw the shape of a canoe and George coming toward us. Helping to pull the canoe on shore, I saw my equipment in the front.

"What took so long?" I questioned George.

"When I first got there, something was happening in the burnt rumble of the house," he said. "Someone was looking for something inside the hole in the ground where the basement once was."

He continued telling us how he hid in some brush and watched what was happening. He never could see who it was, but there definitely was someone or something searching. After about an hour, it stopped and suddenly disappeared as he made his way to our car.

"Okay, let's take a look at that evidence!" George suggested as we carried the gear to his place.

"No! There's no way we're going to look at it!" I told him with conviction and Janet also rejected the idea.

"Well, if we can't look at it, then what good is the evidence," he said in a snappy tone.

Once again I explained what had happened the last time I'd played back any recordings, to include the one in Charlotte that resulted in Steve's death. He seemed puzzled by my explanation, but agreed not to review it for the moment. Back inside the house, we ate some dinner Janet had prepared and didn't discuss the recording any more. Following the meal, George gave us his bed and said he'd spend the night at one of his friend's houses.

When morning came, George knocked on the door early, requesting Janet and I get dressed. Opening the door, he was standing there with two men and I was sure they were going to arrest us.

"I'd like for you to meet agents Miller and Hill," George said while introducing the two men. "They work for the National Security Council and would like to ask you some questions," he indicated as they entered the place.

Seeing two agents made me think it was all over for us and we'd soon be escorted to jail. Instead, they sat down and started explaining the reason they were there.

"Agent Blackwater called us and explained the situation," Hill said and I turned to look at George.

George explained he was an NSC agent and had been watching Doctor Thomas for years. He told us the doctor once worked for the government back in the 1970's in the research Department of Defense. He and several of his colleagues were involved with a *"Project Stealth"* in which they were to make soldiers invisible.

I was totally amazed hearing the agents talk about the project and wondered why they were telling us about it. I didn't have to wait very long for my answer, because Agent Miller said the recording we'd captured could be important evidence against Doctor Thomas.

"I still don't understand what is going on!" I stated to the agents.

George told us that he'd been undercover for more than thirty years watching not only the doctor, but some of the locals as well. Continuing the story, he said Thomas had a falling out with the other scientists working on the project and left the DOD to pursue a private practice in medicine, but not before making sure most of the research disappeared.

"We've always known he was doing further research, we just weren't able to pin it down," Agent Hill spoke up and said.

Janet looked at them and suggested he'd completed the research and was now implementing the plan, saying how she'd witnessed Marsha's transformation.

"That why it's important we review your recordings, to see what we are up against," Agent Hill said.

Knowing viewing the recording could result in a dangerous situation, they suggested we travel to Wilmington, NC to one of their secluded labs. They told us the labs were shielded with metal and would prevent any sounds from escaping the room. It sounded like the first good idea I'd heard in a while, so we gathered up the equipment and drove down Highway 74 to Wilmington.

The laboratory was actually the FBI's facilities and they had made arrangements to use them prior to our arrival. As we entered the building, I spotted a picture of Janet and I hanging from the wall. On the picture, it said we were wanted for the murders of two officers in Bladen County. It also read we were armed and dangerous. One FBI agent, upon seeing us walk through the door, recognized us and ran over with his gun pointed at me.

"Stop right there!" he shouted at me.

"Back off, agent. ...They're with us!" Agent Miller replied and showed his NSC badge.

"But they're wanted for killing one of our own!" he pleaded.

"We know what they are wanted for and it's in our jurisdiction," Miller stated firmly.

The FBI agent dropped his gun and I could tell he wanted to pursue it further, but didn't. Miller led us down some hallways and finally stopped at a steel door. He picked up the telephone hanging on the wall and within seconds, the door opened and we entered a room that looked like a research lab.

"This is where the FBI does its ballistics testing," Hill said to Janet.

In the room, we could see several people working on items like guns and knives. They appeared to be testing them and taking pictures as if they were comparing things. George pointed at a gun over on one of the tables and it looked charred from being in a fire.

"That's the officer's gun that was recovered from Doctor Thomas's place," he said, and my stomach turned hearing those words.

"Rick, I know you are the one who shot the officers, but we also know they were involved with the doctor's activities. Unfortunately, they died before we could catch them," George explained.

Janet reached over and squeezed my hand as if everything was going to be all right, because she knew how badly I felt shooting the officers. Even though it was self-defense, I knew I'd taken someone's life and it was a hard burden to carry.

The agents went into a room and said it was soundproof and nothing could escape that chamber. Hoping he was correct, I removed and set up the video camera and audio recorder. The agent assisting us suggested we run it through some enhancement equipment that would allow him to better review the evidence. He connected some cables and I started the video.

It started off very dark and using his enhancers, we could see Jack Wilson tied to the tree beside Lake Singletary. The image became so clear we could see the fear on his face. The technician set up the audio to play along at the same sequence of the video. At the lake, we could make out what Jack was saying, but not every word was clear.

"God, please get me out of here!" were Jack's screams and his face was terrified.

At the beginning of the video, we did not see the entity appear at the lake, but it suddenly came into view on the screen before us. While looking at it through the infrared lens of the camera during the time it actually happened, it appeared to be seven feet tall and had a large head. Looking at the enhanced video, it had a different appearance all its own. The actual height appeared to be around six feet tall. The remainder was an energy field of some kind surrounding it. The video showed a man who resembled Doctor Thomas and he looked angry with Jack.

The audio was a high-pitched sound that almost hurt our ears to listen to. Nevertheless, it was evident that Jack knew who it was and he pleaded for his life. The technician tuned the frequencies to get a better audio.

"Please, Ray. ...I didn't know," we finally heard after the technician did his work.

Again, Jack begged Doctor Thomas not to harm him followed by a high-pitched noise as if he was talking back to him. Several more exchanges were made and Jack quickly disappeared from the screen. Reviewing the video in slow motion, we could see the energy field completely engulf Jack and he flew into the water. The figure then jumped in our direction and the next thing we saw was it shaking the vehicle Janet was in. The sound was still a high-pitched noise as if it was trying to communicate to Janet. When Marsha screamed, it suddenly moved toward her. In slow motion, the energy field surrounded her and carried her into the lake inside the force field. We could see Marsha's terrified face as she disappeared below the water level.

"That's quite a video you captured, Mr. Parker," the lab technician said to me.

"Yes, it certainly is," I replied.

Agents Miller and Hill left the room indicating to George that we needed to go to the debriefing area. George agreed and escorted Janet and me to another room within the building. We sat there for a while and soon a tall man dressed in a military uniform walked in. On his lapel was two stars and I knew he was a general in the Marine Corps.

"Good afternoon, Mr. and Mrs. Parker," he addressed us. "I'm General Priebe, the head of the National Security Council," he said as he shook our hands.

He stated he was there because of the situation we were involved in. Requesting to know how we had gotten involved, I almost felt we were suspects. Janet got upset and let him know she didn't appreciate the way he was questioning us. He apologized and his mannerism changed.

"We know Thomas was doing experiments on the local animals in the area, because we have been watching him," he said while looking at George Blackwater.

The general stated they knew he was close to a solution, but didn't have the evidence until now. They wanted to arrest him, but he'd disappeared before they could apprehend him. He said they found the tunnel underneath his house that led to the Indian Village. He further stated they found several more tunnels that connected the other lakes together.

"He was using these tunnels to get around without being detected," the general stated.

"So, what is it you want from us?" I questioned him.

He sat across from us at the table and said he wanted us to help catch him. Janet immediately spoke up and said, no. The General looked at us and said we didn't have a choice or we'd end up in jail for killing two officers. He said my fingerprints were all over the gun, and he'd make sure I'd never see the light of day again, and Janet would go to jail as well.

"Besides, you wouldn't want that beautiful little girl of yours to grow up without a Mommy and Daddy, …would you?" he said in the threatening tone.

"You leave our daughter out of this!" Janet screamed at him, and he just stared at her without any emotion.

"That's up to you!" the general barked, and stood up as if he was leaving the room.

I stopped him and said I would assist him as long as Janet was allowed to go home. At first, he stood there and finally agreed to my request. Janet stated she wouldn't leave me there alone and I explained to her that if something did happen, then she needed to take care of Clair. She wasn't satisfied with my reply, but she knew it was the right choice to make.

General Priebe told George to let Janet go and escort me to room 324. He seemed to understand and acknowledged his request. Agents Hill and Miller were waiting for us as we exited the room. George instructed them to assist Janet in any way they could, because she would be going home. I gave her a final kiss goodbye and told her I'd call her later to make sure everything was all right. Tears fell from her eyes as we walked away and it was hard for me watching her go, knowing it could be the last time I'd ever see her if anything went wrong. But I did have comfort knowing she would be out of harm's way and Clair would have her mother.

Chapter 17

HELMUT THE BUTCHER

The walk to room 324 was longer than I had anticipated. We traveled through a series of security checkpoints and I knew I was going into places most non-FBI people wouldn't go. Even George had to get special permission to enter the last room.

Once inside the room, Agent Ronald Roberts greeted us. He informed George he would take charge of me from that point on and George shook my hand giving his good-byes. Agent Roberts sat me next to a table with a model of some type of strange equipment. I didn't say anything to him and waited for him to tell me what was going on.

"Mr. Parker, I've been told you know why you are here," he began saying to me, and I told him all I knew was I had to cooperate with him.

Agent Roberts was understanding of my situation and tried his best to make me feel more comfortable. But it was hard to feel good when you knew there was a possibility you might never see your family again. He could sense my anxiety and said he would do all in his power to ensure my safety.

"So what is it I'm supposed to do?" I questioned him.

"You really don't know why you are here, do you?" Robert questioned.

Pointing at an area on the other side of the room, he explained I was to lure Raymond Thomas into a containment area so they could trap him. I couldn't understand why they needed me, and Agent Roberts said it was because they knew he would go after me.

"Mr. Parker, you've seen him and he knows you have evidence. That's why we know he'll be looking for you," said Roberts.

The more I thought about it, the more I realized he was correct and I'd have to face Thomas. I did know too much and the next time we met, I'd be the one on his table, just like Marsha.

"Agent Roberts, just what is it I'm facing and how did Doctor Thomas become the way he is?" I asked, wanting to know more.

He looked at me and said he figured I had the right to know everything, so he sat down next to me and started talking about the mysteries of the Carolina Bays. This sparked my interest even more, since that was what I'd originally began investigating.

"The story really began in the 1940's when Adolph Hitler came to power in Germany," he began.

He stated Hitler wanted to create a secret army that could invade any country without being detected. His top scientist on the project was, "*Helmut Kiel*." At the time his nickname was, "*Helmut the Butcher*", because of all the experiments he'd done on humans.

Agent Roberts continued telling me that "*The Butcher*" was working on a serum that would make people invisible and control them. Hitler invested a lot of time and effort into this project and became upset when he didn't see the results as fast as he wanted. "*The Butcher*" heard of a plot that he would be killed if Hitler didn't have his invisible army within a few months, so he defected to Europe. The Europeans didn't welcome him either and the Americans offered him asylum in the United States as long as he worked for the government.

Helmut Kiel became a lead scientist working on "*Project Eastland*" during the late 1940's. This was a government project to coat equipment with a special fluid that would cause it to be undetected by the enemy. The intent was to use this on our airplanes to fly into hostile territories. President Truman saw the need to have such a weapon during WWII. The Air Force was in charge of "*Project Eastland*" and given all the resources they required.

The government didn't want to have this information leak out to the public, so the experiments were done at a remote air base located near Holly Ridge, North Carolina, called Camp Davis. It was originally a U.S. Army antiaircraft artillery-training center when it was built in 1941. By the end of WWII, the camp was abandoned and it served to be the perfect place to conduct experiments because of its isolation. While visiting Carolina Beach, a popular vacation spot near Wilmington, he met Mary Thomas. Mary was from Lake Waccamaw and her family owned much of the land surrounding the lake. Mary and Helmut were married not long after they met and had a son they named Raymond. Because of all the hatred for Germany after WWII, they decided to give him his mother's maiden name of Thomas.

Raymond Thomas grew up and became a medical doctor at the young age of 24. He graduated the top of his class from John Hopkins University. It was said he was close to his father until his untimely death in 1969 of a heart attack. Raymond's mother died not long after in 1971, in an automobile accident.

Agent Roberts almost appeared to admire Ray Thomas as he spoke of his accomplishments. He told me the government wasn't that aware Thomas was the son of Helmut Kiel until he was deep into Project Stealth.

"His father had developed the coating and it eventually was used for the stealth bomber to make it undetectable by radar," the agent said smiling.

Raymond Thomas became displeased with the other scientists and quit the program, but not before destroying all the notes he'd acquired over the years. He moved back to Lake Waccamaw and started his medical practice.

"We've had people like George Blackwater watching him to see if he'd continued with his research," Roberts said. "We believe he has perfected a serum that combined his father's work with the genetics of the human body to create the entity that attacked you," he said with concern in his voice.

Agent Roberts said Doctor Thomas used all the folklores and mysteries of the Carolina Bays to allow him the ability to continue his research. Many theories have come from the shape of the bays and writers over the years have claimed aliens created them. Some legends are told of lake monsters living in deep caves that devour people.

"No creature or alien evidence has ever been found associated with the Carolina Bays," he said as he smiled.

The NSC thought Thomas was creating a small group of creatures like himself who one day might attack the very heart of our government, and I knew he was talking about the White House. Agent Roberts' tone changed as he looked over at the device on the other side of the room.

"If we do not succeed, then this country, and perhaps the world, will change," he stated as he got up and walked toward the other side of the room.

Hearing the agent tell me the reason for catching Doctor Thomas, I knew that was what I had to do even at the risk of losing my life. It was from Janet's and my description of what we saw in the doctor's basement that led them to believe he had developed a genetic formula. Somehow this formula changed the molecular structure of the body into an energy field that could think and react on its own. This explained how it was able to move so quickly and even attack people.

"Why hasn't he attacked before now?" I questioned.

"We assume he has been building his army and is close to being ready. ...That's why we have to act fast," he said as he stepped into his device.

I wanted to know more about the machine and how it was to operate. He explained it was like an anti-force field. It was shaped like a cylinder made of iron pipes and about ten feet long. Inside the pipes were wires that connected to a high voltage transformer. A sensor would detect the presence of an electrical energy source and turn on the transformer. Once on, 20,000 volts flowed through the wires to create a force field.

"The theory is, once he's inside our force field, he will be torn apart and that should kill him," Agent Roberts stated, but he didn't sound very convincing.

He explained that a normal energy source worked similar to magnetic fields of the earth. When energy is applied, it creates a north/south pole effect from the energy flow. Using the Earth's own polar energy as a source of direction, they are able to propel themselves in any direction they want to travel. Depending on how much energy is applied, is how fast they can travel.

"This machine will neutralize the force field if we can get him inside," he stated once again.

The plan sounded as if it would work, but I had some concerns on where and how we would lure him into the device. Agent Roberts told me the device would be placed inside one of the ranger's shacks at Lake Singletary. It was my job to lure him into the shack. He knew of my encounters previously while playing back the recordings. Over on one of the benches was my video and sound gear. Another technician was analyzing the sound to isolate the high-pitched frequencies. We stood behind him as he turned knobs and made notes. He had written down the number 27.62— 28.15 GHz on his notepad and I asked him what it meant.

"I believe this to be the range he is communicating in," the technician answered.

He said he was trying to filter out all the background noise to allow him the ability to make better sense of what the entity was saying. The tech implied he might be able to convert it into language we could understand. I didn't know all the details about the equipment he was working with, but he seemed certain he should be able to make it work. Agent Roberts asked how long it would take and the technician told him it could be days.

"We may not have days," replied Roberts, and he led me into another section of the facilities.

We remained in a small conference room until Agents Hill and Miller joined us. It wasn't long after they arrived that General Priebe also came into the room with two other military officers. General Priebe took command and this time he wasn't as harsh as he had been previously.

"Rick, may I call you Rick?" he spoke, and I nodded my head to indicate it was all right. "I realize we are asking you to risk your life and that is exactly what I want you to do. What you are about to do could possibility save this country and our president, and if you succeed in stopping Raymond Thomas, then you will be hailed as a hero," he said, and I knew he was giving me the type of speech that he would give sending his troops into battle.

I looked at him and said I would have done this even without all the threats against my wife and me. The general shook my hand as if he had accomplished his mission and instructed one of the other officers to brief me on the plan of attack. After giving the orders, he saluted me and exited the room. Seeing him salute made me feel like a soldier that was about to go on a suicide mission.

"Mr. Parker, my name is Colonel Long and I'm going to brief you on the mission," he said in a deep voice.

He laid some diagrams on the table explaining it was the layout of the park at Lake Singletary. Another page showed a blueprint of the building they wanted to install the device in. I asked what the name of the device was and he looked strangely at me, saying they had not had time to give it a name. I suggested we call it "*Marsha*" in honor of Marsha Johnson. They didn't seem to care what it was called and everyone in the room agreed.

"At least we will know what to call it in the field," Agent Hill spoke up and said.

Continuing to explain the plan, Colonel Long talked about how they were going to assemble "*Marsha*" piece-by-piece inside the cabin and run the attaching cables to the structure next to it for the power requirements. My job was to lure Thomas into the cabin and get out before it automatically turned on.

"Once it turns itself on, you have less than two seconds to get out or you will be cooked instantly as if you were in a microwave oven," the colonel said, and that wasn't a pleasant thought.

"Well, at least the dogs will have a hot meal," Agent Miller gestured, trying to be funny.

No one thought it was funny and he apologized to me. The colonel gave a few more details and asked if there were any questions. Agent Roberts tapped the back of my shoulder and said I was truly brave to perform the mission. Roberts also wanted to know why I had to do it and why couldn't an agent play the sounds to attract Thomas.

"Thomas is too smart for that and we know he wants Parker for his own army," the colonel said.

"He's been there before and it has to be Rick who will lure him into the trap." These were his final words before leaving the room.

Agent Roberts took charge of me and transferred me to a motel for the evening. The agency had arranged for me to stay in Wilmington at the Hilton located next to the Cape Fear River. He said it would take the lab folks a full day to get "*Marsha*" in place and working, so I could have a day of rest and pleasure. I didn't know what kind of pleasure he thought I would have until I opened the door to my room. Inside I saw Janet lying on the bed and she jumped up to greet me as I entered the room. She explained General Priebe had set it all up and wanted it to be a surprise. It was the best surprise of my life at that moment. They had called Janet before we left the bureau and she had ordered room service. Sitting on the table was a wonderful steak dinner and I was starved, since I had not eaten all day.

"Rick, let's sit down and enjoy our dinner together and what time we will have prior to you leaving," she said and gave me another wonderful kiss.

During dinner, Janet kept grabbing my hand and I felt as though she thought it would be our last night together. It was difficult holding a conversation, because we didn't know what to talk about. It's strange when you think it could be the last moment you'll ever spend with the one you love and you can't think of anything to say to her. Finally, I pulled Janet up from the table, picked her up and carried her to the bed. Gently placing her down, I kissed her and let her know she meant more to me than anything else in the world. Looking into her teary eyes, I said to her that if it meant I would lose my life to save hers and Clair's, then I would gladly sacrifice my life for theirs. She openly cried as she squeezed me tightly to her chest.

"We know the danger, so from now to the time I have to leave, I want us to enjoy each other," I said as I pulled her up from the bed and led her to the bathroom.

The bathroom had a large Jacuzzi and I wanted to take advantage of it. Janet smiled as she turned on the water and poured in something from a bottle she retrieved from a basket next to the tub.

"This is *Gardens of Kyoto* and it will arouse your senses with the mixture of the Fuji apple, Asian pear nectar, Chinese star jasmine and bamboo," she read as she was pouring the first bottle. "And yes, these bottles called *Reflect, Awaken,* and *Plains of Serengeti* are for stress, concentration, emotion, and will revitalize your mind, body and spirit," she again read while empting the small bottles into the tub.

It had been a while since Janet and I had been alone, and I didn't need the assistance of those aromas to arouse my senses. Just watching her remove her clothing was all the motivation I needed. Janet smiled as she dropped the last piece of clothing to the floor, because she could see the excitement in my eyes. She knew I had not looked at her that way for a while and I think it pleased her. The aroma from the scents did enhance the moment as I first got settled into the spa and then assisted Janet. As she submerged in the water and settled in my arms, the touch of her body against mine felt wonderful. There was a peacefulness of the moment, so we decided not to turn on the jets of the spa. My fingers rubbed her soft skin and I wasn't worried about anything else in the world, because I wanted to enjoy every second of the time we were spending together.

"Rick, I love you and I want to tell you, if something happens..." I put my hand over her mouth, because I didn't want to ruin the moment.

"I love you, Janet," was my reply, and we didn't say another word although we both knew what the other was thinking.

We sat in the tub long enough for our fingers to get water-logged and wrinkled. Janet got out first and met me with a towel when I stood up. She slowly dried me with the towel and asked me to turn around so that my back was facing her. As she slowly moved the towel down the middle of my back, she kissed the back of my neck and I felt the tips of my toes tingle. With her long fingernails, she scraped down my back barely touching my skin, and I thought she had touched every erotic sensor on my back. She knew what she was doing and grabbed my hand, leading me into the bedroom where she laid me down. With her hair, she brushed my chest up and down until I couldn't take it any longer and pulled her to me. Without taking the time to pull back the covers on the bed, we made passionate love.

The next morning the telephone rang and it was Agent Roberts informing me the schedule had been moved up because there had been another disappearance near Lake Singletary during the night. When I asked him who was missing, he said it was a teenager by the name of Chad Class. I got knots in my stomach, because this was the young man I'd assisted near White Lake when he'd run out of gas.

"Isn't his father one of the park rangers at Lake Singletary?" I asked Roberts and he seemed surprised that I knew this information.

"Do we know where he was taken?" I asked, knowing Doctor Thomas's house had been destroyed by fire.

Roberts told me they didn't know and that was one of the reasons for moving the schedule up sooner to try to trap Thomas. He indicated George Blackwater would meet me in an hour and would drive me to the ranger's station. Janet and I had barely finished our breakfast when we heard some-one knocking at the door and it was George. I said my goodbyes to Janet and she wanted to go with us, so I quickly explained again why she didn't need to go. She understood, but cried as I closed the door to the room.

On the way, George told me the workers had disassembled "*Marsha*" during the night and were in the process of installing her in the cabin. He also told me the geeks back at the lab were able to interpret some of the information I'd recorded. When I asked him what they were able to make out, he just said it didn't make sense.

"The force that we had identified as Doctor Thomas said some words that they couldn't make out," he stated. "But what I interpreted was him saying, 'You...Violated...The Twelve Men,'" George said in a puzzled manner. "It was immediately after that Jack was ripped from his position next to the tree. There were some more things spoken while it was shaking the car, but they couldn't make any sense out of it," he said, continuing down the road.

Turning to enter the park, I started feeling sick to my stomach. I was sure it was my nerves knowing what I was about to face. But I knew I had to remain strong and didn't want to show any emotion as we stopped at the main cabin. To my surprise, General Priebe and Colonel Long were standing on the porch and greeted me as I walked toward them.

"Mr. Parker, once again on behave of the President of the United States, we want to thank you for your cooperation," General Priebe said, and again I felt he was trying to make me feel honored to die for my country.

"General, I only wish that you make sure my wife and daughter are taken care of if this goes badly for me," I replied, and he nodded his head in agreement.

Inside the cabin, both men gave me one more briefing on the mission. Colonel Long explained where I needed to be positioned so I could escape and still trap the entity. As I studied the layout, it was obvious to me that I wouldn't have very much time to jump out of the machine before it turned itself on. The more the colonel talked about the plan, the more I realized they didn't want me to make it out alive. I was sure it was their intention for me to disappear along with Doctor Thomas.

"If I succeed in getting Thomas, what about all the others still out there?" I questioned them.

"They will fall without their leader," the general barked with a sense of arrogance.

The door opened and one of the technicians from the lab informed us that "*Marsha*" was ready for action. Following him to the cabin where "*Marsha*" was located, I could see several men looking at me as if it was the last time they'd see me. From the plans I'd heard a few minutes earlier, they could very well be correct, I thought to myself. It was amazing to see the cabin and how they had placed the device. Just inside the front door was where the grid began and it ran to the other side of the wall. The only exit I could see was a small window at the opposite side of the room.

"All you have to do is watch the light," said one of the technicians, pointing at a place on the ceiling.

"Once it illuminates, the device will be activated and you will have three seconds to get out," he again said.

Standing inside the device, I could see cameras and microphones. I thought to myself there would be evidence of my demise if it came to that. On the ceiling and in the middle of the room was a speaker. The tech told me that my recordings would be played through that speaker in hopes it would attract the "*Ghost*." Hearing him chuckle and call it a ghost made me think some of the workers really didn't have a clue as to what was going to happen.

Colonel Long met me back outside the cabin and told me that we would be testing the system in about ten minutes. To me it meant I was being placed on the hook awaiting the big fish to strike. Only a few people remained at the site and they were the ones monitoring the equipment. As soon as the last vehicle left the park, Colonel Long hollered out that it was show time. I walked into the cabin ready to begin the process.

"Remember, you only have three seconds to remove yourself from the room once it detects another energy source," Blackwater said as he shook my hand and wished me luck. "Watch the light!" he barked as he exited the room.

I knew he was referring to the red light next to the speaker. When it lit, the transformer would turn on, applying current to the coil of wire inside the ribs. The knots in my stomach seemed to go away even though I knew I was in danger. My fears turned into revenge, hoping to stop Doctor Thomas from doing any more harm to anyone. The thoughts of Chad were in my mind and I was hoping he was still alive.

"Okay, let's do it!" I shouted, telling them to begin the playback noises.

Chapter 18

I Think We Got Him

Shortly after pressing the button, a familiar, high-pitched sound came through the speaker in the room. Its sound made goosebumps pop up on my arms. I stood waiting for a burst of wind to come through the door, but nothing happened. For ten minutes I remained as motionless as I could with my eyes focused toward the door. Just when I was beginning to leave thinking nothing was going to happen, the door moved. At first, I thought it was one of the workers, but no one entered the room or said anything.

So, it must have been a breeze, I thought.

Still thinking I was alone because I didn't see the red light come on, I moved toward the exit. The door immediately slammed closed and I felt the presence of something next to me. The red light did not come on and I knew I was the one trapped inside the cabin. Obviously, the sensors did not work and "*Marsha*" wasn't going to work either.

The sensations that I was getting from this entity seemed a little different from the past ones I'd experienced. For whatever reason, I didn't feel threatened, but I could definitely feel it beside me.

"Jump through the window. …We're turning it on!" I heard through the speaker.

The red light came on and I knew I didn't have time to waste, so I jumped as fast as I could through the small opening in the wall. As I made my move, I heard the sound of the transformer applying voltage and it sounded like a jet engine starting up. The workers had placed some cushions outside on the ground and I landed safely on them just as I heard a cracking noise come from behind me followed by a flash of light.

"I think we got him," Colonel Long hollered, running from the ranger's cabin.

"Good work, Rick!" was followed by George Blackwater as he helped me get up off the ground.

Everyone was cheering as if I'd scored the winning touchdown. My fears were that we'd missed Doctor Thomas and it was someone else inside the room at the time the device was turned on. The entity didn't appear aggressive like my last encounters.

"Can we view the video?" I requested to one of the techs.

"Yes, let's look at it so I can see Thomas's face!" General Priebe insisted.

The general led the way to the cabin with all the surveillance equipment inside. Agents Hill and Miller were reviewing the videos along with several other technicians. The general wanted to know whether or not they had recorded the event and Agent Hill let him know that they had.

"Then let me see it!" he ordered.

On the monitor sitting in front of us, I could see myself standing in the room staring at the front door. At the time, I didn't think I was nervous, but seeing myself on the screen showed the fear in my face. There were two videos showing the front door, indicating one camera was behind me. The other video showed the room view from the door angle. As he began playing the video in slow motion, the image jumped as if something had hit the cameras. Camera number one also captured the door being opened. The next couple of frames showed the energy source just inside the doorframe. As it approached me and they enhanced the video, I clearly saw Marsha's face on the image of the creature inside the force field. It was obvious she was trying not to harm me, but something or someone was controlling her. When the red light came on, she looked in that direction as if she knew what was about to happen. I jumped through the window and she made no effort to move. A couple of frames more and she disintegrated into a million tiny pieces.

"That wasn't Thomas!" General Priebe yelled, and I couldn't get out of my mind the look on Marsha's face. "I want a complete analysis of the recorded sound," he snapped at the technician. "How long will it take before you can tell me what she was saying?" he again commanded.

The tech told him he'd have the sound deciphered within the hour and the general left the room as if he was defeated. When Colonel Long indicated the device had proved to be successful, Priebe screamed it wasn't successful until Thomas was dead. To all of us remaining in the room, it appeared the general had a personnel score to settle with Doctor Thomas.

"What the hell is going on here?" Agent Miller said to Hill.

"I don't know," was his reply.

The technician turned knobs and looked at waveforms on the scope in front of him for the next 30 minutes. Each time he replayed the sound, it became a little clearer. A few more tweaks and we were able to hear exactly what she said.

"Rick, …please forgive me," Marsha spoke while standing in the doorway. "I don't want to do this. …He is forcing me!" she said, and on the video she moved next to me. "Please don't make me do this!" was her plea and the red light came on. "The …Twelve…Men," we could barely make out. "God, have mercy on my soul!" were the last words she said before the winding noise of the transformer was heard.

I turned away from the video because I didn't want to see her vanish again. This was the second time I'd dealt with her death and it was hard for me to accept. Agent Hill wanted to know what she was referring to when she mentioned "*The Twelve Men.*" The other agents in the room did not know its meaning either. I remembered hearing something about it, but I too, could not remember the significance.

"What have you got for me?" the general barked as he entered the room for his briefing.

Not wanting to hear her begging again, I walked out of the cabin and to the lake. George Blackwater soon joined me next to the pier. For a minute, neither one of us spoke, because we both understood the reality of the events earlier.

"Rick, you know the general is going to request you do it again," he finally said to me.

"I know George and this time I'll be glad to participate, because I want Thomas dead, too."

It wasn't long before General Priebe was shouting my name, requesting I return to the cabin. As George predicted, he wanted to do it again. One of the techs told him that he needed some time to fix the sensor and Priebe said he only had 30 minutes.

The tech replaced the sensor and explained it should function properly as I reentered the cabin for the second time. Because it was getting late in the day, it was dark inside. The overhead light had been replaced with the speaker and sensor, so I wasn't able to see anything in the darkness. General Priebe insisted it wouldn't matter and to do what I was there to do.

In almost total darkness, the high-pitched noise came from the speaker. Like before, I stood motionless for almost five minutes. I moved a little closer to the window, because I just made it through the last time. Suddenly, the door ripped from its hinges with a powerful force of wind. The red light was flickering and that told me it had not completely entered into the cabin. I wanted to jump out the window, but knew I couldn't until the light was steady. Then from behind me another gust of wind hit me, sending me to the floor. From my vantage point, I could see the red light turn completely solid. The force or forces inside the room were very strong and I knew I wouldn't make it out in two seconds. During this short second of time, I thought my life was about to end and I was prepared for the worst.

With the force of a tornado hitting the cabin, the place burst into pieces sending wood flying like shrapnel into the air. I knew it was my life ending and it wasn't what I had expected. For whatever reason, I assumed it would be less violent. A few seconds later, I was still lying on the floor looking at the stars above me. One piece of wood struck me in the upper arm and I was bleeding. The cabin had been completely destroyed from a source inside and I knew there had been more than one entity present.

"Are you all right, Rick?" I heard from one of the technicians standing over me with a flashlight shining the beam in my eyes.

The force of the blast had me dazed and I couldn't make myself reply to his question. George Blackwater grabbed my arm and helped me off the floor and to the ranger's cabin. He gave me first aid to my arm and told me I needed to have a doctor look at it, because the wound was pretty deep. He did manage to stop the bleeding and after a short discussion with General Priebe and Colonel Long, George transported me to the local hospital. The doctor gave me a few stitches and said I was lucky, because it had just missed my main artery. As we were leaving the hospital, George got a call from Colonel Long.

"Looks like we're going back to Wilmington," he mentioned following his conversation.

"Why?"

"All I know is they want you back at the FBI laboratory tomorrow morning," George stated.

By now, I felt like I'd fulfilled whatever obligation I needed to for the government. What more could I do? I thought to myself.

We didn't say much on the way back to Wilmington. Neither one of us knew why Colonel Long wanted me there, but I also knew I didn't have much of a choice. George let me know that Janet was still at the motel and she had been informed I was on the way. This made me feel a little better, because I wasn't sure I'd be seeing her again when I had left her crying in the doorway.

"Rick!" Janet screamed as she jumped into my arms at the motel.

It was obvious from the look in her eyes that she had not expected to see me again. The hug was tighter and the kiss was very passionate as if she had not seen me in a year. Janet's tears of joy wet the left side of my face, and I finally had to pull her apart from me because my body was sore from the explosion. Seeing my reaction, she wanted to know what was wrong with me and I showed her the wound on my arm.

"Okay, tell me what happened," she insisted as she led me to the bed. As I removed my shirt exposing the injury, I explained the circumstances that had taken place at the ranger's station. When I told her how I'd seen Marsha and I knew the machine had destroyed her, she openly wept. I was the one who had gotten her involved in the first place and the guilt was weighing heavy on my heart. We talked about her for a while and Janet reassured me it was Marsha's decision to do the investigation. Knowing she chose to come didn't make the guilt go away. The rest of the evening, we stayed in the room enjoying each other's company. We both knew it wasn't over, we just didn't want to ruin our evening by talking about it.

The next morning, I received a call from Agent Roberts and he stated they were working on another machine. He informed me it would take almost a week to complete the construction. Hearing this, I asked if it was all right for Janet and I to leave the area, because we felt like prisoners. He hesitated for a moment and finally agreed, as long as we stayed in touch so they could reach us if needed. Janet was in the shower during my conversation and I wanted to surprise her with the good news. But before she finished, I made one more call to make some plans.

"What would you like to do today?" I said to her as she came through the bathroom door.

"I don't care, baby. Do you think we can walk next to the water and do some shopping?" she questioned and I just smiled.

"I think walking along the water would be great," was my reply and I was still smiling.

"What are you smiling about?"

"We are going to Myrtle Beach for a few days to spend some time with Clair at your parents," I responded and she paused for a moment as if she couldn't believe what I'd said.

When the reality finally sunk in, she became elated and questioned how I'd manage to make it happen. She was worried that I might be running away and this would have the FBI chasing us again. After explaining how I'd gotten permission, she rushed as quickly as she could to get ready for the trip. The call I'd made was to her parents to let them know we were coming. I'd told them not to let Clair know, because I wanted it to be a surprise. I had not seen her in a while and I really was looking forward to the reunion. Just as we were about to walk out the door to our room, the telephone rang. Janet reached to answer it, so I yelled for her not to pick up the receiver and we quickly made our exit.

"Who do you think called?" Janet questioned as I headed toward Myrtle Beach.

"I don't know and I really don't want to know," I replied, pointing the car in the correct direction.

Chapter 19

IT IS REQUESTED THAT YOU COME WITH US

The trip from Wilmington to Myrtle Beach only took about an hour, but the road seemed to get longer and longer as we traveled. The anticipation of seeing Clair made me forget all about the danger I'd faced just a day earlier. Janet's parents didn't know what we were involved in and they believed I was working on a newspaper article. We had told them I was doing research on the mysteries of Carolina Bays, but they didn't know how deeply involved we had become and how we almost became a statistic ourselves.

The look on Clair's face was worth a million dollars as we drove up into the driveway and she was playing in the yard. When she saw Janet and me, she jumped into the air and ran over to the car. I was the first person she ran to, and I opened my door to give her a big kiss and hug. Seeing her, I couldn't keep from tearing up from the joy of having her in my arms.

"Daddy! I have missed you so much," she said, still squeezing me tightly.

"Hey, what about me?" Janet pleaded and she turned me loose running around the car to the other side to greet her mother.

It wasn't long before Janet's parents came outside hearing all the noise. Janet's dad and I once had a strained relationship shortly after we were married. He didn't like the fact that I was a writer for newspapers and traveled all the time. He never felt I would make his daughter a good husband, and he was the type of man who spoke his mind. There was one trip I made overseas to Bangkok, Thailand that I thought would break up our marriage because of him. I was investigating a report on the last great

American refuge during the Viet Nam War. The *Soi Cowboy*, as it was known, was a bar in Bangkok that American soldiers went to let off steam. It was well known for its prostitution and many GIs lost there lives there, not to the enemy, but instead to other soldiers fighting over the women. Janet's father was in the Army and a Viet Nam veteran, so he knew of the place.

"You get over there around them women, don't you bring nothing back and give it to my daughter," he preached to me before I departed on that trip.

I knew exactly what he was talking about and at the time, I felt Janet wouldn't worry about the situation. But while I was gone, he told Janet a lot of stories about married soldiers cheating on their wives and how easy it was in those bars in Thailand to get women. The problem for me came when I called Janet from Bangkok just outside the bar and some of the girls were standing behind me soliciting tourists. At the time, I didn't hear them in the background, but Janet did, and she thought they were with me. I knew Janet became angry and it took two weeks before I finally found out why she was mad.

What changed everything was when my article came out in a world news magazine and it was about young girls and women being utilized as prostitutes or "*comfort women.*" What started out to be an article on the bars American soldiers visited turned out as a world report of the mistreatment of women. Many girls were bought and sold before the age of 15 to abusers and brothel owners. Most of these girls were from the age of 10 to 19 when they were introduced to the industry. If these girls tried to escape and were caught by the local police, they were taken back, because the government understood the importance of the trade. Thailand's official position was that prostitution did not exist because it was illegal, yet allowed. Only brothels were considered illegal, so the business of having a "*comfort woman*" was allowed in bars, massage parlors, restaurants, motels and tea houses.

Many of the other countries in the region have long understood the need to regulate and control prostitution. The spread of AIDS has influenced many of the country's politicians to enforce the policies of the governments. But Thailand's four-billion-a-year sex industry has flourished. One of the biggest reasons was because prostitution is the highest paying job for these women, and that's why my report forced economic development reforms for the country.

When Janet read my report in the magazine, she knew my trip had not been chasing women in the bars as her dad indicated. In some respects, I believe it strengthened our trust in each other. Her dad never apologized to me for his thinking and I've never brought it up in any of our conversations.

Some things are just better off to let die on their own.

Wanting to spend time with Clair, we went to the beach and some of the amusement parks in Myrtle Beach. I don't believe we'd had that much fun together in a long time, and I didn't think about Lake Singletary. This was a family vacation spot and we were enjoying all the amenities it had to offer. On the third day, I was standing watching Janet and Clair on a ride when two men approached me.

"Excuse me, Sir. ...Are you Mr. Richard Parker?" one of the men asked me, and I started not to reply.

"Yes, ...I am and how may I help you?" was my answer.

"It is requested that you come with us so we can take you to Wilmington," the other spoke in a low voice as not to be heard by anyone.

"What about my family?" I questioned and they grabbed my arm as if they were going to drag me away if I didn't comply with their request.

"We must leave immediately, Sir!" the first man said in a harsh tone.

"Not before I can say good-bye to my wife and daughter," I said as I jerked my arm from their grasp.

I figured they would handcuff me and pull me away, but they didn't. Since they were trying to keep a low profile, they agreed to allow me to speak to them. Janet saw what was happening and she knew why they had come for me. We didn't want Clair to feel frightened, so she calmly walked over to me after they got off the ride.

"Clair, something important has come up and I have to leave," I said to her as I hugged her.

"Are you in trouble, Daddy?" she asked, looking at the two men standing next to me.

"No baby, there's an important event in Wilmington that I have to cover and these men are going to take me there so you and your mom can continue having some fun." I smiled as I spoke to her.

Janet wasn't smiling and I could see that look on her face again as if it could be the last time she'd ever see me. As hard as she tried not to tear up, she couldn't prevent them from flowing down her cheeks. I stood up and gave her a kiss and said good-bye. She grabbed my hand and told me to be careful. Not wanting to delay any further and possibly upsetting the men, I turned to walk away.

"It's all right, Mommy. ...He's coming back soon," were the words I heard from Clair, and I was glad she couldn't see the tears streaming down my face.

On the way to Wilmington, I found out the two men were FBI agents who had been instructed to find me and take me back to their bureau. When I asked how they knew where we were, one said Janet's father had told them. I was surprised to know they knew we were in Myrtle Beach, because I didn't tell anyone before we left the motel.

"How did you know we were here in Myrtle Beach?" I asked.

"We knew exactly when you left the motel. This is Agent White and I'm Agent Chase. We have seen every move you've made since you arrived," he replied, and this time he smiled as if he had tricked his mother.

He handed me his cell phone after pressing a few buttons. On the other end of the line was Agent Miller. He explained the reason for the sudden trip to Wilmington and it was because the new device was ready. He wouldn't say much more than I would be used as bait once again to trap Thomas.

At the bureau, Agent White escorted me to the laboratory where the device was located. There waiting for me was Ron Roberts and Colonel Long. Roberts greeted me warmly, but Long was all business.

"Show him how it works and let's get on with it!" he snapped at Roberts.

A technician started showing me a machine similar to the last one. This time it was totally enclosed inside a military van. The box was made out of metal and they said it was reinforced so that it could withstand a blast similar to what the last machine received. To me it looked like a death trap. There was only one way in and one way out of the box.

"I suppose you want me to lure it into the box. ...Is that the plan?" I questioned everyone in the room.

"That's exactly it, Parker!" I heard coming from General Priebe standing behind me.

"And how am I to escape before it destroys your Doctor Thomas, even if I'm lucky enough to get him inside?"

"Not my problem, ...it's yours!" I knew he was serious.

The technician explained that I had ten seconds this time to slowly maneuver myself around the entity and jump through the main door. If I didn't make it in the ten seconds, then the door would automatically shut trapping me inside with the creature.

"What do you mean, ...trapping me inside with the creature?" I asked the tech.

"What he means... is, we are going to catch Doctor Thomas within this containment box instead of destroying him," Priebe blurted out.

The engineers had reinforced the van with steel and it was laced with coils of wires to induce a force field strong enough to contain the entities, or at least that was what they were saying. General Priebe and Long left the room and I did not have the opportunity to probe for more information about the box. The tech seemed very cooperative, willing to tell me everything. I asked him why he was so sure it would be able to withstand the force of the entity.

"We analyzed the data from the last encounter and found out how much energy it generated from the explosion. Our device has been designed to withstand a force that is ten times stronger than the one recorded," he stated, confident in the ability of the force field.

The trick was for me to get it inside the box and have time to escape. The last device provided me an avenue of escape, but this one did not, and I felt as if I was the sacrificial lamb being led to the slaughter. General Priebe reentered the room and when I complained, he told me that I didn't have a choice in the matter.

"I always have a choice and you can send me to jail if that's what it takes," I said, trying to take a stand.

"Jail? …Hell, that would be easy and you don't have that as an option anymore," he said smiling, and I didn't understand what he meant, so I questioned him.

"Right now there are two of my best snipers sitting across from your wife's parents' house waiting for a call from me," he said staring straight at me.

"So, Mr. Parker, …either you do this or I make a call," and he picked up the phone as if to dial.

"You do one thing to harm my family and …I'll kill you!" I screamed at him, and he hung up the phone still smiling.

"So, do you still think you have a choice?" he questioned and laughed out loud.

The only one remaining in the room during our conversation was the technician and I could see on his face that he was very surprised at our discussion. He looked at me as if he couldn't believe the threats were coming from the general.

"Okay, …get this out of here and to the site, now!" Priebe hollered at the technician and he jumped hearing this command.

The general called someone and left the room while agents Hill and Miller were entering. They informed me it was their job to escort me back to Lake Singletary and I asked where George Blackwater was, because he had taken me before. I was told George had been taken off the case and this made me worry even more, knowing he was the one person I thought I could trust.

During the trip to the lake, no one spoke a word. Everyone knew the importance and reason why we were going there. Only once did they mention to me that this would be more dangerous. They did wish me luck in getting out in time. I knew they were under orders, but somehow hearing them wish me success made me feel a little more comfortable hoping some-one would look out for my back.

We stopped at the ranger's cabin and waited for the rest of the team to arrive with the device. The old cabin that had been destroyed was gone and the area was clean of debris. We sat on the porch overlooking the lake and it seemed strange how peaceful the lake appeared. I had to remind myself there wasn't a monster from the deep that we were trying to catch, but rather an evil scientist who had gone insane. I turned to the agents and indicated how nice the area was for people to go on vacation. They both looked at each other and shook their heads as if they would not go there. There was a look as if they knew something more about the area that I was not aware of.

"Is there something you haven't told me?" I questioned Agent Hill. He did not reply and I asked him the same question over.

"What you don't know is twenty more people have disappeared in the last several days and we believe Doctor Thomas is responsible," he finally responded, and we all agreed Thomas was massing his army.

The three of us tried to theorize what the possibilities could be that Thomas could actually accomplish the takeover or demise of the Federal government, and why? However, after being witness to the wrath of his power, I knew it was certainly a possibility. We understood the urgency to stop him, but General Priebe acted as if it was personal.

The sound of the trucks coming down the long dirt road could be heard and I knew it would not be long before I would face death again. The technicians and helpers worked feverishly to get the military van in place and working. As they completed the last checks, General Priebe, along with Colonel Long drove up to the cabin.

"Is it ready to go?" Colonel Long shouted as he exited the vehicle.

"It's as ready as it's going to be," one of the techs replied.

"Then let's do it!" ordered Priebe as he entered the ranger's cabin where all the monitoring equipment was located.

He stopped, turned to me and reminded me about the snipers. I yelled back at him to call off his men, because I would do it without him threat-ening my family. After the discussion I'd had with the agents, I knew Thomas had to be stopped and wanted to do whatever I could. Priebe, hear-ing me agree to cooperate, smiled and gave me a little salute as if he was proud of my decision.

It took all the will power within me to enter the box, but I did as I turned on the overhead light so I could see. The speakers where mounted to the side in front of me and I felt as though I was standing in a tomb. Perhaps that was exactly what I was standing in. I just hoped there was enough time to jump out before the doors shut. A warning light flashed and I knew it was show time.

The sound I heard wasn't quite the same as the last time, and through the communications speaker, I asked the techs what it was I'd heard. One quickly answered it was a recording from my last encounter. When I questioned why they were playing it, the same tech told me General Priebe had ordered it to be played. It seemed a little strange, but I did not pursue it any further. The sound seemed loud to me and I pushed the button to tell them to turn it down, when there was the burst of wind hitting me from the direction of the door. I froze in place and looked up at the warning light they had installed on the ceiling. The light flickered a few times and then turned solid red, indicating I wasn't alone. It had caught me off guard, because I wasn't expecting anything to happen so soon.

The feeling of someone's hot breath was on the back of my neck similar to what I'd felt before. Whether it was Doctor Thomas or someone else, there was someone or something next to me. I knew I didn't have long before the door would close trapping me inside, so I had to make a plan of escape. With my finger still extended on the button, I pushed to talk.

"Rick, what is the matter?" I heard from the speaker.

My plan worked and the entity, hearing the sound, reacted by moving toward the noise source on the wall. I ran and jumped straight out the door at the same time it slammed shut, barely missing my toes. There was a loud noise from something hitting the door from within the container, and I knew it was trapped inside. The whole box shook from the entity thrashing the inside of the mil van. General Priebe and Colonel Long ran out from the cabin and Priebe was shouting, "We caught that son-of-a-bitch!" Agent Miller came over to me and asked if I was all right, and became concerned when I didn't immediately answer him. Several more times he questioned me and I did not reply, because I was still entranced with what had just transpired.

"It really worked!" I finally spoke in amazement.

"You're damn right it did!" Priebe acknowledged, hearing my words.

The pounding inside the military van continued as if it was searching for any available exit. After about 30 minutes, everything calmed down. One of the techs motioned for us to go to the cabin where he was located. Inside was monitoring equipment and we could clearly see the figure of someone inside the box. Using the same procedure he'd done on the last video, he enhanced the monitor and we saw the shape of a man's body.

"Is that Thomas?" Priebe questioned as we gazed at the screen.

"It doesn't appear so, Sir," replied Agent Hill.

"Then who have we caught?"

"I don't know, but we'll find out," he answered.

General Priebe was not happy knowing Thomas wasn't the entity inside the van. He demanded they destroy it and try again as he walked away from the cabin. Long followed him out and indicated for the techs not to do anything until he returned. While we waited, they continued enhancing the video and sound for clarification. It wasn't long before we could clearly make out the face of the man inside. It was also obvious something was happening to him as well, because he appeared to be in pain. Through the speakers, we could hear sounds as if he was trying to communicate with us. The lead technician attached another piece of equipment and said it would translate what it was saying. He said he'd finished the machine right before we came to the lake and was ready to see if it worked.

Even after hooking everything up, there wasn't any change. He told us to cross our fingers as he pushed a button on the front of his machine. Red and blue bars on the front started bouncing up and down, and one by one they turned green. He said when all of them were green we should be able to communicate. I have to admit, it was exciting as the bars continued to turn green. With each bar, the sound also changed. As it was down to the final set of bars, we could make out a few words.

"H...lp me, pl...e...elp me," we heard, and it was the first time it was slightly understandable.

"Please Hel...Me!"

From the look on his face and the few words we could understand, we knew he was begging us and asking for help. I asked if we could communicate back with him and was told the machine could only translate its words and wasn't advanced enough for us to talk back.

"Please Help! He's making us do this! Please Kill Me!" we clearly heard from the translation.

I raised my hand to indicate to him that we understood what he was saying. Seeing my gesture through the small television screen inside the van, he moved closer to the camera as if he knew we were watching him.

"Thomas is controlling us," he stated. "We can't stop ourselves from obeying his wishes. He's going to..."

Watching the monitor, he started shaking violently and the force field that surrounded him started turning hazy making it harder to see the man inside. The energy level of the field was dropping as we watched a different indicator monitor the electrical field.

"What's going on?" came from the general's voice standing behind us, and none of us had realized he'd entered the room.

"I don't know, Sir. ...Its energy level is dropping," the tech responded.

The more the level dropped, the more violent his shaking became.

This continued for a few more minutes until the force field disappeared and a disfigured man was standing inside the box. Seconds later, he collapsed to the floor and upon impact, a bluish liquid burst from his body. It appeared to be the same liquid that Janet and I saw back at Thomas's house.

Seeing what happened to the man, everyone just stood there staring at the screen. No one understood why he suddenly disintegrated. One thing we did see, was him pleading for help. He was clearly being forced against his will to act the way he was. It was obvious Doctor Thomas was able to control them after he injected the blue serum. Colonel Long wanted to get a sample of the liquid and ordered one of the technicians to go get it. When he refused because he was terrified of the remains, Agent Miller said he would get it. Grabbing a knife and a plastic bag, he went to the van. The tech opened the door and we could see him enter the van through the cameras. As he walked in, he waved at the camera and we heard him say it was a mess inside there.

"This stuff is splattered all over the walls," he said while pointing everywhere. "I'll have no problem getting this evidence," he said and suddenly he was knocked to the ground by an outside force entering the van.

Agent Miller was slammed against the wall and we could see it stunned him as he fell to the floor. The light was bright red and an alarm was going off inside the cabin where he was located. From the camera monitor, we could see there were at least three entities inside the van and the energy-monitoring gauge was pegging.

"Get them out of there!" I hollered at the monitor, knowing he was still dazed.

"Close the door...now!" screamed General Priebe, and the tech pushed a button on the console.

The doors to the van slammed shut and I knew Miller was trapped with the entities inside. The tech started adjusting his video to get a better look at the individual force fields. As Miller became more conscience of his surroundings, he realized his predicament.

"Open the door and let me out!" he yelled, looking at the camera and knowing we were watching.

"Don't you touch that button!" Priebe screamed at the tech. "I'm not about to release them and Miller knew the risks."

"You really are a son-of-a-bitch!" I said to him, still pleading to Miller.

"Yeah, ...I am, and that's what keeps this country safe," he said, staring me down.

Miller stood up with his back against the wall and there was terror on his face. The tech had honed in the correct settings and we were able to see who the three entities were.

"We got him!" General Priebe hollered as the tech focused on the force field closest to Miller.

Looking at the monitor, we could plainly see Doctor Thomas was inside the van. He was standing next to Miller and it was as if he knew the camera was on. His mouth was moving and we could hear him talking, but couldn't understand his words, because the tech had not turned on the translator device.

"What's he saying?" Priebe questioned, and the tech pushed the power button on.

The bars started moving and they slowly turned green until all were solid. Thomas's voice became clear and he was threatening to kill Miller if we did not open the doors. With a quick movement, he sliced open Miller's face and blood shot out everywhere.

"The next time it will be his throat!" Thomas informed us as Miller pleaded for mercy.

I again implored to Priebe to open the door and we would catch Thomas later. He ordered me to shut up and said I'd be escorted out of the cabin if I opened my mouth one more time. He wasn't about to release Thomas, even if it meant losing Miller. Thomas asked if we could understand him and to blink the lights inside the van to indicate we were able to interpret his language. The technician flashed the lights on Priebe's orders.

"Who is in control of this operation? Is General Priebe observing this?" Thomas questioned, and the tech flashed the lights two times to imply a yes command. "I knew that bastard was responsible for this," he said. "You can tell the twelve that I did it," he said and the rest of us did not have a clue as to what he was referring. "Now open the door!" he commanded, and Priebe ordered the tech to reply with one flash of the light to indicate a negative response. "Have it your way!"

As quickly as before, he ripped open Miller's throat and we could hear him struggle to breathe. The horrified scene was more than I could watch, and I turned away from the monitor. Everyone else in the room except Priebe gasped after seeing what happened, and Hill yelled out Miller's name.

"Turn it on...now!" Priebe shouted, and the technician knew what he was ordering.

Reaching for a red button on the side of the console, he pushed it causing our lights to flash. We could hear the high-pitched sound of a transformer as it was applying voltage to the coil inside of the van. On a voltage meter close to the button, the tech watched as it increased.

"It's approaching force field level, Sir," the tech indicated to Priebe.

"Good! ...He's done for now," Priebe replied.

Viewing the monitor, it was clear that Thomas knew something was happening. He told Priebe to stop or everyone would die. Priebe ignored his threats and told the tech to continue applying power. As the power increased, I could see the energy level meter peg and it bent the needle, indicating it was more than the van was capable of handling. The technician instructed Priebe he could not predict how the force fields would interact, because the levels were so high. At one point the tech reached for the stop button and Priebe hit his arm, knocking it away.

"You touch that button and I'll kill you," Priebe shouted, pulling a 9 mm pistol from the holster on his side.

Inside the van, Thomas, realizing we were not going to turn off the force field, looked into the camera and mumbled his last words. "I'll see you and The Twelve in hell, ...Priebe!" and with that there was a huge explosion.

The blast was so powerful it blew the van into pieces from the inside outward, making the metal van act like shrapnel from a bomb. The walls of our cabin were not very thick and it tore apart as pieces of the van ripped through, striking everything in their path. I jumped behind the console for protection and felt hot metal piercing my legs and right arm. Agent Hill fell on top of me, trying to find refuge as well. Within a few moments, the cabin was virtually ripped apart from the force. The dirt and dust from the debris was so thick that I could not see further than five feet away from me. Hill had been hit in the head with a rather large piece of metal and I could see he was bleeding heavily. To stop the bleeding, I tore my shirt and made a bandage, tightly wrapping it on the wound. He was able to communicate with me, so I knew his injuries were not life-threatening. Looking around, I saw the technician lying in a pool of blood and I knew he was dead. Colonel Long had taken a direct hit in his chest and was gasping for air. Even with my own injuries, I crawled over to him to see if I could administer some aid. Just as I reached him, a burst of blood flew from his chest as air escaped and I knew he had died. I began CPR until I realized his lungs would not expand.

Knowing Priebe had been in the room, I searched to find him, but he wasn't in my view. I called several times, hoping he would hear my voice and let me know where he was located if he needed medical attention. It was not long before I saw him over by the van area and even though he was bleeding, appeared to be all right.

He must have known Long needed help! I thought to myself.

Scanning the area, all the cabins had been destroyed from the blast and not a single unit was standing. Several more workers were lying on the ground and it was obvious they had been killed from the blast. The remaining workers appeared stunned and in shock. General Priebe pushed the twisted metal away from the van as if he was searching for someone.

"Did we kill him?" he screamed aloud. "I want evidence that he is dead!"

The workers who could help, assisted the general, and I continued giving aid to Agent Hill. His wound was deeper than I had previously thought and the bleeding wouldn't stop, so I had to apply pressure to the area. It seemed like hours before medical help arrived and one time I thought Hill was going to bleed to death. The ambulance transported Hill and me to the hospital for further treatment. I didn't know if General Priebe was transported, but I didn't see him at the hospital. My injuries were not serious and after some stitches and bandages, they released me. Hill was sent straight into surgery and I was told a piece of metal got lodged in his brain.

They had taken us to Elizabethtown, because that was the closest hospital to Lake Singletary. I was without transportation and was about to call for a taxi when George Blackwater walked into the lobby.

"I heard what happened at the lake," he said as he came over to my side. "Maybe now, it will be over," he said as he touched my shoulder.

George offered to take me home and I agreed to allow him to drive me to Myrtle Beach. On the way there, he told me that General Priebe had rushed back to Washington. I questioned why and he did not know the reason for his quick departure. George said he never trusted Priebe, and Long was just a "yes" man for him to do his dirty work. He said Priebe dismissed him when he became too close to me.

"Priebe had instructed us to kill you once this operation was over," he said. I looked at him and wondered whether he would have followed through with his orders.

"Don't worry, I'm not going to shoot you," he said with a smile on his face.

"Do you really believe it's over?" I questioned him.

He explained it would not be over if Priebe thought Thomas was still alive. George didn't know why it was so personal for Priebe to catch Thomas, but it was. Driving along, I suddenly remembered the snipers positioned at Janet's parents' house. When I questioned George, he told me there never were any snipers and that was a tactic Priebe used to get me to participate in his scheme. Hearing this made me feel better and it wasn't long before we pulled into the driveway.

I had not had time to call before we left the hospital, so Janet wasn't expecting me. Her parents' car was gone and no one was at the house as I knocked on the front door. It was around 10:00 p.m. and I was hoping they had gone out to eat and would soon be home. George told me to stay low and he thought it would be a good idea for us to go somewhere on a vacation so we couldn't be found. I knew he was talking about Priebe and the possibility he might use me for further events. After thanking him for all his help, I sat on the porch in one of the two rocking chairs and waited for their return.

For two hours, I stayed on the porch and I was beginning to think they had all gone out of town. It was close to midnight and I was getting sore from the injuries earlier. Just when I was about to get up and walk down the road to find a telephone, the headlights of a car lit up the front of the house and it was them. Clair saw me sitting on the porch, jumped from the car and ran to me. When she saw all the bandages, she screamed and wanted to know what had happened to me as Janet quickly followed.

"Daddy! What happened to you?" Clair said, touching my arm.

"It's all right, sweetie. I was close to a building that exploded and I'm fine," I replied and gave her a hug.

Janet didn't say anything, but her father couldn't pass up the opportunity to give his opinion. He just shook his head and said I had no business running around the world chasing criminals while leaving my family behind. Janet told her dad to shut up and they went inside along with Clair. Sitting next to me in the other rocking chair, Janet wanted to know all the details. I explained what had happened and she wanted to know if it was over and could we finally go home.

"I hope so, baby, …but I'm not sure it is," was my response.

That night we went to bed and the thoughts in my mind were of having to deal with Priebe again. The events of the day haunted me and I found it hard to sleep. So as Janet slept, I thought about what I could do to end this nightmare of a story I'd gotten us all involved in. Over and over in my mind, I kept hearing Thomas tell Priebe, "I'll see you and The Twelve in hell."

"Who was this Twelve he was referring to?" I said one time aloud and thought I'd awakened Janet.

The more I pondered it, the more I knew the answer would be in finding what information I could about "*The Twelve Men*." At first, I thought it meant other officers like General Priebe, but that didn't make any sense, because Colonel Long did not appear to know who the twelve men were.

"It's got to be scientists like Thomas," I said again aloud, and Janet jumped up in the bed from my outburst.

"What's wrong, Rick?" she questioned, thinking I was in pain.

I told her I'd had a nightmare and everything was all right. She kissed me on the cheek, lay back down, and shortly fell back to sleep. Morning came and Janet packed up our clothes to return home. We had been gone for a while and the thought of home sounded good to me. Shortly after eating breakfast, we left and went back to Comelius. Seeing our home as we drove down the road, it seemed peaceful and that was just what the doctor ordered. Lady almost tore the screen door down when she saw us and I was glad to see her. Janet refused to let me do anything and made me rest on the deck. Looking out at the lake made me wonder if we had managed to stop Thomas, but for now, I didn't want to think about it because I wanted to enjoy my family again.

Chapter 20

WELL YOU STILL HAVEN'T SOLVED THE MYSTERY

The next couple of days were nice, just to be able to relax. Other than going to the store for food, we didn't do much. Janet catered to my every wish and made me feel like a king in my own home. Clair was glad to see her friends and spent the third night away from home. This gave Janet and me the opportunity to spend some quality time together without any interruptions. Janet cooked a wonderful candlelight dinner and even though it was a warm summer night, we got into the spa just before sunset. I'd turned down the heating elements and it was warm enough for Janet, and not too hot for me.

Sitting in the spa without the jets turning and Janet lying in my arms, we watched the beautiful sunset across the lake. Many times before, we had enjoyed our view from the deck, because the sunset was straight across the lake from our house. The rolling hills enhanced its beauty. One of the reasons why we fell in love with the place was the hills, and tonight it was never more beautiful.

"Isn't it a beautiful sunset?" Janet spoke in a soft voice.

"Yes it is, …but it's not as beautiful as you," I replied, and I could feel her squeeze my arm.

Many times in the past while investigating stories, I'd been in dangerous situations where I came close to being shot or killed. Each time made me appreciate life and not take it for granted. However, the experience of the last few weeks made me truly understand what is important in life and that is my family. Thinking there was the possibility snipers could have shot them wouldn't leave my mind, and I just could not hold on to Janet tight enough as we enjoyed the evening.

We sat in the spa long enough for the stars of the night to light up the dark sky. I found myself smiling while staring at them and Janet wanted to know what was so funny.

"What started out to be the mysteries of the Carolina Bays, evolved from aliens to our own government conducting experiments," I chuckled, thinking about how farfetched it sounded.

"Well, you still haven't solved the mystery," she replied and I knew she was correct in her statement.

The rest of the evening could not have gone any better. Following the relaxing soak in the spa, Janet fixed us some cheese and crackers to go along with the wine she'd opened earlier. The evening finished with us making love and I didn't want to fall asleep, because I loved having her lay in my arms. For a long time, I gently stroked her soft skin and watched her sleep. Nevertheless, her words from earlier in the evening began to haunt me. She was right when she said I had not solved the mysteries of Carolina Bays. I knew the disappearances were not alien related, but I still needed to discover how much the government was involved and what exactly happened.

The next morning following brunch, Janet went into town with Clair for some items. I took the opportunity to search for information on the Internet. I wanted to see if I could find anything on *"The Twelve Men"* Thomas referred to several times. My search had me chasing many different avenues and nothing steered me where I wanted to go. Janet and Clair returned home from their shopping trip and Janet wanted to show me all the things they had purchased. She noticed what was displayed on the computer monitor and she wanted to know what I was doing. I explained I was researching more information on the Carolina Bays and had just done a word search while using one of the Internet search engines.

"You just can't give this one up, …can you?" Janet said in a concerned voice. "I guess you won't be happy until your dead!" she said and walked into the bedroom.

Janet was visibly upset knowing I was still pursuing the story. As I was about to turn off the computer, I noticed an article listed talking about the *"Carolina Charter."* The title didn't impress me until I read the short description below that mentioned something about the *"Colonial Twelve Men."* Knowing that I should do some damage control with Janet, I still clicked on the link to the article.

The piece was from an old newspaper article dated in 1729 called, *"The Monthly Journal."* The newspaper was an independent publisher out of Charleston, South Carolina. The article talked about an organization called, *"The Twelve Men."* Accordingly, this was a secret council of the thirteen colonies that served their own kind of justice. There wasn't a lot of detail in the story, but it stirred my interest. Continuing my search, I found more sites and information about that period of our history dealing with the subject.

At that time, a governor who directly represented the Crown of England controlled the colonies. The governor had command of the militia and appointed officials and judges. Many of the governors were honest men, but others, and perhaps the majority, used the offices at their disposal and cared little for the welfare of the colonists. Appointed officials were having their way without any fear of reprisal from the judicial system. The citizens became more dismayed and it was the State of Virginia who first began administering its own justice through a secret group called *"Regulators."*

The word of the *"Regulators"* spread quickly throughout the colonies and gained momentum. A few renegade groups in Georgia abused the authority and the other colonies saw the need to organize, and created the first *"Liberty Council"* made up of twelve members. *"The Twelve Men"* as they came to be known, acted as an arbitrary government who pronounced their own judgment as they saw necessary. All twelve members had to agree for any person or persons to suffer the penalty that would be due or executed.

The more I searched, the more fascinated I became. The members became very powerful and six signed the Declaration of Independence on July 4, 1776. Even with the birth of our country and an established government, the *"Liberty Council"* remained active over the years to follow. It was said that several presidents knew of this secret council and more than once used them for covert activities. The first such president was, Thomas Jefferson, and it was reported he hosted many meetings at his Monticello home. Some believed Harry S. Truman was once a member and during his inaugural address given on Thursday, January 20, 1949, he pacified the council when he said:

"We are aided by all who wish to live in freedom from fear—even by those who live today in fear under their own governments."

I wasn't able to find any references to the council after Truman's tenure, and it appeared as if the council had been disbanded. Hearing Thomas mention *"The Twelve"* made me believe they were alive and well. If they were still together and powerful, then General Priebe was somehow closely related to them and I wanted to know more.

"Are you going to ignore us the rest of the day?" I heard from Janet, and it wasn't a pleasant tone.

I'd been so entranced in my research that I had not noticed three hours had passed from the time they came home from shopping.

"No dear, ...I'm finished and I'm sorry," I said, hoping to amend myself.

Still doing what I called damage control, I suggested we all go out for dinner and they jumped at the opportunity. Clair had invited a friend to spend the night and they wanted to go to a local pizza place. It wasn't my favorite stop, but I wanted to make everyone happy, so I agreed to go. We all went and even I had a good time playing games with them. Janet became angry when I beat her in air hockey, but she got her revenge on the second game.

Arriving back at home, there was a message on the answering machine. It was George Blackwater and he requested I call him. Janet did not want me to return the call, because she feared the worst. Once everyone settled down and the girls went to Clair's room to play, I called George.

"George, this is Rick Parker," I said upon him answering the call.

"Rick, ...I want to talk with you, but not over the telephone. Can we meet tomorrow?" he asked me and I agreed.

The following day, George and I met at a rest area just off the Interstate. He seemed nervous as we greeted each other and sat down on one the benches at the picnic area.

"What's going on, George?" I began the questioning.

"It's Priebe. ...He is back and I'm not sure what he's up to," was his reply. "You need to get your family to a safe place until this blows over," George said, giving me tickets and passports with aliases.

He went on to tell me that he thought Priebe was cleaning up the mess caused at Lake Singletary. By that, he meant make anyone associated with the event disappear. George let me know that Agent Hill had been killed in an automobile accident and he feared for his life as well. As we discussed options, I told him about my research and how I believed a group called "*The Twelve Men*" were responsible and pulling General Priebe's strings.

"The only way we can ever be safe again is expose them to the public," I suggested, and for a minute, George didn't respond.

"They are too powerful for us and if they find out we are investigating them...your whole family would be in danger," he said.

I explained to him that I understood the risks involved, but my family was all ready at risk, and exposing them would be the only choice we had of staying alive. George agreed and we discussed how we could find information. I wanted to go to the national press with what we already knew, but he said any and all evidence had been destroyed or relocated to a secure location. With his access to all governmental documents, we thought the first place to begin was to trace Priebe's chain of command. This meant George had to go to Wilmington to gain access in the FBI's computer network without anyone becoming suspicious. My first agenda was to get Janet and Clair out of harm's way once again, and I knew that wouldn't be an easy task.

Janet immediately questioned me as I returned home. She wanted to know why George needed to talk to me in private and I explained the consequences facing us. When I requested she and Clair leave, Janet became upset and wouldn't agree to go, just as I'd predicted. We exchanged a few more words and I finally told her that we didn't have a choice and she needed to think about protecting Clair. Janet knew I was right and reluctantly, she packed what necessary clothes they required for travel. I gave her the tickets and passports for them to travel to Paris, France, and their flight was to leave in four hours. Clair was excited to go to Paris, but Janet still wanted to stay with me. A few hours later, I watched my family depart the Charlotte airport and I wished I were aboard.

Traveling to Wilmington, I checked into a motel and called the number George had given me. As soon as he answered the phone, he told me to hang up and he would come to my location. Several hours passed and I was worried something may have happened to him similar to what had happened to Agent Hill. A knock on the door made me think George had finally arrived. Opening the door, I was surprised to see a stranger stand there and ask if my name was Richard Parker.

"Yes, …I'm Rick Parker," I replied, very leery of this person.

"Here, …this is for you," the man said as he handed me a large folder.

The man immediately left after giving me the package and I never found out his name. Opening the folder, I saw a handwritten note and it was from George.

"Rick, …I'm sorry I couldn't come, but I think I'm being watched and I didn't want to put you in danger. The man delivering the package is a courier and he knows nothing about what is inside. This is what I have been able to find on Priebe and I think you will find it interesting. If something happens to me, then you get out of here and join your family." It was the last thing he wrote and this made me fear for his life.

The folder was thick with all kinds of printed materials. George had personal information on people that I had never heard of. Some looked to be business people and a few could have passed as government officials. The one picture that caught my eye was of John Dent. I did recognize him as a United States Senator from the State of Virginia. Looking through his profile, I saw he was on many Congressional Committees. He was a standing member on the Armed Forces, Energy and Natural Resources, and Judiciary Committees. He also served on the Select Committee on Intelligence. Just below his name, George had written the number, "3." On each of the other names, he had also written a number that began with the number "1" and ended in, "12." Another person I recognized was the name "*Doctor Raymond Thomas.*"

"*The Twelve Men!*" I spoke aloud.

Somehow, George had managed to trace Priebe's origin to John Dent. It was obvious he was Priebe's puppet master and pulled his strings. It was also unusual for a military general to work directly for a senator, so I knew this had to be Priebe's boss. Also inside the folder was a document entitled, "*Project Stealth.*"

Project Stealth was written on a notebook at Doctor Thomas's laboratory, so I opened the document. Stamped all over the first page was a government "*Top Secret*" seal. I was curious how George managed to get his hands on the document, but continued reading. The document was a detailed process on how to create an army of soldiers using a serum laced with radioactive materials. By following the formula using materials like Strontium 85, Uranium 235, Tritium, Phosphorus, Iron 55, Plutonium 32 and Chromium 51, a person's molecular and genetic structure would change. The Uranium 235 provided power for the skeletal force field and it acted as a shield. By using the Earth's own magnetic fields, they could quickly move from one point to another. This explained the sudden burst of wind each time I'd encountered an entity.

The document showed pictures of some gruesome bodies of experiments conducted over the years. The experiments began in the early 1950's and I was surprised to see the name of Helmut Kiel as one of the first scientist to perform the research. This was Doctor Raymond Thomas's father, and even in some of the pictures, Thomas could be seen standing beside his father as a child. When Thomas began working on "*Project Stealth*" in the 70's, he began where his father had left off, and over the years succeeded in accomplishing his father's dream.

Even knowing how the process had been used for evil, I was totally fascinated with what I was reading. A formula of the proper mixture of the materials was bombarded with Alpha waves that changed the molecular structure of the internal organs, muscle tissue and skeletal bones. Beta was used to change the outer layer of skin for the energy field. The correct combination caused the body to produced Gamma radiation or X-rays. The Gamma radiation produced is electromagnetic radiation like visible light, radio waves, and ultraviolet light. The amount of energy they produced is directly related to the electromagnetic radiation. Doctor Thomas had redesigned commonly used X-ray machines in hospitals to saturate the mixture before injecting it in the blood stream of his victims. This explained why I noticed the lights flashing at his house the night I rescued Janet.

Now that I knew how the serum worked, I wanted to investigate the *"The Twelve Men."* So far, I knew Dent and Thomas were part of the council, but I had ten more to find. I put the project book to the side and leafed through the folder for answers. I didn't look far before I found a name and the number "9" beside it.

"General Steven Tyler …works for the Under Secretary of State for Arms Control," I read to myself. "Number 4, Henry Thornton III," I spoke aloud.

He worked for the Bureau of Nonproliferation and I wasn't sure I knew what this department for the government managed. However, looking further, the Nonproliferation Bureau leads U.S. efforts to prevent the spread of weapons of mass destruction (nuclear, chemical, and biological weapons) and their missile delivery systems; to secure nuclear materials in the former Soviet Union; and to promote nuclear safety and the protection of nuclear materials worldwide. It also leads U.S. efforts to promote responsibility, transparency, and restraint in international transfers of conventional arms and sensitive dual-use technology. The Bureau has primary responsibility for leadership in the interagency process for nonproliferation issues; leads major nonproliferation negotiations and discussions with other countries; and participates in all nonproliferation-related dialogues.

George Blackwater had compiled a list of names to include: 12—Peter Duncan—Scientist;10—Mark Windsor—Business; 8—David Mueller—Major Newspaper Editor; 6—Charles Seaver—Business; 5—Avery Moore—Foreign Relations; and 7—Jefferson Arden—Science and Technology Advisor to the Secretary of State.

Listing the names by the order of the numbers beside their names, I counted ten members. The number one and two names were not in the folder George had given me. Thinking I had missed them, I revisited every page again, searching without results. The names that I did have were all influential people in their own rights. They were all high-ranking government officials or predominant executives. Each one seemed to be wealthy and well respected in their community.

Why would they want to create an army of such power? I thought to myself.

"Who are the number one and two people on the council?" I said aloud and the telephone rang.

The only one who knew where I was located was George Blackwater, so I wasn't afraid to answer. But when I put the receiver to my ear, there was a loud pitch coming through the earpiece almost piercing my eardrum.

"What the hell is that?" I questioned while looking at the phone. "Oh Damn!" I screamed as I slammed the phone on the hook.

The high-pitched noise was still present as I ran as fast as I could out of the motel room and jumped over the guardrail into some bushes. Within seconds, the room I'd just departed exploded from a powerful force entering the room, and I knew it was one of the entities. The telephone had been used to locate me and it was a homing signal for the entity to zero in on. I didn't move a muscle and I heard loud noises as if it was destroying everything inside. A few seconds later, the blast of glass flying brought people running out of their rooms to see what was happening. One man, who had run out of his room, suddenly flew through the air landing on top of a parked car. A woman screamed seeing what had happened and this seemed to scare it away, because I heard the sound of strong wind passing not far some me overhead. The folder was still clutched in my arms and I was glad I'd grabbed it, because everything in my room was destroyed.

It wasn't long before the sirens of the local police and emergency squad were heard screaming at a distance. The last thing I wanted to do was explain what had happened to the local police department. Therefore, I quietly hid around the corner of the motel as several police cars pulled into the motel. The manager met them and I could see he was giving them as much information as he could about the occupant of the room. I barely heard him tell them he did not believe anyone could have survived the blast and he assumed I was dead.

Not far from the motel was a sports bar, so I went over to try to call a taxi. With the police all around the motel, I knew I could not get to my car, so I figured a taxi would be my best available mode of transportation. No one seemed to care that I was dirty from the fall to the ground, because they were busy standing outside talking about the explosion. When the taxi arrived, it took me across town to the FBI building. It was early in the morning, but I was hoping the security guard would page George Blackwater for me, knowing he was the only one I felt I could trust.

"Good morning. ...I need to talk with Agent George Blackwater," I aid to the guard entering the building.

He looked at me strangely for a minute and started typing on his computer terminal.

"There is no Agent George Blackwater listed as working in this bureau," the guard replied, and I asked him to check again, because I had talked with him earlier in the evening.

"Sorry, but like I said, ...there's no Blackwater in this building," he again responded, and I could see from the look on his face that I did not need to pursue it any further.

Thanking him, I exited the building hoping the guard would not become suspicious of me. Seeing another motel not far down the road, I began walking down the street. Just as I was about to turn and enter the check-in counter of the motel, I heard tires from a car hitting its brakes next to me. At first, I thought a police car was pursuing me, but quickly looking to see who it was, I saw George Blackwater.

"Get in Rick, and hurry!" he ordered me, and I jumped into the front seat as he sped quickly away.

"How did you know where to find me?" I questioned George.

"I heard about what happened at the motel and when I didn't hear on the local scanner that you'd been killed or captured, I figured you would come to the bureau looking for me," he replied.

I explained to him the security guard said there wasn't anybody by his name working at the FBI and he laughed.

"That's because my real name is, Cheveyo Lomawaima, and it stands for Spirit Warrior. I'm listed by that name in the FBI directory," he explained.

George said he changed his name to Blackwater shortly after he moved to Lake Waccamaw and saw the dark water of the lake. He also said it made it easier for people to pronounce, but he'd never had it changed legally.

He took me to a remote house not far from Lake Waccamaw. He said it was his place of recluse when he didn't want anyone to find him. As we traveled, I explained what had happened at the motel and how the high-pitched noise was used as a homing beacon for the entity. George thought the courier might have been followed to the motel and that was how they knew I was there. It was his belief Priebe was responsible and I questioned his reasoning. I was shocked when I heard him say that Priebe had another team of scientists that had successfully conducted experiments similar to Doctor Thomas's.

"Why do you think Priebe wanted to stop Thomas?" he said. "He's in it for the money and nothing else, …just like the *Twelve Men*," he said as we pulled up to the small cabin next to Lake Waccamaw.

As we settled down after the long ride, I wanted to know more information, but he suggested we get some sleep, because it was early in the morning and it would be daybreak soon. It had been a long night and I quickly fell asleep on the small sleeping bag George provided me.

The sun shown into my eyes as George opened the door to the cabin. I had not realized I'd slept until noon. He had gone to a local restaurant and brought back some coffee and cinnamon buns. It had been a while since my last meal and I was ready to eat something.

"What did you mean that Priebe was in it for the money?" I questioned him as I bit into the warm bun.

Picking up the folder he'd sent to me, George started talking about the men sitting on the council. One by one, he described how they fit and what their jobs entailed. Each one had influences in their areas of control. By using their power, they could gain the technology and means to conduct covert experiments. George said he gained his information from several sources and he feared he was in danger as well.

"Who are the number one and two men on the list?" I asked him.

"I don't know. ...I was in the process of finding out when I felt the heat and had to stop my investigations. The top two men are the ones who we need to expose in order to stop this insanity," he said and poured me another cup of coffee.

We talked more about the individuals on the list and I wanted to know about Priebe's experiments. It was obvious to me that he could also be creating his own army, but I did not understand why a military general would betray his own country. George explained once again that it was a money issue and the *"Twelve Men"* would all become wealthy.

"Just imagine being able to snatch the President of the United States from the oval office in the middle of the day with all his security surrounding him," he suggested. "Could you place a price tag on such an army that could overtake any government and possibly the world. ...That's what they will soon be able to offer to the highest bidder," he stated, and the magnitude of this was more than I could comprehend.

"What would stop Priebe from using the army for his own purpose?" I suggested.

"Nothing!" he said in a fearful tone.

Chapter21

WE NEED TO EXPOSE THEM

For most of the morning, George and I tried to come up with a plan to discover who the last remaining members were on the council. We both agreed they had to be in a high place in either the government or business. Neither one of us felt safe in his cabin, so I suggested we relocate to Charlotte, because I knew someone there who would hide us and assist us in our investigation. Soon after we got onto the main highway, I called my friend.

"Hello, Bob. ...Hey, it's me," I said, hearing Bob Chandler's voice.

Bob was my publicist for one of the magazines I wrote for. I knew he would help us, because he had helped me in the past on several occasions. George was apprehensive at first, but I convinced him that Bob could get us access to sensitive information.

"Rick, where have you been? ...I've been calling your house for weeks!" Bob yelled into the telephone.

"I'm working on a case and I really need your assistance," was my answer to his question.

I didn't want to say a lot over the phone and he agreed to meet us at his place not far from Lake Norman on the west side of Charlotte. When we arrived, he was standing on the deck looking like an eagle getting ready to strike on its prey. We shook hands and I introduced him to George, and told him we'd explain everything and why we needed his help. Since we had worked together many times before, he welcomed us into his place. Bob's wife, Joyce, hugged me as I entered the kitchen and wanted to know where Janet was. All I said was she and Clair had gone to France and I would be joining them as soon as my latest story was complete.

"Bob, can't you live without his story for once so he can be with his family?" Joyce drilled Bob.

"It is not me, this time," he replied, and she gave me a look of disappointment for not going with Janet.

Bob was ready to hear what I had to say and we went into his study to talk in private. It was customary for him to conduct business there, so Joyce was not upset when he closed the door.

"Okay, what gives?" he said, staring at us as we sat down.

For the next hour, George and I took turns explaining what was going on and why we needed his help. Several times, I could see he must have thought we were out of our minds as we talked about invisible entities that could kill. During one of the conversations, I stood up and showed him the wounds on my back and side. After seeing the evidence of an attack, he became more attentive.

"So, what is it that I can do?" he said after hearing our story.

"We need to figure out who the top men are and we need to expose them so they can be stopped," George said sternly.

Bob agreed to help and suggested we go to his office, because he had access to resources within the government. About an hour later, Bob escorted us inside the large 80-story building located in downtown Charlotte. His office was on the 72nd floor overlooking the downtown area.

"This is a secure line and will allow you to search almost anywhere," he said, pointing to a computer on a table in the corner of the room.

George sat at the computer and began typing away. Soon he was in sensitive FBI files and I was amazed by the information displayed on the screen. He began doing a comparison of the known names of the "*Twelve Men*" to find any connections. He said it would take a while for it to match all the possible relationships and suggested we get something to eat. Bob did not want to leave the office and ordered food for everyone. While enjoying our lunch, George looked over at the computer and jumped up, seeing something pop up on the screen.

"Look! I believe we are about to see who the top guys are," he said, pointing at several names scrolling across the screen.

Bob and I moved closer to read the names. Most of them I did not recognize, but one was a major actor who was one of Hollywood's largest producers. The comparison list stopped and there was a match of 22 names that had ties with all the other members.

"This gives us a start," George stated, and began doing a search on each name listed.

There wasn't much Bob and I could do other than watch George look through all the information flashing on the monitor. The editor in Bob made him want to know all the details of past events. He and I sat in the next room as we watched the data on the monitor. I started at the beginning and told Bob all the small details of our findings. His reaction was one of disbelief and he soon wanted to expose the *"Twelve Men"* to the public.

"You are going to publish your results in my paper, ...aren't you?" he asked, seeing the opportunity to be the first to break the story.

"That's why I called you," I responded, and he was ready to do whatever it took to disclose the covert operations.

It wasn't long before George yelled for us to come back inside to join him. He was busy printing out information and started reading aloud.

"John Henry Lewis. ...Does that ring a bell?" he said, reading from a piece of paper he was holding in his hand. I had no idea who he was. "John Leary is his professional name," George said, and I knew he was the Hollywood producer and actor I'd seen earlier on the screen.

George informed us that he thought Leary was the second man on the list. He printed out all the business holdings and associates he was able to find. The list was long with many recognizable names on it. I asked if he had figured out who the top name was and he said he had been unsuccessful in his endeavor. The day was getting late and Bob insisted we stay with them.

Back at his house, Joyce had fixed dinner, knowing we were on our way. I knew Bob did not want us to get out of his sight. Before we settled in for the evening, George entered some more data into the computer and said it would run all night long, and if we were lucky, we'd have the name of the chairman for the council. I was still tired from all the running around the night before, so it didn't take long to fall asleep once my head hit the pillow.

When morning came, I entered the study and found George sitting at a computer terminal. Bob told me he'd been at it all night, never once taking a break.

"George, ...did you find anything?" I questioned him.

As he looked up through his bloodshot eyes, he shook his head to indicate no. He said all he could find was the name of *"Themis."*

"It must be a code name of some sort," George said exhaustedly.

Sitting next to him were several sheets of paper. I could see what appeared to be a flowchart with all the members listed and their relationships. It was apparent that the numbers beside all the names indicated the position they held within the council. John Leary's name was written in the second block from the top. George had written *"Themis"* in the top slot and we knew this was the man we were after.

Joyce fixed breakfast and a fresh pot of coffee, so as we ate, we discussed who the top person could possibly be. He had to be in a powerful position and the name must have been an alias so as not to disclose who he was. Sipping on the coffee, I kept repeating the name of Themis.

"I know that name from somewhere," I said aloud.

"That's a Greek Goddess. ...I believe the Goddess of Justice," Joyce said as she entered the kitchen then walking outside. We all looked at each other in amazement, because we knew she was right.

"That's right, the Goddess of Justice and Law," I relayed to all of them.

George immediately stood up and headed for the computer. He did a search on the Goddess of Justice and Law. Within seconds, the figures of the three statues of Justice at the Supreme Court Building appeared on the screen. What caught our attention was the Justice without a blindfold in one of the courtroom friezes done by Adolph Weinman. The description stated the robed Justice was the focus of the allegorical story of the battle of Good versus Evil. His defying stare and posture in the direction of the forces of Evil indicated he was ready to do battle to protect the forces of Good. The sword was in a hilt position, ever ready to strike if needed.

Doing more research on Weinman, we found out he had done many other statues that were proudly displayed on Pennsylvania Avenue. Born in Germany, he came to the United States in 1880 and studied at New York's Cooper Union and the Art Students' League. He was an assistant of sculptors Daniel Chester French, Olin Warner, and Augustus Saint-Gardens. After opening his own studio in 1904, he was commissioned to do many of the sculptors displayed in the District of Columbia.

Every sculpture listed in Washington done by him, appeared somewhere in each of the Twelve Men's folders. The more we studied the sculptures, the less sense it made to us. What we did understand was the number one man on the list had something to do with the Judicial System of the United States.

"It must be one of the Supreme Court members," Bob expressed.

"Maybe, but who?" I replied.

We studied the names of all the Court Members, trying to collate any relationship to the other men on our list. None of the members seemed to have more than one or two dealings with anyone.

"If it's not a Supreme Court Justice, then what other judicial department of the government could it be?" Bob said, puzzled.

"The Attorney General!" Joyce again answered as she entered the room.

I'd known Bob and Joyce for a long time and I was surprised by the knowledge Joyce had of the Judicial System. When I inquired how she knew so much, she smiled and said she practiced law for 11 years. My degree was in journalism and other than a few basic courses in college, I was ignorant about the judicial process.

Joyce explained that the Attorney General's duties were to prosecute and conduct all suits in the Supreme Court in which the United States shall be concerned, and to give his or her advice and opinion upon questions of law when required by the President of the United States or heads of any department. The Attorney General heads the world's largest law office and oversees the central agency for enforcement of federal laws.

"Roger Themer!" we all shouted at the same time.

"Themis must be his codename," George injected while doing a search on the computer.

We now believed we knew who all the Twelve Men were, but we still did not know why they would want to create an army. Together, they almost ran the country, so why have an army? George insisted that he and I take a trip to Washington in hopes of finding more clues. He stated he knew some agents we could trust who could help us. However, I felt uncomfortable knowing someone knew I was still alive and wanted to kill me. They missed at the motel, but the next time I might not be as lucky.

The drive to Washington took about seven hours and we went straight to the Supreme Court Building. George wanted to get a better look at the frieze of Justice on the top of the west wall courtroom. He flashed his FBI badge and that gained us access to any room we wanted to go into. At first, it looked like a normal craving without any unusual markings. But George stopped a maintenance man and asked him to go get a ladder so he could get a closer look at the frieze. Perched atop of the ladder, he started rubbing just below the thumb of the right hand holding the sword.

"What do you see?" I hollered to him, knowing he was reading something.

He continued brushing away dust and dirt from the frieze, never stopping to answer me. I didn't want to disturb him, so I stood back and watched as he started writing something on the back of his hand. Several minutes later, George came down the ladder and wrote some letters and numbers on a piece of paper.

"LC76-07-04-12," George read as he wrote the sequence on the paper.

"What does that mean?" I queried him, and he did not know.

We went to some of the other statues to look for clues or writings, and no other figures had anything written on them. Some had a date of when the statue had been carved, but none had any writings similar to what George had found. We assumed it was a code and all we had to do was figure out what it meant. For hours, we tried to decode the writings without success. At one time, we thought it might have been the combination to a secret vault and of all the theories we came up with, this made the most since.

Taking a chance of possibly being caught, George suggested we go to the J. Edgar Hoover Building a few blocks away on Pennsylvania Avenue in hopes of finding some information. Still able to use his identification card, he took me to a room and said it housed all the central records for the FBI.

"Use this code and you can have authorized access to data by other government agencies, law enforcement, general public records, informants, witnesses, and all public source materials," he instructed me as I sat in a small cubical space with a computer and monitor.

"What if someone comes in and wants to know who I am?" I questioned.

"Just tell them you are a field agent doing some research," he suggested, and started to leave the room.

When I questioned him as to why he was leaving, he told me he was going to a different part of the building to talk with the agents that could aid in breaking codes. He said he'd be back in an hour and if he wasn't, to exit the building.

Using the code George had given me, I began looking for anything to do with the Twelve Men. My first attempt returned over 10,000 items related to my subject, and I knew I had to narrow down the search. I couldn't find anything related to what I wanted to see, and I began to get discouraged. George was working trying to break the code, so I had not really thought about finding a solution for it. My search wasn't going anywhere, so I typed in the information we found on the frieze. The screen seemed to be frozen and for a while, I thought I'd locked up the computer. Just as I was about to reboot, the screen flashed and there was one item listed.

"Liberty Council—Constitution," I read from the screen.

Clicking on the link, it was a letter written in 1937 and it talked about a secret council of Twelve Men who administered a special kind of justice not done by the law enforcement agencies. The name and address had been blacked out, but it was clear the author was writing to someone important. The letter did not go into many details, but did refer to a charter document for the Liberty Council that was referenced on a frieze located in the Supreme Court Building.

As I was about to continue my search, George came into the room and said we should leave the building as soon as possible. From his mannerism, I knew to follow him and not ask any questions. We didn't leave the same way we had entered, and exited on the opposite side of the building. George was looking all around as we entered another building across from the FBI's location.

"Meet me at the National Archives Building in two hours and don't let anyone follow you!" he insisted and took off in an opposite direction.

I walked down the long hallway of the building until I saw an exit sign leading me back onto Pennsylvania Avenue. George was nowhere in sight and I continued several blocks toward the National Archives Building, all the while looking over my shoulder. Several times, I stopped to observe my surroundings to see if I noticed anyone following. When I felt safe, I entered the building to meet up with George.

The minutes passed by as I stood in the rotunda waiting for George to appear. There before me was the Declaration of Independence, the Constitution and the Bill of Rights proudly displayed in their altars. All the original writings that still govern our country were under the same roof. The nation's historical data were also within the walls of this building and I found myself entranced for a moment.

"The charter must be somewhere in here!" I unexpectedly said aloud.

While staring at a picture of the men who signed the Declaration of Independence, someone tapped me on my shoulder and it was George. He said he thought he had been followed and that's why he was late arriving.

"I'm not sure I lost them, so let's go," George instructed, and I followed behind him as we entered a restricted area.

A security guard stopped us and George quickly flashed his FBI badge allowing us access. It wasn't long before we entered a room that reminded me of a large high school library. Inside was an older lady who I would have said was my high school librarian, because they favored each other. George explained to her that we were doing some research and needed to find a document in section 12, location RC483.5—L5.1867. The lady began typing in the information on her computer and it wasn't long before she told us where and how to locate the document.

"This is FBI sensitive information and any disclosure of our research will be punishable up to five years imprisonment," George told her as we headed in the direction she instructed us to go.

"Can she be arrested?" I asked as we turned down one of the bins.

"No, but she does not know that," he said smiling.

When we first entered the room, I had no idea it was so large. Nevertheless, turning down section 12, it looked as if there was no end to the row of books and documents. I asked George why we were looking for this particular document.

"If my information is correct, this will be the charter document we are searching for," he said, and suddenly came to a stop.

Looking at the piece of paper the librarian had given him, he started pointing at some of the old documents and reading the numbers. As I heard him read off the last two numbers, he carefully removed a binder matching the numbers on the paper. We went to a nearby table and he opened the binder to reveal the first paper.

"Charter of Freedom for the Liberty Council," was the first thing written and dated July 4, 1776.

The author of the document was George Mason and from reading the information while standing in the rotunda on the Declaration of Independence, I knew he had written the Bill of Rights adopted by the Virginia Constitutional Convention on June 12, 1776. It was obvious that he was one of the first members of the Liberty Council and helped enlist the remaining 11 members. Originally, there were supposed to be 13 members representing the 13 colonies, but Rhode Island elected not to send anyone to join the council. The remaining members of the council became the proprietors of all the colonies.

Reading through the document, it read like the Bill of Rights for the United States of America. It talked about how all men are by nature equally free and independent, and have certain inherent rights. The government instituted to common benefit, protection, and security of the people, nation, or community against the danger of misadministration. Neither George nor I saw the necessity of the charter until we read section 8.

"That in all capital or criminal prosecutions a man has been deemed guilty of the evidence against himself and the governmental agencies can not execute punishment, the unanimous council shall administered any and all punishment."

The document continued, describing the powers of the council to do the dirty work of the government. On the last page of the document, it listed the order of authority for the council members. The number one person on the list was Edmund Randolph, the first Attorney General of the United States. The charter stated he could, and would, use the power of the office to execute the council's judgments. With the Attorney General as the head of the largest law office and overseeing the enforcement agencies, it was easy for him to have the resources to carry out the punishment.

Along in the document were accounts of actual incidents that had happened throughout our history. Attorney General William Wirt was the one who aligned the council with the executive department and President Monroe. One letter he wrote to Monroe in 1870 explained how the council had taken care of one of Monroe's political enemies. The details told of a hired assassin shooting the man in the head as he slept.

To become a member of the council, you had to be nominated by another member, voted on and unanimously elected. Membership was a lifetime appointment and only upon one's death could he leave the council. There was one account of the murder of John Breckenridge, the Attorney General from 1805—1806. The document stated he became concerned with the power of this secret council and threatened to expose them to the public. The other 11 members held a secret meeting and determined Breckenridge to be a danger. On December 14, 1806, he was found dead of mysterious causes in Lexington, Kentucky. In 1806, the charter was ratified to state that any member who threatens the sanctuary of the council would be executed. With the advent of this amendment, no other records of mutiny were recorded.

The most shocking revelation, was reading about the death of our twentieth President, James A. Garfield. On July 2, 1881, twice Charles Guiteau shot him as he made his way through the Washington railroad depot on his way to catch a train for a summer retreat on the New Jersey seashore. One bullet grazed his arm and the other lodged in his abdomen. According to the document, the Liberty Council considered Garfield a risk to the nation because of his political affiliations. They voted to assassinate him and Charles Guiteau was hired to complete the task. Guiteau had been in trouble with the law and Attorney General Wayne MacVeagh issued the order for the assassination. Until his death, Charles Guiteau maintained that God had ordered him to kill the president. Reading the document before me, it was obvious the Liberty Council or "*Twelve Men*" gave him the order.

It wasn't Guiteau's bullets that were responsible for Garfield's death. The first doctor on the scene, Willard Bliss, inserted non-sterile probing instruments into the wound. He never retrieved the bullet and caused further damage. It was determined that the president would be dead within twenty-four hours, but to everyone's amazement, he hung on. This worried the council members and they put a second plan in place. A young inventor at the time by the name of Alexander Graham Bell rigged up a crude metal detector to aid the doctors in finding the still hidden bullet inside Garfield's body. As his condition grew steadily worse, the surgeon decided to cut him open to remove the slug. They never found the bullet and it was discovered that the metal detector had located a metal spring under the mattress instead of the bullet. When it was over, the three-inch wound turned into a twenty-inch canal becoming heavily infected. This surgery resulted in massive infection and blood poisoning from the lead bullet, which led to a heart attack that killed Garfield on September 19, 1881. The surgeon who performed the operation, was not the physician Garfield normally saw. He was sent there by the council to ensure a successful end to his life.

In the 1900's, the activity of the council seemed to slow down. There was mention of only a few more times they followed through on executions. The members seemed to use the council for their own benefit to take care of personal enemies. Council members in 1945 became displeased with President Truman's handling of the country. This was when they began planning the development of an army that could take over the country if the need should ever arise. A major shift of members occurred in the 1960's. At the time, the country appeared to be heading down an immoral path, so the scientist of the group convinced the council to enact Project Stealth. Although the technology had not been developed, they wanted to pursue the possibilities.

Having read the entire charter, it was clear the number one person on the list had to be Roger Themer. Themer was the present Attorney General and we were sure he was controlling General Priebe. George told me that Doctor Thomas was the first to perfect the serum and started creating his army. General Priebe wanted to use military solders and Thomas refused, sighting it would be easier to control the civilian populous. Because of their differences, they departed on separate paths.

"Priebe found it hard to except Thomas's direction and wanted him stopped," George told me as we ate dinner at a restaurant in the Georgetown section of town.

"Why didn't he just kill him?" I questioned, chewing on a tender piece of steak.

He said Priebe had tried on several occasions, but failed. Thomas was able to detect his assassins and kill them before they could get close. He used his army to locate and attack Priebe's men. The concern now was Priebe creating his army of soldiers and what were his intentions might be.

"Do you think Themer is involved in Priebe's plans?" I questioned him once again.

"I don't know, but that's what we're going to find out," he said, finishing his meal.

Chapter 22

He Didn't Seem Surprised

For the next several days we focused on devising a plan to get to Roger Themer and confront him with our findings. We both knew this would be dangerous and needed to move slowly. If he were involved, then we would be walking into a trap. On the other hand, we needed to know if Priebe was planning to use the resources for personal gain. George used his means to find out Themer's schedule of events. He'd been out of the country with the Secretary of Defense to Italy and was due back in Washington in two days. Having this information allowed us to coordinate our plan with Bob Chandler back in Charlotte. Bob was very interested when I told him to come to Washington in support of our plan.

Bob met with George and me at his hotel the following day. He always stayed at the luxury Hotel Monaco located in the historic 1839 Tariff Building. Bob once told me that he never stayed in a hotel unless it was luxurious. Most of the motels that I was used to staying in didn't come close to the plush sophistication and style this place exhibited.

"Okay, what is this plan of yours and how can I participate?" Bob asked as he poured us a glass of champagne.

For the next hour, we told him how we'd read the charter of the Liberty Council and our reasons for wanting to speak with the Attorney General. He listened as we talked about the "*Twelve Men*" and I showed him a list of who they were.

"My God, David Muller is on this list," he said in disbelief. "David and I have been friends for a long time and I can't believe he would be involved in such a surreptitious organization."

Of the twelve men on the list, he knew or had a business relationship with nine of them. As he described the relationship with each one, he also began to see a correlation between them. It finally dawned on him how these men could easily manipulate the judicial system and the government.

"I knew Roger Themer even when he was a lawyer working in New York and I was a reporter for a local television station. And I just can't believe he would be a part of any plot to overthrow the government," Bob stated convincingly.

"I hope you are right, Bob," I said, taking a sip of the champagne.

We explained the need to meet with Themer and he picked up the telephone. George and I stared strangely toward each other as he pushed the numbers on the phone. We had no idea who he would be calling in the middle of our briefing.

"Hello Genoa, this is Bob Chandler. How are you doing today?" Bob spoke into the receiver. "How are the boys doing? I'll bet they are almost grown," he said and we had no clue who he was talking with. "Yes, I'm glad to hear that. When is Chaser coming back into the office?" he asked, and later said Chaser was the nickname he gave Roger in New York because he was a malpractice lawyer. "That sounds just like him and my number is 555-3254." Then he hung up the receiver.

Bob informed us he had called the Attorney General's office and spoken with his secretary. Themer had returned home a week early from his trip, but was keeping it a secret. He was in a meeting and she would have him call Bob at the hotel. George and I were impressed by his ability to pick up the telephone and talk directly to the Attorney General. Even with George's FBI status, he would have to go through a lot of red tape in order to meet with him.

After enjoying a fine lunch at the hotel, we returned to Bob's room. The telephone was ringing as we entered and it was the Attorney General. Bob exchanged some jokes and old memories with him, and we heard him ask if he could find time in his schedule to meet with us. There was a pause and I was sure he would be too busy, but Bob gave him his room number at the hotel and hung up the phone smiling.

"Okay, he'll be here in about an hour," he said, again smiling as if he was proud of his accomplishment.

My nerves were already on end when I heard the knocking on the door. Bob greeted him and immediately introduced us to Roger Themer. Bob started out by telling him that we had some information of national consequences and he seemed very concerned. George began explaining the circumstances involving Doctor Thomas and General Priebe. He told of the invincible army they were creating and how we thought they were going to possibly use them to overthrow the government. The Attorney General sat there listening to every word George said. When he heard about the entrapment of Thomas at Lake Singletary, he didn't seem surprised, and that made me feel uncomfortable. Not one time during the conversation did he ask me any questions as to why I was involved. George finally explained my reason for being in the room and Themer didn't appear interested.

Bob could see what was happening as well, and he looked at me as if we needed to discontinue the conversation. Themer removed his cellular phone from his pocket and pressed a number. All he said was the hotel and room number.

"What are you doing, Roger?" Bob questioned.

"I've called for some security agents to join us in this discussion," he replied, and we knew they were coming for us.

"Before they arrive, let's talk about your membership in the Liberty Council," Bob snapped at him.

Roger looked puzzled and at first tried to deny knowing of any organization. Seizing the opportunity, I told him how we'd found the writing on the frieze, which led us to the National Archives and the council charter.

"We know of your organization and I have a copy of the charter hidden in a safe place along with all the names of your members," Bob stated. "If anything happens to any one of us, it will hit every news organization in the country," he said threatening Roger.

"And just who do you think will believe such a story, Bob. …We control the news," Roger said, almost laughing at us.

From the names on the list, it seemed very possible, but Bob didn't earn the reputation as an intimidator for no reason. I knew he was playing a game and his poker face was on.

"You don't control all the news. …Remember, I own my own distributing companies located *all* over this country and they are ready to print front page news," Bob said, pointing his finger at Roger.

"What do you want?" Themer said after a short time, thinking over Bob's words.

"I want you to…" Bob said in a stern voice, but never finished.

The glass window of the room shattered from a strong force and I knew it was one of the entities in General Priebe's army. It flew into the room knocking over tables and lamps. A few seconds later, I felt myself flying across the room hitting the side of a wall. George was also tossed across the room and I could see he had sustained an injury. I was hurt, but I didn't think anything was broken. Roger was touching Bob's shoulder and this seemed to prevent the entity from attacking him.

"All I have to do is give the command and you will be destroyed," Roger said to Bob in a forceful tone.

The haze from the force field surrounding the entity was barely visible but I could see it standing directly behind Bob. It didn't phase him knowing his life was in danger. Bob stood tall as if he dared Roger to give the command.

"Roger, you do this and before the next sunrise, you and your council will be exposed to the world. As a matter of fact, if I do not make a call within the hour, the presses will begin turning with your picture leading the front page," Bob defiantly said.

For the first time since Roger entered the room, he looked concerned. He didn't say anything and only stared at Bob, George and I. Bob again asked him what his plans were for us and he remained silent. Roger reached in his right pants' pocket and pulled out a small device that looked like some kind of remote unit. Pointing the device in Bob's direction, I thought it would signal the entity to attack. Instead, after pushing a button, the sound of air rushing out of the room was heard and I could see the entity was gone.

"Make the call!" Roger demanded.

"How do I know you will not call it back to finish us off if I do make the call?" Bob inquired.

"You don't, but if you refuse to call, then I can assure you, …you'll die!" he stated, and I could tell it was the final card laid on the table.

Bob picked up the telephone and dialed a number. I was puzzled as to whom he was calling, because I knew he had been bluffing. Roger stood there listening with his finger resting on the device as if he was ready to recall the entity.

"Hello Dalton, do not print the headline story in today's edition," he said over the telephone.

"But if something happens to Richard Parker, George Blackwater or me, then forward it to every news agency in the world," Bob spoke and quickly hung up the receiver.

The reaction from Roger made me think he was pushing the button, because he quickly moved as Bob slammed down the phone. Bob still did not budge and stood firm and defiant.

"Well, we still have a problem, …don't we, Bob?" Roger said. "You may have prevented me from killing you now, but remember, I am the law in this country," he stated as if to intimidate us.

George was moaning from his injuries and I figured he had internal problems or broken bones. I made my way over to him to see how I could assist. Roger hollered for me to stop, but I continued making my way to him. His arm was broken and I could see a bone protruding.

"George needs to go to a hospital," I insisted, trying to comfort him the best I could.

"No one is going anywhere!" Roger shouted in my direction.

With the limited knowledge that I possessed from my days as a life-guard in college, I grabbed George's arm and tried to reset the bone. He screamed from the pain, but thanked me while I used a sheet from the bed to make a sling.

"You are right, Roger. ...We do have a dilemma here," Bob said to Roger in a vigorous voice.

Bob suggested to Roger that we calmly sit down at the table to discuss some options. He agreed to his request and I helped George to his feet. George's pain seemed to ease after I reset the arm and he joined us at the table. Bob started explaining to Roger that we knew of the secret council and their plans to create an army using the technical advances from Project Stealth. Realizing how much knowledge we possessed, he began to talk about all the members and their roles.

"The plan to create the army was first devised by Avery Moore, the Foreign Relations member, more than ten years ago," Roger explained. "This was before I was on the council. Two years ago when my predecessor died suddenly in an automobile accident, I became a member," he said as if he was unaware of the council's involvement.

Roger said General Priebe had been Project Stealth's program manager for the last ten years. It was Priebe, who pushed the program and solicited Doctor Thomas's help. Once the transformation was possible, Priebe wanted to use the army as his own. Thomas was actually trying to stop Priebe's plan by creating an army of his own.

"Why didn't you stop Priebe?" Bob asked.

"Because the other members of the council were on board with him and I was the new guy. You read the charter. ...John Breckenridge, the Attorney General from 1805—1806 was killed when he did not go along with the other 11 members. John Dent, as you know, insinuated I'd better approve of the council's activities or I'd be the next Breckenridge," he said as he looked through the broken window.

Roger stated that General Priebe had attended several meetings with the council and easily convinced them his army was needed for the security of the United States of America. The council, knowing the hostilities facing our country from all over the world, agreed with his plan and funded the project.

"Thomas visited me shortly after I became Attorney General and told me of Priebe's plan to use the army for his own political gain. I secretly funded Thomas in hopes of neutralizing Priebe. Priebe heard of Thomas's success and you know what happened because you were there," he finished saying.

Bob and he talked more about Roger's involvement with the council and how he had wanted to stop Project Stealth. He apologized for calling Priebe earlier to arrange the visit from the entity. His reasoning was because Priebe and the council would kill his family if he did not go along. Listening to him, almost made me feel sorry until I remembered how close we came to dying an hour earlier.

"I'm in this too deep, but it's not too late for you," he indicated.

Roger suggested that we disappear out of sight for about six months and Priebe would be either stopped or successful in his plan. He said he could arrange through one of his agencies for us to go under the witness protection program. Bob instantly agreed and I thought it was unusual for him to give in so easily. As Roger exited the room, he stopped and shook our hands.

"God be with you and our great country!" he spoke and closed the door behind him.

My first reaction was to leave the hotel, because I did not trust Roger after what had taken place. It took some convincing, but Bob agreed and checked out of the room. Bob informed us that he had a friend who owned a place on the Potomac River and we could stay there until we figured out our next move. As it turned out, his friend was a doctor and later that evening he set George's arm properly.

The next couple of days, we sat around discussing what our options were. We were careful not to go anywhere that someone would recognize any of us. We knew General Priebe was not the kind of person who would stop searching for us. The following day, Saturday, I went to retrieve the morning newspaper and almost dropped it as I read the headlines.

"Attorney General Dies In A Freak Accident!"

The article said Roger and his family died in a mysterious fire in his home while they slept. The cause of the fire was unknown, but it appeared to have been started from an explosion. One neighbor reported hearing a strong burst of wind just prior to the house exploding.

"This is it. …Now's the time to strike!" Bob said, reading of Roger's demise. "We have all the information we need to expose them and now with Themer gone, let's go for it," he said with conviction in his voice.

All three of us began calling different news agencies. Bob called his editors and told them to begin a special printing of the Sunday morning edition. George and I called the national television networks and told them to get a copy of Bob's newspaper, because a story of national interest would be printed. Bob was still a businessperson and wanted the exclusive to the story. As long as it made the headlines, that was all we wanted. For the rest of the day, we called news magazines and talked to some of their publishers.

After eating dinner, I called Janet in Paris, because it had been several days since I had spoken with her and Clair. She knew the danger I was in and seemed glad to hear that I was all right. She told me they had made reservations to return to the States the following day. I tried to convince her to stay another week or two, but I couldn't persuade her. When I talked to Clair, she was also ready to come home. So I told them I loved them and to have a safe trip, and I looked forward to seeing them.

Chapter 23

OUR JOB IS DONE

It was difficult sleeping, knowing how we would change history the following day. Around 3:00 a.m., I walked out on the pier and sat staring at the lights and skyline of Washington. I thought to myself the first run of the papers were hitting the streets and soon people would be reading our story. For the first time, I became worried we might cause total chaos as people read past history and the methods of the Liberty Council. Soon I was joined by George, who was also having difficulty sleeping. With his right arm in a cast, he shook my hand and thanked me for all I had done.

"It will be worth everything if we are successful stopping Priebe," I said while shaking his hand.

The sun was beautiful rising across the river and it reminded me of Lake Waccamaw with its sunrises. Even though I did not mind sharing the moment with George, I truly missed Janet. We both loved watching the sun come up together and I missed her. However, the excitement of the day was just beginning.

Walking toward the house, we could hear the television and it was loud from the sounds of newspersons talking about the morning news. Once inside, I could see all the national morning shows dedicating their attention to the story. Some were reporting from Roger Themer's house, showing the destruction, while others stood in front of the Supreme Court Building.

Everyone was referencing the Liberty Council and the "*Twelve Men.*" One by one, the names of the members were read. One reporter was talking to Jefferson Arden, the advisor to the Secretary of State and number seven on the list. Arden denied the allegations, stating it was the most ridiculous story that he had ever heard.

"This is certainly an attempt by some of the terrorists operating in our country to undermine our government," he stated while entering his office building.

One news station reported that General Priebe could not be located and this began to worry me, knowing he was the very person who needed to be exposed. All through the morning, reporters indicated Priebe could not be found. Shortly after noon, the Presidential Press Secretary held a press conference at the White House and it was carried live on all the networks.

"*Ladies and Gentlemen,*" Press Secretary Arlie started out saying, "*The president is deeply disturbed from these allegations and will conduct a thorough investigation. Any and all perpetrators will be brought to justice,*" and with that he turned and walked away.

"Our job is done," Bob said, but I did not feel the same sense of completion as he did.

That afternoon, a news flash appeared on the television and it said a Boeing 747 had suddenly exploded over the Atlantic Ocean. The plane had departed Paris, France in route to New York City when it disappeared from the radar screen. The GPS system indicated it was 200 miles off the New York coastline coming in on its final approach when the accident occurred.

"Janet!" I screamed, because I knew from the identifier, it was the flight they were taking.

"No,... God! ...No!" I cried aloud, and Bob and George grabbed me as my knees buckled beneath me.

The thought of losing Janet and Clair devastated me as I sat glued to the news reports. A network was reporting one of our military aircraft had shot down the plane. Some of the other stations reported the same theory.

"It appears there was a bomb stored on the Boeing 747 jet, American flight number 121, and a military F-18 fighter jet shot it down, according to Jeff Arden. Mr. Arden is an advisor of the Secretary of State," the reporter said.

We knew that Arden was one of the twelve members of the council, and I was positive he was the one working with General Priebe. Priebe, with Arden, could have easily ordered the attack on the 747 and covered it up. They must have located Janet and shot down the plane to get at me. This was when I realized that all of our families must be in danger.

"Bob, call Joyce and tell her to get away until this is over!" I screamed at him.

He dialed his number and she didn't answer. Bob tried calling his neighbor's house and was told her car was parked in the driveway. He pleaded for them to go check on Joyce and to call him at the number I heard him give over the telephone. A few minutes later, the phone rang and Bob answered.

"Oh God! No!" he cried into the receiver and dropped the phone.

George steadied Bob while I talked with the person on the other end of the line. The neighbor explained to me how he found Joyce lying in a pool of blood and her throat had been cut. The trauma of the news was more than either one of us could handle. Dealing with my own sorrow I felt worse knowing I'd gotten Bob involved.

"Bob, please forgive me. ...I'm so sorry," I said while comforting him, but he didn't reply.

The strong-willed man that I knew was in shock from hearing the news of his wife's murder. I think I was in a state of denial, because I refused to believe my family was gone. We both sat watching the television as more stories of the morning paper exposing the council were still being reported. Then as if someone had turned off the story, several stations stopped talking about it. Only one network station mentioned Priebe's name and that was to say he'd been located in Washington at the Pentagon Building.

"If that son-of-a-bitch thinks he's going to get away with this, ...then he better watch out for me!" Bob suddenly hollered.

Bob picked up the receiver to the phone and began calling. He was loud and demanding, and I knew he was talking to one of his staff. He ordered them to print some headline news and started dictating what he wanted printed. The last instruction he gave them was to print it no matter what happened to him. Along with his own company, he called several more people who I did not know and told them story of the day's events.

"Now if we can survive the night, then we'll see what happens tomorrow," Bob said as he left the room and headed for the bedroom.

For the rest of the night, we did not see him. I remained awake thinking about the reality of losing Janet and Clair. I called the hotel in France where they had been staying and was told they had checked out earlier in the day. My hopes of seeing them again were now fading and I knew I had to face the facts, they were gone. George tried to use his influence to gain information to the passenger's list, but wasn't able to attain any names. All night I sat on the pier watching the stars flicker in the sky. Sometime around four in the morning, I stopped crying because there were no more tears left.

"Janet,...I love you." I said while focused on a twinkling star. "Clair, take care of your mom and I love you." Then I collapsed on the deck of the pier from exhaustion.

The events of the day and the emotions of losing my family were more than I could handle. With the morning sun shining into my eyes, George shook me to wake me up. He wanted me to come into the house and see what was happening on the news. Still exhausted, I really did not care to move, but he insisted I go.

Bob was sitting in the chair as I entered the house. He was pointing at the television and there was a sense of confidence about him. On the screen, I saw General Priebe taken into custody by two secret service agents. The reporters were saying Priebe had been arrested for his involvement in the murders of 337 passengers and crewmembers of the Boeing 747. It was his direct order to the fighter pilots that brought down the plane.

The television was almost jumping from the reports of the secret council, and I knew it was no longer suppressed. Bob almost smiled as one by one, each member of the council was either shown or reported arrested. When he saw David Mueller's face appear on the screen, Bob jumped up from his seat and pointed at the screen.

"I got you, ...you bastard!" he screamed. "He's the one who tried to silence the story we printed in my newspaper. ...You won't stop me now!"
.

Mueller was the owner of the largest publishing company in the world and he controlled most, if not all, of the largest news organizations. He also owned controlling stock in the major networks, and that was how he managed to halt the first reports of the secret council.

"If he is so powerful, why is he being arrested?" I questioned.

"The Associated Press and a few close friends," he replied.

Bob explained the Associated Press was the information backbone of the world. It served thousands of daily newspaper, radio, television and online customers. It is the largest news organization in the world, serving more than a billion people a day. I still was curious how he had managed to persuade this non-profit organization to print his story.

"You see, in 1970, the AP sent news copy from a computer in Columbia, South Carolina to Atlanta, to which it was automatically relayed back to South Carolina over a broadcast wire," he stated. "This was the beginning of the electronic age of computers to replace typewriter and teletype setters."

"Okay, what does that have to do with my question?" I queried him.

"Well, it so happens that in 1976, Keith Fuller became the General Manager of the Associated Press and revolutionized the world with this new technology," he said, and I was still confused by his reply. "Keith Fuller and I were best friends in college and that's who I called last night on the telephone," Bob finished saying.

It was Keith Fuller, who called the President of the United States at 2:00 a.m. and told him that the story of his military shooting down a friendly aircraft was going to hit the airwaves if he didn't do something about it. This time the story could not be stopped from reaching the entire world. He also informed the president that General Priebe was plotting to topple his office and this would put the country in turmoil.

The president informed him that heads would roll and called his secret service, instructing them to round up all the men identified as members of the Liberty Council. Priebe was captured in the Pentagon as he tried to escape the Mission Planning Room. He used his authority to start mobilizing some of the Special Forces troops around the country so they could shut down and capture any opposition to his plan. As the Commander —in —Chief, he called the Secretary of Defense, along with his National Security Advisor, for an emergency meeting at the White House. As the morning progressed, the results of the meeting were plainly shown on television, as many buildings in Washington and around the country were surrounded by military. It appeared as if the country was in a state of chaos watching our soldiers stand guard over the nation's judicial and legislative buildings. At noon, the president held a press conference and explained why he had mobilized the military.

"My fellow Americans, this country has averted an attempt by some to undermine the very fundamental principles of our founding fathers," **he started out saying.**

"I'm sure you have heard by now reports of a secret council to overthrow the government for their own political and financial purposes. We have discovered a secret project to create a new kind of soldier that would be able to go undetected anywhere in the world, without any resistance using today's technological methods. Thanks to the actions of some concerned citizens, we were able to locate and destroy the secret laboratory this morning located just south of Washington.

"I assure you once this threat has been completely neutralized and all perpetrators have been caught, our country will return to the great nation that it is."

For the first time in a while, I finally felt safe knowing Priebe had been captured. We all were happy we'd been able to prevent the coup, but the reality of losing our loved ones in the process hit home. Bob stood up and said he needed to return to Charlotte, and we all agreed it was best. I made one final attempt to call the motel in Paris, but the events of the day had all the telephone lines tied up and I could not get through. After an hour of trying to reach the airline, they informed me there was not any information available on the passengers that went down on the 747. George called some other airline officials and tried to use his FBI status, but he wasn't successful either.

The travel to Charlotte was long, because the roads were crowded with slow moving military vehicles. We understood and that did not bother us. George had arranged for someone to meet us at Interstates 85-40 intersection so he could return to Lake Waccamaw. We thanked him for all he had done and wished him well as we continued our journey. A few hours later, we pulled up to Bob's house and the police caution tape was still stretched across his front yard. Bob's neighbor met us and provided more details of the tragedy. He explained to Bob how the police had a suspect in custody from the security cameras located around the outside of the house taken the night of the murder. A man could be seen entering the house from the back and breaking a window to gain access. He had managed to disable the alarm, so Joyce never knew he had entered the premises.

"The police found the tape and identified the suspect," his neighbor stated. "They want you to call them as soon as you can," he said and we entered the house as the evidence of her death remained on the kitchen floor.

Bob never said a word and only stood there staring at the pool of blood. A wilted rose was lying on the counter, and he slowly picked it up and clinched it to his chest. He could no longer hold back his tears and wept as he kissed a rose petal.

"I gave this to Joyce the night I left for Washington and told her to think of me and hold it next to her heart as a reminder of how much I loved her," he said through his tears.

Hearing Bob talk about his love for Joyce made me think of Janet, and I couldn't hold back my tears of sorrow. Together we held each other and shared memories. Soon the telephone rang and it was a police detective asking Bob to go down to the station. Bob informed the detective he'd be there soon and asked me to go home, because he knew I needed to deal with my own loss. He offered to go with me for support, but I declined, stating I would be fine.

Using one of the cars Bob had loaned me, I traveled the short distance to Comelius. Driving around the last curve, I could see our house and it looked very strange to me. Knowing Janet and Clair would not be there made it seem unreal, as if it was not my home anymore. Pulling into the driveway, something was very wrong. The door was open and I knew someone was, or had been, in the house. Thinking the adventure might not be over, I grabbed whatever I could find as a weapon and make my way up the stairs to the house. Just as I was about to open the screen door, I was startled by the sound of a barking dog and it was Lady. She had not seen me in a long time and jumped up into my arms.

With Lady in my arms, I slowly walked through the kitchen, because I didn't hear anyone else in the house. The only thing I could imagine was Joan, our neighbor, must have gotten Lady from the kennel and was watching her. Joan loved Lady and would dog-sit her on occasion for us. However, the back door had been left open and I did not believe Joan would have left it that way. Putting Lady down, I moved through the house ready to strike anyone who should not be there. Even the door leading to the deck was open, so I did a quick scan of our items to see if anything was missing and everything looked in its place.

Walking down the hallway toward the bedrooms, I noticed the door to Clair's room and our bedroom was closed.

Whoever was here could perhaps be in one of the two rooms, I thought to myself.

My emotions were running high and I could not make myself open Clair's door and possibly seeing her things destroyed. Moving further down the hallway as softly as I could walk, I turned the doorknob to open the door to my bedroom. As the door opened fully, I almost fell to the floor with what I was seeing. Lying in the bed asleep was Janet and seeing her made my eyes flood with tears.

How could this be possible? I thought and slapped myself to make sure I wasn't dreaming.

But I wasn't dreaming and she was there before me in all her glory. I could not move and just stood there crying like a baby, staring at the true love of my life as if she had returned from the dead to me. Lady came running into the room and jumped up on the bed before I could grab her. Janet turned from the sudden movement of the bed and saw me standing before her. The tears were steadily flowing down my cheeks and she jumped up from the bed into my arms, joining me with her own tears. Neither of us said anything and only hugged one another for a long time.

"I thought you and Clair were dead," I finally said, wiping the tears from my eyes. "You were supposed to be on the plane that was shot down. …What happened?" I questioned Janet.

"We were about to board that flight when Clair got sick and had to run to the bathroom," she said as she grabbed my hand and sat me next to her on the bed. "I asked for them to hold the plane, but they didn't, because when we returned, they had already shut the terminal doors. We sat in the airport and waited for the next available flight, which was three hours later," she explained.

Janet told me that she couldn't reach me and it wasn't until she had landed in the United States that she heard about the plane going down in the ocean. She did not know how to contact me and figured the best she could do was to come home and hope that I would call. I thought she had perished in the ocean and never thought to call the house. At this point, it did not matter, because I was so happy to see her. Clair, hearing the sound of my voice, came running into the room and gave me a hug. Holding my child once again, I couldn't stop from shedding a few more tears.

For the remainder of the day, we talked about their trip to Paris and Clair told me all about the exciting things she did and saw. Janet and I did not mention what was going on in our country and we wouldn't turn on the television or radio. We were in a discussion over what to do for dinner, when the telephone rang and it was Bob.

"Rick, how are you doing?" he asked as I answered the phone.

I informed him that Janet and Clair were there and he was relieved to hear the news. I had not told Janet about Joyce, and she knew something was wrong from the conversation over the telephone. Bob let me know that his daughter and son were arriving in town and he was on the way to the airport to pick them up. Knowing he would not be alone made me feel better, and I reassured him we would be there if he needed us.

Janet was disheartened hearing the news of Joyce. She wanted to go be by Bob's side and I convinced her to give him time with his family. We went to our favorite restaurant for dinner and spent a wonderful evening together sitting on the deck overlooking the peacefulness of the lake.

For the next couple of weeks, the news was full of reports about the Liberty Council and all its history. It was surprising to hear how many people knew of the council, but were afraid to mention it in public. Then one evening while watching television, the president interrupted the primetime shows for an announcement.

"My fellow Americans, I come to you this evening to give you reassurance that everyone involved with the conspiracy to overthrow our government have been caught. And I promise you they will be prosecuted to the fullest extent of the laws of this country.

"This country owes a great deal of gratitude to three Americans who had the tenacity to do what was right through personal sacrifices and loss of loved ones. They managed to disclose the evil terrorists who wanted to topple our government and with that, we can never thank them enough.

"May God Bless George Blackwater, Bob Chandler, Richard Parker, and especially the United States of America," the President

said and Clair jumped up cheering, hearing my name mentioned on
television.

For weeks after the president's remarks, the telephone rang with offers
for employment from all over the world. Every major news organization
wanted me to write the exclusive story about the Twelve Men, but I
remained true to my promise and two months later the complete story was
published in the *Charlotte Observer* along with a front-page picture of
George, Bob and myself. Along with the newspaper article, Janet collabo-
rated along with me in writing a book that was to be made into a movie.
With the royalties we were making, neither one of us had to continue working.

Janet and I could afford a nicer house, but we remained at the two-
bedroom place that over-looked Lake Norman, because it was home to us
and nothing else would take its place. Clair was almost out of high school
and would soon be heading off to college, so this would give Janet and I
time to visit places together.

The day Clair moved onto campus at the University of North Carolina
in Chapel Hill, I booked a flight to take us to the Caesars Cove Haven
Resort, located on Lake Wallenpaupack in the Pocono Mountains. Janet
was pleasantly surprised and ready to go as we boarded our plane. She
couldn't believe her eyes as we were escorted to our room that was a one-
of-a-kind. The suite was a four-level setting decorated in shades of bur-
gundy and sandstone with an Egyptian theme. Entering the room, we saw
a seven-foot tall, champagne glass whirlpool bath made for two. In the bedroom, along with a cozy fireplace, was a king-sized bed with a large heart-
shaped pool at the foot of it.

Having all these things at our disposal, we started with the champagne
glass whirlpool. The tiny bubbles created in the whirlpool seemed to elec-
trify our senses, but the tub was too small to enjoy the excitement. We
moved to the heart-shape pool and this was what the doctor had ordered.
Janet and I, excited from the champagne bubbles, made passionate love
completing the voyage to ecstasy.

Lying in the huge, round, king-sized bed, we noticed the ceiling was
celestial, providing the illusion of a starry night. Janet put her head on my
shoulder while I gently stroked her back. I smiled and she wanted to know
my thoughts.

"Looking at the stars, it seems funny now how I thought the disappearances at the lakes were somehow related to aliens," I said, still smiling.

"Well, at the time, it did seem possible and appeared to be the only
theory," Janet replied, and sat up at the end of the bed facing the pool.

"But there's never been any evidence of aliens on Earth," I said back as I stood up beside her next to the bed.

"But that does not mean they're not here," she said jokingly.

I smiled at Janet and told her I was glad she felt that way, because I'd heard of a mysterious creature living not far from the resort in the Water Gap area. The reports said it created an eerie silence followed by hooting noises in the brushes.

"Even experienced naturalists and bird watchers say the hooting is not from a human or any known species of bird," I quoted to her. "I think maybe tomorrow, we'll go up there and…"

The next thing I can recall was suddenly falling into the heart-shaped pool followed by Janet pouncing upon me.

"You are not leaving this room tomorrow, Mister!" she shouted at me, and gave me a kiss as she positioned herself over my outstretched body. "And for the remainder of this trip, …I'm the only story you better be thinking about," Janet said, moving her body closer to mine.

"Oh, you will be darling," I responded as I pulled her next to my body, hugging her tightly, while staring up at the stars on the celestial ceiling. But I could almost hear the faint sounds of hooting noises coming from outside our window calling to me.

Printed in the United States
62688LVS00001B/49-84